for:

**How To Live Happily Ever After
with the Wife and Family You've
Always Wanted**

Take one Attorney/Mother,
one Physician/Father and a "miracle" on
the way.

Add: daily doses of tender loving care
lots of hugs and kisses
boundless romance,
understanding, too
one very sexy back rub
and food to satisfy a craving or two.

Wait nine months...

Neil Cavanaugh, MD

MEN at WORK

✈ —MILLIONAIRE'S CLUB   🐎 —BOARDROOM BOYS   —MAGNIFICENT MEN

🐎 —TALL, DARK & SMART   —DOCTOR, DOCTOR   🔫 —MEN OF THE WEST

🔫 —MEN OF STEEL   🛡 —MEN IN UNIFORM

MEN at WORK

CATHY GILLEN THACKER

HEAVEN SHARED

DOCTOR, DOCTOR

Harlequin Books

TORONTO • NEW YORK • LONDON
AMSTERDAM • PARIS • SYDNEY • HAMBURG
STOCKHOLM • ATHENS • TOKYO • MILAN
MADRID • WARSAW • BUDAPEST • AUCKLAND

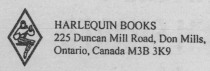

HARLEQUIN BOOKS
225 Duncan Mill Road, Don Mills,
Ontario, Canada M3B 3K9

ISBN 0-373-81017-2

HEAVEN SHARED

Dear Reader,

Like all prospective parents-to-be, my husband and I knew that having children would change our lives—and our marriage—forever. And, as we anticipated the births of each of our three children, we were ready for every roller-coaster emotion!

What we didn't expect was that we'd learn more about ourselves with each pregnancy, or that we'd grow together both as individuals and as a couple.

From the thrill of feeling each baby's first fluttery movement, to the zany excitement that occurred when each baby announced his or her imminent arrival into the world, to the joy we felt when we first held our new baby in our arms, we were together every step of the way.

We learned how to balance careers, family and our marriage to each other in the most fundamental way. And we learned that love is something infinite and enduring, even as it grows and changes.

In *Heaven Shared*, Neil and Ellie Cavanaugh embark on a similar journey. Along the way they encounter a host of challenges that threaten to tear them apart until the love they've always had for each other and the "miracle" they're expecting draws them together again.

I hope you enjoy this book as much as I enjoyed writing it. And if you're a parent or about to be: Bon voyage!

Best wishes always,

Cathy Gillen Thacker

To my brother Steve,
and Dad especially,
for patiently answering all my legal
and medical questions. Thanks, guys.
Couldn't have done it without you.

Prologue

"You trust me, don't you?" The whisper came out of the darkness, low and coaxing, as soon as Neil had turned off the bedside lamp.

Ellie blinked, letting her eyes adjust to the black velvet around them. Moonlight, faint and silvery, tinged the large but cozy master bedroom, offering just enough illumination. Bedtime flirtations were the best, she decided. Intimate and alluring, so full of promise. She folded her hands beneath the nape of her neck and questioned softly, "As a lover?"

Neil turned to her in a rustle of bedcovers, gliding toward her until his bare thigh touched her silk-covered one. Although it was still chilly at night, that early in the Joplin, Missouri, spring, he'd left the window slightly open, claiming that they both slept better when it was cold. She knew for a fact that they cuddled closer under the thick layer of quilts on the king-size bed, taking up only one-fourth of the space.

Outside, the March wind whispered through the trees, the brisk breeze fragrant with the scent of new grass and dew-drenched leaves. Casually Neil propped his head up with his fist and planted his elbow on his pillow, as if to survey her better. Ellie regarded him with whimsy and affection. His smile was slightly lopsided, knowledgeable to a fault and so very sexy. "Or a husband...a physician," Neil finished finally.

Ellie turned and, rolling slightly on her side, snuggled closer to the warm, prone form of her husband. Her fingertips experimentally explored the strong cords of his neck, moved over his broad shoulders, the contours of his muscled chest. "I'd rather answer the first."

His laughter was low and masculine, as he contemplated what she was going to say about his prowess as a lover, prowess that had never been lacking. "Go ahead," he encouraged.

Ellie spun away from him until her back touched the mattress. She propped her hands behind her head in a lazy gesture. "As a lover, you have always had superb judgment."

"And as a physician?" He moved over her, placing a forearm on either side of her, trapping her beneath his weight.

"Your patients all adore you." The lacy hem of her gown twisted between them, heated swiftly with the warmth of their bodies.

"Hmm. And as a husband?" The meter of his breath became less rigidly controlled, as did hers.

"You've been wonderful." Her voice trembled slightly with the confession. Ellie buried her face in the column of his neck, reveling in the masculine scent and feel of him. She swallowed hard, mustering her courage, the reservations she'd not yet had nerve to voice. "But the thought of taking fertility pills scares me, Neil," she whispered honestly at last.

He brushed her hair back away from her face with gentle, soothing strokes. Abruptly he was all confident M.D. again. His lips met hers with gentle promise. He smoothed the hair away from her face, then talked quietly, reassuringly, while still holding her in his arms. "You know I'd never suggest or agree to anything with the probability of anything but a happy ending. When a patient is properly monitored—and you know that under Dr. Raynor's care you will be—the chances of delivering a single child are in the eighty-percentile range."

Ellie smiled. Ever the scientist and medical pioneer, her Neil.

His tone remained gentle, assured. "Ellie, I've used the drug myself in my obstetrics practice. I know that with proper monitoring, the risk of multiple births is minimal."

He'd never had occasion to deliver quintuplets, Ellie knew. Twins many times, but those women hadn't been on fertility pills.

He paused, his expression turning serious as he read her anxiety and realized, apparently, that her apprehension wasn't all due to the prospect of taking menotropins, but of the changes in their lives that were about to be made. "Ellie, I want to have a baby with you."

"I want that, too," she confessed. Perhaps more than she wanted to admit, even to herself. And the past year of trying and failing to conceive had been hell. If she wanted a child, she knew, she had no other choice but to accept the path being offered her.

The tension went out of him. "You'll see. It'll be easier than you think." The flat of his hand slid beneath her to stroke the soft skin of her back. Their legs tangled together, the intimate pressure both familiar and exhilarating. He chuckled softly as he related, "The hardest part of this whole procedure is the homework. Because when the time is right..."

Ellie caught his meaning and laughed, too. "Action must be taken. Promptly," she guessed.

He drew her to him until they were touching in one long, sizzling line. "Think we ought to work on that a little? Just to make sure we've got it down pat?"

Love flooded Ellie, at his patience, his gentleness, his tender regard. Never one to forgo the opportunity to love her husband, she wrapped her arms around his neck. "Dr. Cavanaugh, I'm all yours."

Tenderly Neil pressed a line of kisses from her shoulder to her throat. The softest of shudders went through her as his fingertips followed the path his lips had blazed, his every action, touch and gaze making her feel as if she belonged to him and as if nothing in the future could ever rival what they both felt at that moment. He paused to give her another slow, heartfelt kiss before murmuring approvingly, "Just what I wanted to hear, Ellie Cavanaugh."

Chapter One

"Ellie, you're due over at Dr. Raynor's office in thirty-five minutes," Hazel Morris reported from the door of Ellie's law office.

Ellie glanced up at her secretary, ran a hand haphazardly through the loose natural waves of her shoulder-length golden-blond hair. She'd been on the fertility drug menotropins just nine days now, though it felt like two months. Corresponding physical exams designed to monitor her response to the drug were scheduled every twenty-four to thirty-six hours—which meant she was constantly running back and forth to her obstetrician's office at the Medical Center, a fact that made it very hard for her to continue with business as usual, never mind keep up with her usual work load.

"Thanks, Hazel. I'll be finished here in a minute." Absorbed, Ellie went back to the legal briefs on her desk. Noticing that Hazel was still lingering indecisively, Ellie put her pen down momentarily. "Anything else?"

"Maybe." Hazel hesitated, studying Ellie's wide-set green eyes for any sign of accessibility. As protective as a mother hen about her boss, Hazel could always be counted on to shield Ellie from the more routine vagaries of running a law office. But her concern now was of a different nature. "There's a couple here to see you, the Middletons. They don't have an appointment. Or even, they said, any way to pay you—at least not right away. Added to that, they've got a baby with them that couldn't be more than a couple of weeks old." Hazel clucked her tongue disapprovingly. Although she was a highly trained legal secretary who enjoyed working tremendously, she had stayed home with her three children until all of them were settled well in elementary school, and hadn't gone back to work full-time until they were all of high-school age. "But there's something about them. I don't know what it is. But I—I just feel you should hear them out."

Ellie folded her hands beneath her chin and rested her elbows on her desk. Although she'd only been in private practice for three years, she had more than enough divorces and child-custody cases to keep her busy. "What do they want to see me about?" Another routine house closing she could do without.

"That's why I hesitated. They mentioned something about trouble with Memorial Hospital. I know how you feel about taking on malpractice cases."

"That's right. I don't."

Hazel's face softened compassionately. "They need help, Ellie. They said 'right away,' and I believe them. Mrs. Middleton doesn't look well. And the baby is so...tiny. Premature, probably."

It wasn't like Hazel to be so swayed emotionally, Ellie thought, her attention and interest caught completely. Could it be that there was malpractice going on as they spoke? The woman receiving some treatment that was harming instead of helping her? Alarm bells sounded in Ellie's head. Abruptly she knew that no matter how difficult this case would be for her personally, she had at least to see what it was about, why they wanted to sue.

"I know normally you would simply give them the name of an attorney who specialized in malpractice. And I suggested that. But they wouldn't hear of it. They said they'd already talked to one such specialist and they didn't want to deal with any more 'ambulance chasers.' They looked like they were going to leave right then, and that's when I said... Well, I just thought... I know you've been looking for a case that would really challenge you and—"

"You did the right thing, Hazel." Ellie stood up, straightening her skirt.

"Besides, Neil isn't on staff at Memorial. He works at the Medical Center," Hazel continued, to justify her actions.

"It's all right. Send them in." Ellie's mind was already made up. As a doctor's wife, she didn't want to see anyone sued for malpractice, but that didn't mean she would turn away someone who had come to her in need of help. She would find out what the couple's problem was and refer them to someone else who could help them.

Hazel was halfway out the door before she turned back, recalling. "But your doctor's appointment—"

"Don't worry. I'll make it. This won't take long," Ellie said quietly. "And, Hazel, while I'm talking to them, would you see that I'm not disturbed?"

"Sure thing, boss."

Seconds later the Middletons were ushered into Ellie's office. "What can I do for you?" Ellie asked gently, once the mutual introductions had been concluded.

She noted immediately their well-groomed appearance, their youth. Neither could have been more than twenty-one or twenty-two. Their clothes might have originated at a cut-rate department store, but they were fastidiously clean and well-pressed. The baby was obviously their pride and joy. He was wrapped in a soft blue blanket and sleeping quietly, his newborn skin still flushed pink, his hair black and curly.

Ellie, reminded of her own yearning for a baby, stared quietly at the infant for several seconds, aware of the maternal smile instinctively curving her lips, before she turned back to the Middletons. She was hoping privately that a baby would give Neil and her the sense of family that apparently the Middletons had and she and Neil lacked. Currently, they were almost there, almost a family, but not quite. Neil and she still tended to operate in separate spheres most of the time; whereas the Middletons seemed so firmly aligned, united. It was a closeness she envied and had never experienced as a child—at least in a traditional sense.

Mr. Middleton spoke first. "First off, Ms. Cavanaugh, I want you to know this is very difficult for us. If there were any way out of it, we wouldn't even be thinking about suing."

"Why don't you start from the beginning and tell me what happened?" Ellie said quietly, leaning back in her chair.

Bit by bit, the story came out. "It all started when I was seven months pregnant," Audrey began in a voice that trembled slightly. "I went into labor early. My obstetrician, Dr. Talbot, met me at Memorial Emergency Room. He gave me a shot of a drug called ritodrine hydrochloride, to stop my labor. It didn't work. They knew we were in trouble because Ryan was so early, so the decision was made to move me to the nearest hospital with a neonatal center. The closest facility is in Springfield."

"Dr. Talbot quickly arranged to have a neonatologist standing by there," Stu Middleton continued. "He didn't accompany us to the hospital, but a nurse and an intern from Memorial were sent along with Audrey in the ambulance. En route Audrey's membranes ruptured."

Audrey picked up the story. "That was a very bad sign. The decision was made to start me on antibiotics right away. They gave me a drug containing cephalosporin, without noting that I was allergic to penicillin." She winced, remembering. "We later learned from a friend of ours who is a pharmacist that the two drugs are very similar and that people allergic to penicillin are often allergic to cephalosporin, too. The drug manufacturers know this, and they issue written warnings with all drugs containing cephalosporin. Our pharmacist friend gave us a pamphlet that is issued with the specific drug I was given." She reached into her purse and handed the pamphlet to Ellie. Ellie read it, noting grimly that the cross-allergenicity warning and the contraindications were clearly stated—that fatal anaphylaxis had resulted in cases where the drug was wrongly or imprudently administered.

"Within minutes, a severe allergic reaction began." Audrey paused to describe symptoms that, though understated, had to have been hellishly uncomfortable, Ellie knew. Audrey continued, still speaking calmly and, Ellie guessed, glossing over all she had suffered because of the improper administration of a drug. "Realizing what had happened, they quickly gave me an antidote, but it didn't...quite work. We got to the hospital, and another doctor took over. They did an immediate cesarean section and moved Ryan into pediatric I.C.U., where he stayed for the next eight weeks until he was ready to go home."

"And in the meantime, Audrey had developed severe exfoliative dermatitis—as a result of being given the wrong drug," Stu concluded.

"Explain what exfoliative dermatitis is," Ellie interjected. "I'm not familiar with the term."

"Exfoliative dermatitis is a severe allergic reaction—a redness, scaling and thickening of the entire skin surface. Along with the change in appearance of the skin, there's severe itching, fever, heat loss because of the increased blood flow to the skin and exfoliation—or peeling. The reaction itself can be fatal in severe cases or can lead to congestive heart failure. It's a very serious illness. The fact that Audrey was already in a weakened state made it that much worse." Abruptly Stu stopped his knowledgeable recitation. Clearly, during the time of Audrey's illness, he'd learned much about the specific nature of her malady, as would have any concerned husband. He swallowed hard, looking as if he were about to break down at any minute. "She spent three weeks in the intensive care unit, almost died several times. It was a very difficult time for all of us."

Ellie nodded sympathetically. Fortunately Audrey had recovered, from an appearance standpoint. There seemed to be no lingering physical scars. Ellie was grateful for that. The poor woman didn't need to deal with any additional trauma after all she'd been through. "Did the doctors admit to you that a mistake had been made?"

The Middletons glanced at each other in frustration. "No. Everyone involved medically verified that Audrey is allergic to cephalosporin—and that she should never have any medication containing cephalosporin again—but no one mentioned to us the cross-allergy problem. Not directly, anyway. Audrey remembers some shifting of the blame while she was going into shock as the intern and Dr. Talbot communicated via ambulance radio. But once we arrived in Springfield, everything was hushed up. It was as if they were hoping we wouldn't figure out for ourselves that what happened could very easily have been prevented altogether."

A conspiracy of silence seemed de rigueur in those cases, Ellie knew from her reading. A proven malpractice charge against any doctor could mean that the physician would have his license revoked; at the very least it would shoot his own insurance rates, and possibly the hospital's, too, sky-high. "There's no doubt in my mind both doctors were very upset and sorry about what happened," Audrey said quietly. "It was a very frantic, tense situation. And I know in my heart, odd as this sounds, that they were doing their best to save Ryan and me."

"The real problem," Stu revealed, "is that we have no medical insurance. We were prepared to pay the routine birth and delivery fees, perhaps a little more. But nothing like this." He unfolded an envelope from his pocket and handed it to Ellie. Inside were medical bills that totaled fifty thousand dollars. "That's why we came to see you today. We need help. Even if we worked the rest of our lives—I'm a computer operator and Audrey was a file clerk for an auto repair shop—we'd never be able to pay those off."

Considering the circumstances, they shouldn't have to, Ellie thought, further incensed that the hospital would even have the gall to bill them for complications and subsequent hospitalization for what was caused primarily by its staff's mistake. Everyone involved should have been grateful that the Middletons weren't angrily suing them for all they were worth, and in the process putting the entire hospital out of business. Instead, the hospital had slapped them with a bill they couldn't expect to pay in a million years. Ellie loved Neil, but her faith in the medical community lagged just a little. Where were those self-regulating processes Neil always talked so much about?

"You said the doctors knew Audrey was allergic to penicillin?" Ellie needed to ascertain the facts carefully. She tried her best to remain emotionally unswayed by the details of the case—a feat easier tried than accomplished.

"Yes. It was noted on the records."

Ellie marveled at the ease with which the Middletons were able to accept the ordeal they had lived through. After several more questions, she asked, "And you harbor no ill will toward the hospital or doctors responsible?"

The couple exchanged an apprehensive glance. Stu spoke for both of them, "If we thought they'd been intentionally negligent, it would have been different. But they weren't. They were kind and attentive, and they did what they could for us in a very tense, life-threatening situation. They also saved our baby's life. The fact that a mistake was made wasn't terrific, but Audrey's okay now—still recovering, but okay. We just want to get out from under the medical bills, get on with our lives and forget about it. We don't want a million-dollar settlement or so much as a penny over the amount we absolutely have to have. We're not here to put the hospitals and the doctors out of business."

Audrey smiled wanly. "Knowing that, do you still want to take the case?"

Ellie smiled in response. "That's the only way I would. But I'll be honest with you. I'm still not sure I should take the case. My husband is an obstetrician for another hospital here in Joplin."

"We know," the Middletons said in unison, exchanging a glance.

"That's one of the main reasons we came to you," Audrey continued persuasively, "aside from your excellent professional reputation. We figured that if anyone would understand we had no intention to hurt the doctors involved and simultaneously see that the case didn't get out of hand, you would. We really don't want to hurt anyone."

Ellie knew that in the hands of another, less scrupulous lawyer, a case like this could be disastrous for the hospital and the physicians involved. More telling still, though, was the inner knowledge that had she not been married to Neil, she would have jumped at the chance to represent the Middletons. The case they had presented her with was a young attorney's dream come true, a chance to act on principle for the common good, not for personal gain, and in the process earn a reputation for herself as a true representative of the common people. That was something she had always wanted, the entire reason, really, she'd become a lawyer. And though she had never planned to make a name in malpractice suits, or even to handle a single lawsuit of that nature, taking the Middleton case would give her invaluable experience and help her make a name for herself.

Darn it, Ellie thought in sudden fierce frustration, knowing how long she had waited for just such an opportunity, how could she not take the case? She would just have to talk to Neil, make him put aside his disapproval of all malpractice suits and understand why she was doing what she was. But could she do that without betraying the Middletons' professional confidence? Ellie wondered. Probably not, at least at that point. She'd just have to wait until after the suit was filed, when it became public knowledge, before talking to Neil. He loved her. He knew how important her career was to her, how hard she had worked to achieve what she had, and how much further she still wanted to go. He would understand...wouldn't he?

With a glance at her watch, she saw that she was almost late for her appointment. Ellie glanced up to see Hazel hovering in the doorway. Hazel pointed to her watch officiously, sent Ellie a mother-hen look. Ellie paused momentarily, sent her secretary a beseeching glance, then held up a hand, traffic-cop style, as a signal to everyone to stop everything momentarily. "Hazel, please call Dr. Raynor's office for me. Tell him I've been unavoidably detained," she directed calmly, ignoring her secretary's disapproving look.

"I already have." Hazel sniffed, as if maddened that Ellie hadn't given her credit for doing at least that much on her own. "They were *not* understanding. Dr. Raynor's nurse said if you can't make it within the next fifteen minutes, she'll have to reschedule you for first thing tomorrow morning. Dr. Raynor has an emergency cesarean section."

Ellie swore inwardly, then shrugged. If it couldn't be helped, so be it. "Tell them I'll be in tomorrow, then," Ellie decided.

Reminded that they had dropped in without an appointment, the Middletons looked dismayed.

"It's perfectly all right," Ellie said, ignoring Hazel's shake of the head. Soothingly she continued, "The appointment was nothing that couldn't be put off for another twelve hours." Beyond that, though, she knew she would be in trouble.

Hazel left. Ellie gave a sigh of relief and sat back more comfortably in her chair. *Back to the business at hand,* Ellie thought, reaching for a yellow legal pad. Calmly she warned the young couple, "Before I can file suit, I'll have to conduct an investigation of my own, verify facts, look at the medical records, talk to the medical personnel involved. I'll also need, aside from your written consent to do so, some further information from both of you." She buzzed Hazel on the intercom and instructed her to bring in a steno pad. "As well as depositions from each one of you."

UNFORTUNATELY FOR ELLIE, Neil was called into emergency surgery later that afternoon. By the time he'd finished, another of his patients had gone into labor. Despairing about when they would ever find time to be together again, or make their schedules mesh on a regular basis, Ellie, instead, spent the evening working on the Middleton case. Unhappily, that only made her feel worse. Several times she almost called Neil at the hospital. She wanted badly to talk to him—in confidence—about the case. But her allegiance to professional ethics stopped her. By the time he came home, she was already asleep. She awakened long enough to make love with him, and then fell asleep in his arms. He left again early the next morning before breakfast—another emergency, a cesarean section this time. When she saw him again that evening, exciting news from her doctor had eliminated thoughts of all else and unexpectedly had given her a reprieve from further taking, that month anyway, of the fertility drug.

"So, you're ovulating," Neil said with a grin as he walked in the front door.

So this is what it takes to get the man's attention, Ellie thought wryly. She was beginning to think that he was always going to be a stranger to her, that they'd be closer, in categorization, to long-distance lovers than to man and wife. But having a baby together was going to change all that, or so Neil had vowed. He'd promised that once she was pregnant and more in need of him, he would slow down, decrease his patient load, find a way to make more time for her and the child. Still, Ellie worried about the practicalities of combining a career and motherhood. She worried about keeping Neil interested. Not an easy feat, when one considered what a dynamic man her husband was and, medically speaking, at least, how very much in demand.

"Appears that way, yes." Ellie blushed. Inwardly she'd already begun to wonder what would happen if she didn't conceive. She knew how desperately Neil wanted a child—their child. What would happen if she didn't get pregnant? Would he still love her? Deliberately she pushed the thought away. Neil was not going to desert her as her father had. She had to stop thinking that way, to believe and trust in her husband.

Oblivious of her thoughts, Neil grabbed her around the waist and drew her to him for a long, ardent hug. Beneath her cheek, she could feel the hammering of his heartbeat. He seemed every bit as excited as she. "I managed to get the whole night off. Jim Raynor is going to be taking all my calls. And deliveries." His eyes, when he drew back, were fever-bright.

"Hallelujah!" Ellie cried happily. Decisively, she put the Middleton case and her missed obstetrician's appointment from her mind. There would be time to tell him about both events later. Right now she wanted to concentrate on Neil and the precious time they had alone. And on nothing, no one else.

"Amen to that. As to the other, I think this calls for a celebration, don't you?" Lacing an arm around her waist, he drew her toward the living room sofa. They sat side by side on the sofa, mutually weary from a long day.

Ellie nodded her agreement as she kicked off her shoes and rubbed her tired arches.

"Dinner out?" His hands closed around her shoulders and intimately massaged the tension away.

"I'd love it." Ellie leaned back into the circle of his arm when he'd finished, resting her cheek against his shoulder. She relished the time they had together. Unfortunately, it was a commodity that always seemed in short supply. Would that change when they had a child? It would have to, wouldn't it? They both couldn't keep going as they had been. Yet, again, she was loath to bring the question up. It was like putting the cart before the horse. They would get to the problem when they reached it, not before. In the meantime, she didn't want anything to spoil their celebration.

An hour later they were seated in a quaint country inn, twenty miles out of the city. A favorite haunt of theirs, the small, cozy restaurant sported soft lighting, a magnificent view and down-home Ozark cuisine. Dishes like pan-fried chicken and roast beef, home fries and crisp salads and luscious calorie-laden desserts. Neil ordered a bottle of champagne and they sat back to sip it slowly before ordering dinner. The sounds of country-and-Western music surrounded them, that and the welcoming feeling of homespun creature comfort, coupled with the intimacy and love flowing freely between them. Ellie savored the serenity of the moment, watching Neil surreptitiously as he looked over the menu.

Had she ever not been in love with him? It didn't seem so. Though not classically handsome, he was very good-looking and carried himself with the assurance of a professional, while at the same time not losing his innate aura of accessibility. He had dark-brown hair, brown eyes and a complexion that tanned well and evenly at the drop of a hat. He was tall, with a spare, athletic build; he had played tennis competitively when he was a kid, on school and country club teams. Now it was his major physical form of relaxation. His hair was thick and full, cut agreeably short above perfect, sexy ears. His face was more oval than square, with features all clearly defined. He had thick straight brows, a nose that was straight and long, a full, sensual mouth, an implacable chin. But it was his eyes that caught and captured a woman's attention, Ellie knew. Eyes that seemed to understand, empathize and soothe, all without half trying. A physician's bedside manner? she had often wondered in the three years since they had met and later married. Or just a sensitive man's innate understanding of others' feelings? She couldn't discern; she only knew she had never met a man like him or loved anyone half as much.

But her affection for Neil, though admittedly enhanced by the chemistry between them, was not limited to a strictly physical level. No, Neil was much more than a lover or a friend to her; he was a man to be admired, respected, revered. Even in the relatively brief time she'd known him, she'd watched him accomplish miracles, on one memorable occasion sliding by and around an administrative taboo at the hospital to allow an extra person in the labor and delivery rooms when a patient, distraught from the recent unexpected loss of her husband, had needed the emotional support. She'd watched him soothe and calm expectant fathers into some semblance of normalcy at a second's notice when the Big D—delivery date—had arrived. And she'd benefited greatly from his own gentle assurances and patience, the comfort and solace he offered her after a long, tiring day. He was never too busy to hear her problems, never too busy to be there when she really needed him. And she had tried to give him the same steadiness, the same quality of spousal support. She knew she didn't want to lose him, not ever. Yet it was a possibility that stayed with her constantly. Maybe because she was a lawyer and worked daily with the aftermath and preparation for events that changed people's lives irrevocably.

"So, how was your day?" Neil asked conversationally at length, when the waitress had disappeared with their dinner orders and the instructions to delay the meal for at least an hour. The two of them had been so busy talking about the medical results of Ellie's checkup on the way to the inn that neither had discussed their day.

"Busy, as usual."

"Anything interesting happen?" His eyes met and held hers.

Ellie thought of the Middletons. Apprehension churned inside her without warning. She fought to contain a desperately unhappy look. She knew he'd never approve of her involvement in any legal action against the medical community. He felt, as did many other doctors, that only physicians had the knowledge and the right to govern and watch over themselves. The fact that they didn't always do so was no reason for lawyers to get involved. Or so Neil, the successful, caring, competent physician, thought. No, now was not the time to tell him she was preparing a lawsuit against one of Joplin's hospitals. Or that every physician was not as adept as he. That life-and-death mistakes were made. That Audrey Middleton and her baby both could have died, but hadn't, and now, miraculously, the Middletons only wanted absolution from a staggering medical bill.

"Hectic," she said honestly at last. "I've had some particularly difficult cases referred to me lately."

"Anything you want to talk about?" Neil asked.

"Not right now. Maybe later, when it's all over, a matter of record."

He seemed to know, without her ever saying so, that she had much on her mind, much she needed and wanted desperately to share with him. "Sure?" he asked softly. His hand snaked across the table to capture hers. His touch instantly evoked a thousand memories and the promise of the night to come.

"I'm sure." Ellie forced a smile, banishing the disturbing thoughts about her work, the possibility that there might be a conflict of interest on her part, albeit a personal one—one related to her marriage. Without warning she had the sudden feeling that he wanted to share something with her. "How about you? How was your day?" Curiosity brightened her tone.

"Well, as a matter of fact, I do have an announcement to make." He sat up straighter, looked inordinately pleased. "Jim Raynor called me into his office this morning. He's announcing his plans to cut back on both his private practice and his work at the hospital at the staff meeting tomorrow. Naturally, they'll be looking for someone to replace him as chief of obstetrics. He's going to recommend that I be his replacement."

"Neil, that's wonderful!"

"I thought so, too."

"How long before you know whether you get the position or not?"

"Another month or two, probably. First, the board will post the opening with the state medical society. Though standard policy is to promote from within, it's possible some highly regarded colleague from another part of the state or a teaching hospital will want to apply for the position, too. After a set time, the board of directors will screen and interview all candidates, just to make sure they're qualified. When that's done, all candidates will speak before the obstetrics-gynecology staff. A vote will be taken. Whether I get it or not, it's quite an honor even to be considered. And to have Jim recommend me personally...it means a lot."

"I'll say!" She lifted her glass of champagne. "To the next chief of obstetrics."

Quietly, he added his own toast. "To the soon-to-be-accomplished conceiving of our child."

"Mmm." Ellie grinned and sipped her champagne. Briefly she wondered if her involvement in the malpractice case would affect Neil's getting the position. Surely not...would it? After all, the Middleton lawsuit was against another hospital, one where Neil wasn't on staff.

Neil paused. He gave her a strange, searching look. "What's wrong?"

"Nothing," Ellie lied. How could he have noticed that first instant's tension, she wondered, when she had just herself begun to truly comprehend the complexities of their situation? Because deep within her, she was beginning to see that her involvement in the case might mean more than just a single argument between her and her husband. It might mean a complete polarization—a possibility she didn't even want to contemplate.

"Something's bothering you," Neil observed.

Ellie took a deep breath, met his gaze and was able to say honestly, "I want you to get the position, Neil. I want you to get everything you deserve."

"And?" he waited tensely.

"And I want career success for myself, too."

His expression relaxed into confidence, in her and her abilities. "You're getting that."

"Not as fast as I'd like," Ellie confessed.

"It takes time to build a legal practice."

"That's what worries me." The words spilled out before she could stop herself from saying them. "I worry that I'll have a baby before I've really made it, and shortchange what I could have accomplished." Yet in terms of timing, physically, she didn't have any choice. Her biological clock was ticking away at breakneck rate.

"I want you to continue to work after the baby is born," he said softly.

"I know that. It's just that I've worked so hard and so long to build up a reputation, and I'm still handling mostly divorces and real estate closings. Not that I'm undermining the importance of that. I enjoy working with people. Part of being a lawyer is being a sensitive and skillful negotiator, and in that sense, the experience I'm getting is great. But I also long to do something more complex, more challenging and problematic. Something that will use every bit of skill and bargaining power I've got.''

''Your chance is going to come soon, Ellie. And when it does, I have no doubt you'll meet the challenge as admirably as you do everything else.'' He laughed softly, captured her hand and squeezed it tightly, but he was only half joking as he continued, ''Believe me, if I could go out there and rustle you up a truly exciting case myself, I would. Hell, I'd have potential plaintiffs standing in line outside your office, all waiting to see you. Except, of course, if I did that—'' his voice lowered caressingly, mesmerizing her with its intensity ''—it wouldn't leave you much time to spend with me.''

So he felt their absence from each other acutely, too, Ellie thought. ''Then you'd better forget that, for the moment anyway,'' she teased in response. He was so confident at that moment, so sure of her, that Ellie relaxed. Neil would understand what she'd done and why.

''There's nothing I wouldn't do for you. You know that, don't you?'' he asked, his grip tightening affectionately, possessively, on her hand.

''I do,'' Ellie said. She turned the talk once again to the position at the hospital. ''What would you like to see accomplished that hasn't already been done?'' Ellie asked. There was no limit to Neil's philanthropic and professional dreams. His compassion for the problems of his patients was his most endearing quality.

''I'd like to see the hospital someday institute a residency program, become a teaching hospital. Maybe increase the medical education programs offered to patients.''

Neil and Ellie talked happily of their dreams as the evening drew out languorously. By the time their dinners were served, they had dropped all talk of their respective careers and were instead contemplating where they might vacation the following summer and exchanging the latest news of their mutual friends. They lingered companionably over coffee, waiting for the last effects of the alcohol to abate before embarking on the journey home. Hence, it was after midnight when, sated and happy, they returned home. Out of habit, Neil locked up and switched off the lights downstairs while Ellie went upstairs. He was beside her in the bedroom moments later, helping her with the clasp of her necklace.

"Did I mention how much I liked that dress?" As the silver choker fell away and was placed in her jewelry box, he let his hands drift down to her shoulders. His eyes followed the path of his hands, lingering on the transparent silk-and-chiffon T-shirt over the black chiffon T-shirt-style dress. Thin and exquisitely cut, the simple dress hugged Ellie's curves softly, sexily.

Ellie bent to kick off her thin-strapped evening sandals; finished, she wiggled her stocking-clad toes in the soft oyster carpet. Several feet away, the smoky blue-and-silver jacquard satin coverlet on their bed beckoned invitingly. "No, but I could tell, the way you were looking at me all through dinner."

"Did you mind?" Hands on her shoulders, he turned her toward him and moved her forward, centimeter by centimeter, until they were touching, shoulder to shoulder, leg to leg.

A thrill of magical awareness shimmered through her. She was inundated with sensations—the slightly rough surface of his palms caressing her skin, the lingering scent of his after-shave, combined with the always-clean fragrance of his skin. In the meantime, he worked with the buttons at her back, freeing them effortlessly one by one.

Her breath was shallow, her pulse racing, as she admitted in the same teasing tone, "I enjoyed your visual salutation."

Neil parted the cloth by degrees, until the fragile fabric hung open past her waist. "Always glad to be of service, milady." He mocked her with a courtly bow, then found out firsthand how very little she wore beneath the dress. He paused on a short intake of breath, his hands circling around her rib cage, beneath her breasts. "Now, how else may I be of service?" His hands found the soft undersides of her breasts, cupped them gently.

Suddenly he wasn't the only one who was finding it hard to breathe. She let him dance her backward toward the bed, realizing it wouldn't be long at all before her legs would turn to butter, refuse to support her weight. "Knowing you, Neil," she teased, "I'm sure you'll think of something."

"Mmm," he murmured distractedly, amiably dispensing with her dress, assisting her with the scattering of his clothes. In a heavenly cloud of sensation, they cozily found their way into the sheets. His dark gaze reflecting all the love he felt in his heart, Neil clasped her to him ardently. *We're making a baby tonight,* she thought, *creating a new life. A part of him, a part of me.*

She closed her eyes and gave herself totally to the experience and to him.

Chapter Two

"Neil? Got a minute? I have something I need to talk to you about," Jim Raynor said.

Neil handed the chart he'd been glancing over back to the nurse, murmured a polite thanks and, with an acquiescent nod, followed the silver-haired physician down the hall and into his private office. Oddly, once the two men were alone, Neil's mentor looked unswervingly grim, as if he were about to be the bearer of some very bad news.

"I just heard about the lawsuit being brought against Memorial Hospital. I'd heard rumors, of course, but I had no idea Ellie was involved," Jim informed Neil worriedly.

Neil was half expecting some news about Ellie's medical condition, and it took a moment for him to accept that his boss was talking about his wife's career. "What are you talking about?" Neil asked. Exhausted, he sank down into an armchair and stretched out his long legs. Still clad in surgical blues, he'd had five straight days of nonstop surgeries and deliveries, and very little sleep. He'd not seen Ellie much during that time, granted, but he'd known that she was busy at the office, too. Inordinately busy, he thought with a jerk. He vaguely recalled that she was researching some new case. A change of pace, she had explained haltingly when asked. But they'd never gotten into the exact details, largely because she hadn't seemed to want to talk about it. And Neil, as exhausted and overworked as he was, hadn't thought to pursue it.

Jim expelled a long breath. "Ellie is the attorney in the case against Memorial. It's all in the evening paper." Jim handed him a copy, folded over to reveal the article on the front page, featuring Ellie's picture in front of the courthouse steps. "Surely she told you about it!"

Neil scanned the headlines and article, his sense of fury and betrayal growing with every word he read. Finally he said, "She probably felt to do so would be a conflict of interest on her part." His outward demeanor was cool, but inside, Neil's temper was fast scaling upward of the boiling point. How could Ellie have done this to him, made him look like such a fool, in front of his colleagues, no less? Didn't she realize what she was taking on, bringing suit against any hospital in the town where they both worked and lived? Damn it, Ellie knew how much he detested malpractice suits. He'd thought she felt the same.

"I see." Jim sat down in the swivel chair behind his desk. He folded his fingers together steeple fashion and rested his elbows on his desk. "I always liked Ellie. I admire her prowess as an attorney. But to be perfectly blunt, Neil, an action like this on her part could hurt your chances of being voted chief of obstetrics."

"How so?" Neil rubbed his hand across his jaw, feeling the imminent five o'clock shadow.

Jim frowned, continuing carefully. "Department heads are privy to much...private information, much of which could be construed as controversial, on the surface, anyway, by an outsider to the medical profession. As husband and wife, it's only natural for you and Ellie to exchange confidences."

Jim didn't need to say any more. Neil understood full well what he was getting at, that the board would worry that Ellie would use her connections to Neil to find a basis eventually to sue the Joplin Medical Center as well. Neil's saying that she wasn't morally capable of such a dastardly deed wouldn't help one whit. "Obviously we haven't exchanged confidences lately, at least not about this," Neil said sourly, tossing the paper aside.

"I'll do what I can when it comes time to vote," Jim offered lamely. But they both knew that all things considered, it probably would do little good. Ellie had just lost the opportunity for him.

Neil finished up at the hospital swiftly and drove home, not

bothering to change out of his rumpled and sweat-stained surgical clothes. He found Ellie in front of the television. She was
wearing a sporty white linen suit and low-heeled shoes. She
looked as if she had come straight from the office. Her shoulder-
length golden-blond hair was no longer twisted up into the loose
French knot she'd worn earlier in the day, but loose and free,
down around her shoulders, as if she'd arranged it with her fingers but neglected yet to find a hairbrush. Typical Ellie—casual,
sporty and windblown.

Seemingly unaware of his presence, she was absorbed in
watching the end of the six-o'clock news. Featured was an interview with the Memorial Hospital administration and then herself. The intern, senior physician and nurses involved in the case
had all declined to be interviewed. Photos of the Middletons and
their infant son were also shown, though currently they were
being shielded from outright interviewing by the press. Neil
knew instinctively that it was Ellie who was protecting the Middletons. Why hadn't she thought to fend for him as well?

Ellie looked up guiltily when she saw Neil framed in the doorway of their living room, his shoulder wedged against the frame,
one ankle crossed leisurely against the other. She started nervously, getting slowly to her feet. There was no doubt, judging
by the expression on her face, that she knew exactly what she'd
done to him. *Damn her anyway,* he thought. The anger he'd been
holding in check came out full force.

"That's right, jump," he said bitterly, stalking forward, his
hands resting loosely on his hips. "After all, it wouldn't do to
have your doctor-husband witness your maligning of the entire
Joplin medical community." His thumb tapped his sternum for
emphasis. "A community I just happen to figure prominently
in."

Carefully, she slid her glasses off the end of her nose. "It's
not like that," she said circumspectly. Yet her ivory skin, min-
imally made up as always, had abruptly acquired a sudden pink
tone, and her clear green eyes were avoiding his. She looked up
at him pleadingly. "Neil, I wanted so many times to explain."

"Why didn't you?"

"I wanted to wait until the suit was filed. If it's any consolation, I don't think it will go to court. The malpractice insurance company has already contacted me, to set up an informal meeting; it'll be held once they've had a chance to review the case and gather their own data.''

''And how long will that be?'' There was some relief in knowing she intended to settle out of court, or at least try. His anger at being kept in the dark still flowed readily. He advanced on her furiously, aware of a muscle clenching and unclenching convulsively in his cheek.

''Six to eight weeks.'' Briefly, she told him about the Middletons, the mix-up in medication, the resultant life-or-death complications, the huge medical bill.

''How long have you known about this?''

She looked guilty again, distressed. ''Over a month.''

''A month,'' he repeated numbly.

''I was going to talk to you last night.'' Her tone lowered defensively, ''But you got called back to the hospital.'' Still avoiding meeting his gaze, she began gathering up papers and briefs.

''And the nights before that? I know I'm gone a lot, but you must have had a dozen times to tell me.''

''I tried, Neil. But we were always talking about the possibility of a baby now that I've started ovulating again. I didn't want to spoil it.''

''Then you knew how I'd feel.''

''I...guessed.''

''Yet you took the case, anyway, without even bothering to discuss it with me.''

Anger flared in her face, as virulent and destructive as his own rigidly impatient tone. Her voice was crisp to the point of being insulting. ''Yes, I did. I'm a professional, Neil. Just like you. I don't call you up from the office to ask your permission to take a case any more than you call me up at the office to ask if it's okay if you take on a new patient!''

''A rotten analogy, Ellie.''

Her eyes held his, steadily, furiously. It came to him then that he wasn't the only one who felt betrayed. He pushed the faint, nagging tendency toward guilt away and concentrated on holding on to the anger. "It's the only one I've got," she responded in a flat, icy tone. Abruptly all the fight went out of her. She spread her hands in a self-effacing gesture. "Look, can't we sit down and discuss this like reasonable, rational adults?"

"That depends. Was that with or without reporters?" His sarcasm grated between them.

She stepped back as if he'd attempted to strike her. Beneath the surface calm, she looked faintly shocked. He was dimly aware that she'd never seen him like that before. He'd never felt that way, either, as if he'd been pushed to the limits of his endurance, physically, emotionally—and worse, betrayed by the person closest to him, the one and only person he had supposed he could always count on.

"That's not fair and you know it," she said finally. At his silence she sighed and tried again. "I didn't know the reporters were going to be at the courthouse today. Evidently someone had tipped them off."

"Who?"

"I don't know!" Agitated, Ellie ran a hand through her hair and paced back and forth.

Neil's eyes were drawn to the flash of calf beneath her skirt. Desire was the last thing he wanted to feel for her at the moment. He looked away, at the ceiling, the windows, the fireplace—the place he'd called home with Ellie since the day they were married. His haven from the pressures of outside life. Only now...now it felt more like prison than sanctuary. He resented her for destroying that most of all. Hadn't he been a good husband to her, given her everything she could have wanted? Hadn't he tried to be understanding, tried to be supportive of her career? But this malpractice suit was something he could never condone, no matter how much she explained, no matter how much, in his heart, he wanted to listen. It was wrong, dead wrong, for lawyers to think they could regulate the medical profession. And Ellie knew full well how he felt; they'd been over it hundreds of times. She knew how he felt on a gut level about lawyers who took malpractice suits. Yet she'd gone ahead and done it, anyway, the knowledge that she'd felt she couldn't even come to him after all they'd been to each other. Or had that been another surface image, like the reflection one saw of oneself in the water? Surface bright...but nothing beneath. Was that what their marriage was, the intimacy he'd thought they'd shared? Nothing, just images, surface-deep? Neil only knew for certain that he was exhausted, too exhausted to be dealing with this.

Ellie, not knowing the maelstrom of his thoughts, was trying to explain to him and herself how the newspapers had known to be there. "I've been quietly researching the case for weeks. Anyone at Memorial or Springfield General, even the ambulance service, could have mentioned it in passing or called the paper to deliver a hot tip. I just don't know." With effort, she lowered her voice, "I can only tell you that I didn't want them to know, nor did I plan to put myself in the news—"

"Didn't you?" he accused harshly.

"No, I didn't. And if you don't believe that, you don't know anything about me."

"After this—" Neil picked up the paper and flung it at her "—I don't know what to believe about you anymore. I do know what it feels like to be called in on the carpet and told by my superior about my wife's latest legal activities."

Her mouth formed a silent "oh" of dismay. "I'm sorry." She swallowed hard and looked back at him. "I don't know what more I can say. Except...trust me?"

"Trust you?" His answering laugh was harsh. "That's a riot, El. A riot. After what you've done?"

"You must know I'd never do anything willfully to hurt you."

"You just did."

"I almost didn't take the case because of you."

"You should have followed your instincts, El. Because I can't and won't forgive you for this."

"Can't we at least talk about it?"

His glance raked her up and down. Did she really think a simple apology would erase the damage of her betrayal? "Talking won't do any good."

"If you'd just listen—"

"I might have listened last night. Today the paper says it all, doesn't it, El?" He advanced on her, feeling more furious and betrayed than he had ever felt in his life. "Tell me you didn't know how I'd react," he said. "Tell me!"

But about that much Ellie wouldn't evade. He could tell by her manner that she was sorry he was furious, but not sorry about what she'd done; that given the same circumstances, she would react exactly the same. "I knew how you'd feel, I guess," Ellie said tiredly, running her hand over her face. She paused to massage the back of her neck with her palm, as if feeling unbearably weary. "And I also knew that this was something I wanted to do, something I had to do."

"Something you had to do?" he echoed coldly.

She shook her head helplessly, as if not sure she could explain to him what she felt. Calming slightly, he waited. She went on in a voice so quiet that he had to strain to hear her. "The moment the Middletons walked into my office I knew I wanted the case. Not so much because the case was interesting and a step up for me, although that was a major part of it, Neil. But I took the case primarily because I felt an odd sort of connection with them." She put up a hand to prevent him from interrupting. "I know it sounds odd, mystical, and it is. But it doesn't make it any less true. I felt compelled to help them. Maybe because I know, from memory and experience, what it's like to be suddenly and unfairly burdened with bills there's no money to pay. I still remember the first years after my father left my mother and me. I was terrified, week to week. Terrified we wouldn't have enough to eat. Terrified we'd be evicted from the apartment. I didn't want that to happen to them, especially when I knew I could stop it, right the wrong, and still manage to keep the hospital and the doctors involved from being unnecessarily hurt."

"The implication being that because of my safe, secure upbringing, I can't identify with any of that, right?"

"I didn't say or mean any such thing." She gave him a level look. "But now that you mention it, maybe you're right. Maybe you can't relate to that. Maybe that's why you can't understand or condone my taking this case."

"That's a cheap shot, Ellie."

"It seems to be the day for them, doesn't it, Neil?" she answered calmly. Abruptly suffocated by the cozy living room, he turned and started toward the door. He needed a workout, needed to slam some tennis balls around the court. Anything to work off the destructiveness welling up within him.

"Neil!" She swept past him, unexpectedly cutting in front of him and barring his way to the entry hall. "Wait a minute. Don't go."

His breath was coming rapidly. Every muscle was tensed, ready for battle. "You've had nothing to say for the past four weeks, Ellie. Why blow the delicious little secret you've been harboring and start trying to appease me now—when the majority of the damage, as far as my career is concerned, has been done?"

"Wait a minute. What are you talking about?"

"The chief of obstetrics post. Thanks to you, there's not a chance in hell I'll get it."

She looked stricken. His desire to get out of there increased tenfold. He pushed her aside and continued his exit.

She stepped backward with him down the length of the entry hall, as if they were partners in some bizarre dance, then finally cut in front of him at the last minute, barring his way out. Panic constricted her face as she realized what he could have told her beforehand if she'd only confided in him. That success for her on this particular score would only mean automatic failure for him. Add to that the new breach between them, and it was a cost that far exceeded whatever personal gains or satisfaction she would reach by handling the Middleton case.

When her back was against the front door, she reached out toward him, her forearms resting against his chest. "Neil, I'm sorry. I—I should have told you; I realize that now. But damn it, try and understand why I acted as I did." He remained implacable, unsympathetic. With difficulty she went on in a voice that was choked with emotion, hardly more than a whisper. "I didn't want anything to spoil the conceiving of our baby."

Neil's answering laughter was harsh, like something out of a horror movie. Had she been thinking about the malpractice case, plotting it, while they were conceiving their child? How indicative of the state of their marriage! At the moment he felt vindictive as hell; he felt like punishing her as she had just flailed him. With effort he got a grip on his emotions. "You knew how I'd feel..." And she'd still gone full steam ahead anyway.

Damn her again.

Ellie leaned against the front door, her hands behind her, tensely gripping the knob. Once again, they went over the facts. She explained for long minutes, telling him nothing specific and yet everything of her feelings for her clients, finishing, "They don't want any money, no big settlements, just the hospital bill paid."

"Okay. I understand why you took the case." Somewhat mollified, Neil followed her back into the living room and took a seat opposite her. "I hope it can be settled out of court—but by someone else, someone else just as capable. Ellie, I want you to withdraw from this case."

"I can't do that." Her chin lifted stubbornly, as if she resented him for even asking.

Neil's irritation with her was increasing. "It's a conflict of interest." He enunciated every word clearly, pushing each syllable through a fence of teeth. Hadn't the damn lawsuit caused enough trouble between them? Why was she compelled to drag it out?

"If you were on staff at Memorial, it would be different, Neil. Then, yes, it would be a conflict of interest for me. But you're not on staff there."

"Damn it, Ellie, I've been as reasonable about this as I know how. I'm willing to forgive and forget—despite what this little faux pas of yours has cost me professionally and personally—but only if it ends now."

"Maybe you haven't lost the position."

"And maybe bears don't walk in the woods."

Silence fell between them. He felt as if they were playing tug-of-war over a black abyss. One false move on either person's part and it would all be over—everything they had ever worked for, everything they had ever shared. One last time he tried to reason with her. "This case is wrecking the hell out of our marriage."

He could almost see the wheels turning in her head as she responded evenly, cautiously, "Only if you let it."

"If you think that, you really don't know me at all, do you?"

Her chin was as intractable as her gaze. Determinedly she replied, "And then, again, maybe I do. And maybe, just maybe, Neil, in this one instance, I want you to change."

"No way, Ellie, no way." He was on his feet again before she could react.

There was a silence in which she refused to budge an inch. In that instant, he could imagine her as an opponent in court and knew he never wanted to go against her.

"Do you really care so little about our marriage?" he asked finally in a deceptively quiet voice.

"Do you really care so little about what I want, about the development of my career?"

Neil felt like saying "The hell with your career." But he didn't. They'd said more than enough already—much more, and there would be no going back.

With difficulty he kept his temper in check. Distance, he thought steadfastly. A few hours, a few days. Maybe, given time and perspective, they would be able to deal with this problem rationally. Right now, neither was giving an inch or was in the mood to negotiate at all. "That's your final word?" His tone was icy as he asked. "You're taking the case over us?"

Agitatedly she raked a hand through her hair and tried one last time to reason with him. "Neil, I became a lawyer because I wanted to make a more perfect world...to right injustices, to give representation to those who had none."

"I'm not asking you to give up the law. Just this case. For me. For us." Why couldn't she see that? he wondered. Didn't she care? Or was it just that he didn't mean as much to her, they didn't mean as much to her, as her precious career? Suddenly it all fell into place for him. "You knew about this the night we began trying to make a baby, didn't you? That's what that talk about the frustrations you were feeling professionally was about?"

"Yes." Her face was strained, parchment-white. Her hands were balled tightly into fists at her sides.

Neil felt that he was facing a stranger, a woman he didn't know, maybe had never really known. For the second time that evening, she followed him toward the door. Her hand circled his arm. He shrugged it off, but she held tight. He turned to face her. She swallowed hard at his impatient glare. Never before in their relationship had he felt he had to leave her. Until now. She took a deep, tear-choked breath. "Where are you going? Where can I reach you?"

"At the hospital."

"You've got a patient?" she seemed hopeful that that was it.

He found brief retaliatory satisfaction in quashing her misconception. "No. I'm off tonight." With a decided economy of motion, he extricated his elbow from her staying hold. "I've got to get some sleep."

She stepped back. Hurt radiated from her wide-set eyes. He ignored it. At the moment he didn't want to be near her. He didn't trust himself, or his temper, and the exhaustion—emotional, mental and physical—that was tearing at him just made everything worse. He strode forward, reaching the door alone and in silence this time. He shut the door behind him on distressed quiet.

Later, alone in his office at the hospital, he was able to review their situation more pragmatically. Her taking the malpractice case was not the end of their togetherness, as he had rashly first assumed. It couldn't be. Not when they loved each other as much as he knew they did.

He and Ellie had met three years previously at a dedication ceremony for a charity-sponsored children's camp. She had been there to represent the local professional women's organization. Neil had been there simply as a supporter of what he saw as a very worthy cause.

The chemistry between them had been immediate, powerful. He'd started seeing her the same night. Three months later they'd been lovers, soul mates. Almost a year to the day they'd met, they'd been married. Ellie hadn't wanted anything elaborate and neither had he. They'd eloped quietly, returned to Joplin after a two-week honeymoon and settled down. They'd bought a house, furnished it, begun trying to have a baby. They'd both wanted a family, and already in their thirties, had been aware that the time to do it was then.

Up until Ellie had taken the malpractice case, their life together had possessed an almost celestial happiness. Sure, there had been schedule conflicts occasionally. Both were busy, committed to their careers. But they were also committed to each other. Or they had been. Had that changed? Was Ellie signaling an increased devotion to her work? Or was this a fluke, something that would never happen again? Neil found himself hoping for the latter. Their lives were challenging enough as it was without unnecessarily adding controversy and stress. He hoped Ellie would realize that, too. And soon. In the meantime...in the meantime he'd better keep his distance. He was still angry and disbelieving and disappointed enough in her actions to want to lash out. Until he could trust his temper, she'd be better off seeing little of him. Who knew? Maybe their brief physical estrangement would work to the advantage of them both. Give them time to cool off and assess what and where their priorities were.

"ELLIE, DARLING, I hate to bother you at work. But I've been hearing some rumors. Is there anything wrong? Are you ill?" Viv Jensen asked.

Ellie looked up to see her mother standing in the outer office. It was just past noon and her secretary was out to lunch. Ellie had opted to stay and answer the phones and simultaneously finish up some paperwork.

"No, Mom, I'm not ill." Ellie stood up, receiving the light kiss her mother pressed on her cheek. Perfectly attired and coiffed, her mother was as strikingly beautiful at fifty-two as she had been in her youth. "How are things at Temporary Solution?" Ellie asked, trying for some degree of normalcy. Had her mother heard about the fight she'd had with Neil? Ellie wondered. The resulting and unprecedented semiestrangement between them? And if so, how? Ellie had told no one they'd been quarreling.

"That's fine, as always. It's your health I'm worried about. Darling, one of my employees who's been working at the hospital says you have been seen coming and going from Dr. Raynor's office countless times in the past month or so. She didn't want to mention it at first. But she saw you at the dry cleaners last evening, and she said you looked so pale...."

Ellie shut her eyes, removed her glasses and rubbed her suddenly pounding temples. This was a discussion she'd been very much hoping to avoid.

"Is something wrong?" Viv persisted when no explanation was immediately forthcoming.

"Not in the way you think." Ellie bit her lip. With herself and Neil, the answer was yes; their relationship was suffering immensely after the quarrel. Three days had passed since he'd walked out on her. Since then he'd been home to eat and sleep and not much else. He'd said very little to her, but it was very clear from the chilly but potent looks he often cast her way that he expected her to give in on this issue. He expected her to drop the lawsuit. Getting back to her mother's inquiry, Ellie continued calmly, "I've been taking fertility pills, Mom."

Viv's mouth gaped. "You're not serious!"

Ellie squared her shoulders and lifted her chin. She met her mother's gaze directly, with no apology. "Sit down, Mom, and I'll explain." Ellie waited until Viv had complied before continuing. "I didn't mention this before because I didn't want to worry you, but my menstrual cycle hasn't been exactly normal since college. The doctors weren't sure why. The irregularity and the fact I didn't appear to be ovulating could have been due to stress or other emotional factors. I was very honest with Neil before we were married. I told him there was the possibility I might never be able to conceive a child."

"How did he take the news?" Viv looked ashen.

"He couldn't have been more supportive or understanding," Ellie recalled with tender affection. "And like any good doctor, he also took prompt medical action. He lined up an appointment for me with the leading infertility expert in the area, the gynecologist and obstetrician I'm seeing now, Dr. Jim Raynor. At my insistence before we married, I had a battery of tests. It was discovered that there was no physical reason why I couldn't bear a child. So, soon after we got married, I began taking a drug called clomiphene citrate. To make a long story short, there were side effects, and it didn't work. Then we began to consider a stronger fertility drug like menotropins to help the maturation of eggs in the ovary."

"And Neil agreed to this?"

"He and Dr. Raynor suggested it simultaneously," Ellie said crisply, pushing back her desk chair and getting up to pace the small carpeted area behind her desk.

"But what about the possibility of multiple births? Ellie, I know the chances for a quintuplet's survival are slim. I've read in the paper countless times about parents losing not just one of their newborns from a multiple birth, but—"

My initial fears exactly, Ellie thought. But Neil had successfully soothed her about that much. "If a woman on the fertility drug is being properly monitored, it won't happen." Ellie went on to explain exactly how that worked, in very scientific terms. "They've watched me very carefully, Mom. Dr. Raynor has examined me every twenty-four to thirty-six hours. He's also taken constant blood tests to monitor my estrogen level, both while I was taking the medicine and after I stopped."

Viv leaned back until her spine touched the back of the chair. Her facial features relaxed. "And thus far everything has been just fine, you've been monitored nearly every day?"

"Yes," Ellie replied. Except for the one day she'd missed her exam, and that had been her fault. She had since determined never to let it happen again. Fortunately, everything had been fine when Ellie went in to see Jim, but the administration of a fertility drug such as menotropins was a complicated process that required constant monitoring. If, for instance, her ovaries had been abnormally enlarged when she had gone in, a different procedure would have been followed. The second part of the drug therapy, a shot of HCG, would not have been administered at that time, thereby reducing chances of development of the hyperstimulation syndrome. The drug company that manufactures menotropins warned that unless both patient and physician were willing to devote considerable time to the endeavor and conduct the necessary lab studies, the drug should not be used. Ellie had committed to do that; she would have to keep her promise. Her health, and that of any child she and Neil might conceive, depended on her continuing cooperation.

"Well, I don't know if it's a good idea," her mother maintained stubbornly. Viv was modern in every other respect, but she had never moved forward with the medical profession in either technology or thinking—a fact Neil bore stoically and never argued, no matter how much Viv impishly baited him upon occasion, because for every allegedly synthetic remedy Neil had, her mother had a natural one. Indeed, Viv took a handful of vitamins every day to maintain her youthfulness, a habit Ellie and Neil both frowned on. "When will you know if it worked?"

"I'm not sure. Probably another week or two, I guess," Ellie said evasively. Actually, she already had an appointment with Dr. Raynor on Friday morning. But she didn't know when they would be getting the tests back and she didn't want her mother getting all excited. Especially if, as Ellie half suspected, the attempts to impregnate her hadn't worked.

"What if they don't work? Will you continue on this way, every cycle, until you do conceive?"

The sixty-four-thousand-dollar question, Ellie thought. "I don't know, Mom. I may not continue the treatments. Going in to be checked every twenty-four hours is a pain." And with Neil not even speaking to her...well, it had put a damper on the idea of having a child. Ellie still wanted a baby very much. She wanted Neil's child. But she was also realistic enough to know that if the situation between them continued as angrily as it had, there was a good possibility it might never happen.

Furthermore, if this was truly the way it was going to be, with Neil walking out the door whenever they had a disagreement, never to return, or at least not until he was good and ready to do so, she wasn't sure she wanted to stay married to him. The uncertainty was too unsettling. She didn't want a marriage that worked only as long as she didn't rock the boat or speak her mind. She wanted a commitment that was everlasting, that would last through hard times and good times, sickness and health, fertility and infertility. It didn't look as if Neil felt the same. And that worried her. Because, if he could walk out that easily and not come home, then maybe, just maybe, he didn't love her after all. At least not enough. About that fact she was certain. She wouldn't bring a child into an unstable relationship. She knew firsthand how traumatic divorce or the experience of living with perpetually battling parents was on a child. She wouldn't subject her own child to that. Better to be a single mother or, she thought sadly, to forgo the experience of motherhood.

"What about Neil?" her mother asked. "Are they sure the problem isn't his, too?"

Again, Ellie forced herself to keep up the cheerful, carefree facade. "He's fine, Mom."

She saw that her mother was still worried. Persuasively, she continued, "Menotropins is my last hope, Mom. Not to worry. Neil's very enthusiastic. He's used the drug on his own patients and always with good results."

Viv nodded. "What does Neil want you to do if the initial results are not positive?"

Ellie shrugged, reflecting as she looked out on the busy street beyond. "At the moment, we're taking it one day at a time." Or even one hour at a time. However long Neil would stay angry with her.

Realistically, as much as she'd tried to convince herself otherwise, she'd known in her heart from the moment she'd heard about the case that he would be angry with her for taking it. She hadn't bargained on his staying furious for more than a day. But he had. And, tragically, it was beginning to look more and more as though it might be a permanent move on his part. Was he thinking of divorcing her? And if not, even if he came back to her now, what security was that for her, living in the fear that he would become angry with her and walk out again? Suppose they did work their problems out temporarily. Suppose he accepted her taking this one malpractice case. What would happen the next time she took a case he disapproved of? What would happen if the malpractice insurance company stubbornly refused to settle out of court and insisted on a court trial? What then? Even if Neil came back to her, would he leave again every time he got really angry from now on? Simply not speak to her? And how could she stand it? Heaven knew she had hardly been able to function for the past few days, with him constantly on her mind. And yet, by the same token, she'd been almost afraid to phone him, afraid to reach out for fear of being rejected again. So she'd done nothing. And he'd done nothing. And the stalemate between them had continued unbearably.

With effort Ellie pushed her nightmarish thoughts aside, refusing to let herself think about Neil anymore for fear she would cry. She turned back to her mother, but her attempt to put on a breezy face failed. Her mother studied her momentarily, then came to her own conclusions. "It's the Middleton lawsuit that's getting you down, isn't it?"

Ellie nodded, glad finally to be able to talk to someone. She'd been so lonely the past few days. "Neil doesn't think I should have taken it." She rearranged items on her desk.

"It's your career!"

"He understands that." Ellie put her electric pencil sharpener down with a thump.

Viv's silvery-blond brows rose questioningly. "Does he know how essential this case is for you, that it's just the breakthrough you've been working for? My goodness, Ellie, think of it, no more nonstop divorce and custody cases or small-claims court. Winning this will really put your career in high gear."

Just at the time I was getting ready to settle down and have a child. Was that conflict at the root of Neil's anxiety? she wondered. Or was it something more that was bothering him, something deeper? Viv chatted on about Ellie's sure legal victory, and Ellie's mouth curved at her mother's abundant enthusiasm. "Aren't you getting just a little ahead of yourself, Mom?"

"I don't think so. Of course you'll win!" Viv stood and gave Ellie a second hug. She paused a moment, searching her daughter's face and reflecting softly, "I'm so proud of you. You've done for yourself what I should have done for myself long ago."

"Mother, you own your business. That's nothing to scoff at, especially when one considers that except for a brief stint in secretarial school," which Viv had started three years after her father had left them, "you had no formal business education." Before that Viv had worked as a waitress and later as a department store salesperson to pay the rent.

"My training was mostly on-the-job," Viv admitted. "But Ellie, what I admire most about you is your independence, your spunk. I got where I was because I was boxed into a corner and had no other recourse. You've known from the very beginning that you had to make your own way, and you did. Without help from anyone!''

Viv hadn't been blessed with much help, either, Ellie thought. Her mother had raised her single-handedly from the time she was seven.

"There's no difference between us, Mom. I just had a little head start, knowing from the time Dad walked out that it would be up to me to support myself. And I hope, someday, my children.''

"If only all women were so levelheaded,'' Viv said, "the Equal Rights Amendment would have passed!''

Ellie smiled, not wanting to talk about the lawsuit, fertility pills or career demands any longer. Linking arms with her mother, she said, "Can I buy you lunch? It's been so long since we talked.'' Since the fight with Neil, she'd felt very abandoned and alone, in need of nurturing.

"What about the office?'' Viv glanced around, reminding Ellie that she'd always been one to take care of business first. But then, as both women knew, she'd had no choice.

"My secretary will be back any minute,'' Ellie said. As if to echo her, a door slammed in the background. Hazel's voice called in, to let Ellie know it was her turn to take off for a noon respite.

Viv consulted her watch with anticipation as Ellie grabbed her purse. Arm in arm they left the office.

Chapter Three

Ellie was kneeling before the refrigerator, putting fresh fruit and vegetables in the produce bins when Neil sailed into the house early Saturday afternoon. She'd already decided that she wasn't going to let anything he said or did at that point negate what had happened earlier in the week. He was going to have to account for and rescind his behavior before she'd call a truce. To do otherwise would be to chance it happening again. But her decision to stay angry with him, at least for a little while longer, was a resolution that proved very hard to keep when she saw him.

"I heard," he said simply, joyfully. His gaze drifted downward to her abdomen, lingered happily before moving back up to her face.

Ellie felt color flood her cheeks in response. But soon dampening her silent exaltation celebrating her pregnancy was the knowledge of what they had been through and were still going through emotionally. The news of her conception didn't block out all the heartache Neil had caused her, first by walking out on her in the heat of their first major argument and sleeping at the hospital that night, and then by his coolness since, his either-take-the-lawsuit-or-me attitude.

"How did you find out?" she said at last. "Who told you?"

"Jim Raynor." Neil answered, sedately matching his tone to her careful one. "He said you walked out of his office on cloud nine, alternating between laughter and happy tears."

"I was excited," she admitted, pausing for a moment simply

to bask in the happiness she had felt then and felt now. She wanted this baby fiercely.

Neil nodded, his eyes darkening subtly as he appraised her. "I'm excited, too." He took a deep breath. His eyes narrowed as his tone dropped another notch. "I'm less happy about the way I found out about it. When were you going to tell me?" He seemed to be waiting for an explanation. When none was immediately forthcoming, he strode across the kitchen, halting just short of her. Leaning up against the counter, he crossed his arms against his chest.

The truth was that Ellie hadn't known what to say or how to begin to tell him, not with them still manning their "battle stations." She'd been trying to figure out how to proceed with the news when he came into the house. Averting his steady gaze, she continued putting apples and oranges into the bin. "I figured I had plenty of time. Eight and a half months, to be exact. I'm due January first."

A long moment passed in which neither moved. "I see," he said finally. There was another silence, this one emptier than the last. Was he waiting for her to apologize? Ellie wondered, still slightly miffed with him. Or was he still angry with her for taking the Middleton case? She wasn't sure. She only knew that for the first time in their married life they were uncomfortable being with each other, at a loss as to what to say or do. Ellie opened her mouth to speak, then closed it again. She didn't want to talk about the case—yet everything she could think of to say would lead indirectly, eventually, to that very subject. Neil seemed similarly at a loss: happy yet perplexed, wary, unwilling to hurt her any more; yet no less committed to his original stance. They seemed to be at some kind of an impasse or stalemate, Ellie noted unhappily, watching as he reached behind him into the cupboard for a glass and, turning on the faucet, poured himself some water.

Ellie got to her feet, reluctantly taking the hand he stretched out to help her. She dusted off the seat of her old jeans, still not looking at him. Ironically, she wished the news of the baby had come later, after they'd worked out their problems. Worse, her emotions were rocketing up and down like shooting stars. Hormones? she wondered. Or just the craziness after an exceptionally rough week? She only knew that one moment she felt like hugging Neil, begging his forgiveness, the next, pushing him away and going off on her own again.

Her mouth twisted into a cryptic moue, as she related verbally what was bothering her most. "Funny, isn't it, that now that you know I'm pregnant, you've decided to afford me some courtesy and actually speak to me cordially, seek me out." *Had he done that earlier...* she thought, her resentment of his handling of their predicament beginning to grow again. Was this what the rest of their married life was going to be like?

He bit off a quick retort, saying finally, with a carefulness that set her teeth on edge, "I admit I was angry. Considering the way you handled things, I had good reason."

She cocked her head toward him over one shoulder, but said nothing. Yes, there were reasons for his anger, but there were also reasons for her hurt. He'd been glacial to her this past week. So much so that she'd half expected him to be as uninterested in the baby as he had been in her lately. Finding that he wasn't, that he was happy about the baby and somewhat more inclined to try to get along with her now, and not a moment sooner, made her feel even more abandoned than she already had felt.

Neil put down his glass of water on the counter behind him. He closed the distance between them languidly, taking her resisting body into his arms. He held her loosely. His voice was warm, coaxing, when he spoke. "Look, I know I've behaved very badly the past few days. I'll be the first to admit it and I'm sorry. But this trouble between us was the first major fight we've had in the three years we've known each other. This or something like it would have happened sooner or later; it was to be expected."

Not to Ellie it wasn't. The whole traumatic five days terrified her, like a specter from her past. She was petrified at the thought of being abandoned again, as she had been by her father years ago. Dimly she was aware that she was strung up as tightly as a bow.

He released her gently when, as moments passed, she became no less tense. His voice was gentle as he said, "I came home to remind you that the county medical auxiliary dinner dance is this evening. I realize, under the circumstances, it might be difficult for you to attend—''

Did he think she was ashamed of what she was doing for the Middletons? "Not at all." Her tone was calm.

A peculiar expression crossed his face. Again, he said nothing. "Fine. Then I'll be back to change and pick you up around seven." Ellie realized she'd just boxed herself into a corner. In an effort to hide her unease about the evening's festivities, she asked with only mild curiosity, "Where are you going now?"

"Back to the hospital." His gaze raked her up and down. To her inner disappointment, there was no trace of his previous depth of affection, just cool consideration, a physician's attempt to assess visually that she was physically all right. "If you need me, I'll be in my office there. I have some notes I want to go over. Some videotapes to watch."

"Oh."

He turned toward the door but stopped in mid-path, then pivoted and came back toward her. Before she could do more than take in a breath, his arms wrapped around her in a giant bear hug. His mouth brushed against the top of her hair in a brief yet affectionate kiss. He squeezed her again. "I really am glad about the baby, Ellie. Very glad." He released her, stepped back slightly. Magically, unexpectedly, it was as if the hug alone had restored his confidence—in her, in himself, in them as a couple. "We'll talk tonight." His eyes were full of promise.

He left her on that optimistic note.

NEIL DROVE SLOWLY BACK to the hospital, his thoughts in disarray. At the end of their time together, he'd put on a cheerful facade for her sake. But inwardly he was just as confused and—damn it, yes—as moody as she was. How had it happened, he wondered, that he and Ellie had let a simple argument get so far out of hand? Was it stress, overwork, on both their parts? Just the issue of malpractice alone, their polar views, keeping them apart? Or was it more than that? Now it seemed that they could barely talk to each other. She was tense, overemotional, mistrustful. Of course, she had an excuse for her mercurialness. Part of her current moodiness could be blamed on her pregnancy, the resulting hormonal changes in her body, the complex physical changes already taking place within her. But the rest of her unhappiness was all his fault. He had to face it once and for all. The truth was he'd behaved like a self-centered jerk. The fact that she'd made him angry was no excuse. He should have stayed with her that first night they'd fought, as she'd asked. He should have worked out their problems then. But he hadn't. And now...now the emotional climate between them was frigid, uneasy, defensive. He couldn't blame her for not welcoming him back with open arms. And yet he wanted to change her attitude toward him more than he'd ever wanted anything in his life.

The facts were these: They had a baby on the way, a baby they both wanted. She still had her malpractice case to get through. He might not like it, but he could try to leave her alone about it and avoid the subject, try his damnedest not to give her even the slightest chance to bring it up. Added to that, their marriage was in moderate need of repair.

So where did he start? With serious discussions?

Or with fun? Or maybe just a simple reminder of how nice and easy it used to be between them, before all this business with the Middletons came up. Maybe what they did need was a night out. A medical auxiliary dance wasn't exactly apart from their problems. On the contrary, it was like confronting them head-on. But maybe that, too, was what they needed. A little dose of reality, of what it felt like for a doctor's wife to handle a malpractice case by day and then head off into the medical social whirl by night. Maybe if Ellie were exposed to that, she'd begin to see what he was talking about when he told her it was going to be difficult for her on personal terms. And a little dancing, a nice band, a chance to hold Ellie in his arms wouldn't hurt, either. Just holding her those few moments in the kitchen had helped.

Once the first few awkward hours were bridged, well, it would all be downhill from there. They could go home, talk, make love. He'd take it one step further and arrange to have all of Sunday off. It wouldn't be easy, but with work they could get their relationship on solid ground again.

And, strange as it was, he had the baby to thank for putting everything into perspective for him again. Nothing mattered to Neil but his wife and his child, taking care of them, making them happy, making them—the three of them—a solid family unit. He sensed that in her heart Ellie felt the same. With time they could and would work it out.

So where do I start?

Maybe by just acting normally, Neil decided, stopping the car at a traffic light. He needed to go on as if nothing had ever happened to upset the equilibrium between them. His nonchalance might mystify her at first, but after that, it was bound to be catching. Once Ellie's behavior was also back to normal, they could go from there. That decided, he smiled. His spirits lifted optimistically. By the time he got to the hospital, he was whistling, thinking of all the future held, for Ellie, their baby and himself. With love and a little luck they'd manage to build a solid family.

A THOUSAND TIMES that afternoon Ellie regretted her acceptance of his invitation. She should have taken the out he'd given her. But why? So people would think she was a coward? She wasn't ashamed of what she'd done. Maybe it was time the whole medical community of Joplin knew that.

Naturally, he was late, breezing in at five minutes before seven, with an apology about losing track of the time. Ellie, ready to go except for slipping on her dress, stood at the top of the stairs and watched as he threw off his sport coat and raced up the stairs simultaneously. Striding into the bedroom with barely a look at her, he discarded his tie, shirt, socks and shoes. Every item landed exactly where he was at the moment it was removed. "How was your day?" he shouted over his shoulder as he strode buck-naked into the bathroom to turn on the shower.

Seconds later, steamy water poured from the open door.

"My day was fine." In reality, Ellie had been bored stiff. She'd tried to concentrate on the Middleton case, only to have her mind go back to the scene earlier with him, the heartfelt hug he'd given her, the light kiss. Regardless of all the problems they'd recently encountered, he had been happy. Ellie took advantage of his absence to slip off her robe and step into her evening dress.

"Only fine?" With a grin he poked his head around the door, watching as she dabbed Obsession, her favorite scent, behind her ears, on her wrists, at the pressure points on her throat.

"Actually, it was great. Busy," she fibbed, bantering back. "I just didn't want to outdo you." Inwardly she wished the routine of getting ready for an evening out didn't seem so intimate, so normal. Just being with him so easily again had made her want to forget everything and just make love, just go forward as if nothing had ever happened to spoil the tranquil harbor of their marriage.

His smile widened. He shut the glass shower door. Though the steam was rising all around him, she could see him scrubbing away. "I called my folks!" he shouted above the pelting noises of the shower. "They're ecstatic! And my sister's happy, too! She's delighted she's finally going to be an aunt!"

The water was turned off. Neil stepped out of the shower, wrapped a wide bath towel around his waist and stepped up to the sink. He ran the palm of his hand across his beard, grimaced slightly. "I think I need a shave." Without further comment, he smeared lather on his face and began removing the five-o'clock shadow with sure, easy strokes. Lifting his chin to reach better the underside of his jaw with the razor blade, he asked, "What about you, Ellie? What did your mom say?"

Ellie flushed. "I...haven't called her yet."

He looked at her askance, then rinsed his face and patted it dry with a hand towel before briskly slapping on after-shave. "Why not?" Quickly he strode past Ellie, dropped the towel and stepped into skimpy black briefs. Ellie turned her head slightly, trying not to notice how virile he looked—all bronzed skin aglow from the heat of the shower and whorls of dark masculine hair that feathered his arms, chest and legs.

"She wasn't happy about me being on fertility pills."

"But she'd be happy about this." Neil's eyes narrowed slightly.

Ellie floundered. It was impossible to explain the sudden shyness she felt. She only knew that she was in an extremely emotional and vulnerable mood. She didn't want to risk breaking down into happy or anxious tears.

Neil's eyes were sympathetic, gentle. "I'll call for you. The news is already all over the hospital. We'd better tell her before someone else does." He was quiet, first dialing, then listening for his mother-in-law's voice. "Viv, hi? Great news for you... *Grandma*. Yep, that sure is what you're about to be.... Me, too." He handed the phone to Ellie several minutes later, mouthing, "I think she may be crying."

Oh mercy, Ellie thought. She hoped Viv would get a grip on herself before she started crying, too.

By the time Ellie got off the phone, her eyes were indeed misty. Ignoring Neil's steady assessment, she moved swiftly to the vanity in the master bathroom to get a tissue. Delicately she dabbed at the mascara that was threatening to smear. Neil was standing next to the bureau, still dressing, when Ellie walked back into the bedroom. She was preparing to go downstairs when he swore. "Give me a hand with these cuffs?" he asked.

Ellie nodded, after a barely perceptible hesitation. It was getting harder and harder to ignore the sensual feelings stirring within her. She walked over, stood fastening the sterling silver cuff links through the starched white cotton cuffs. Miraculously, to her surprise and wonder, as seconds drew out, it was almost as if the tense week between them had never been. His after-shave, brisk and woodsy, brought back a fire storm of memories, all of them good. His black trousers emphasized the spareness of his hips and his taut abdomen. The pleated white dress shirt made him look elegant and refined, like the country-club member he had grown up to be.

He was quiet as she finished the second cuff. "One more favor?" he asked, moving away from her to grab his black bow tie. With one hand he finished the last of his buttons and laced the tie around his neck. "Straighten this—" he gestured toward the bow he was making "—when I'm finished?"

"All right." *Work through your problems first,* she admonished herself sternly, silently. *Kiss and make up later.* But before they could do either, they had to attend the dinner dance.

He slipped into his jacket before coming back to stand in front of her. As always, Neil had managed to get the tie correctly put together but not quite centered. Even with her high heels, Ellie had to stand on tiptoe. He lifted one palm behind her to rest against her waist and steady her as she finished. Stepping back, she looked him up and down with a critical eye, nodding. "That should about do it."

His appreciation of her efforts was reflected in his gentle regard. "We're going to be late," she cautioned, grabbing her wrap and her purse.

The dinner dance was proceeding nicely when they arrived. Doctors from Joplin's three hospitals were in attendance, as well as members from the medical community county-wide. As at previous auxiliary events, Ellie and Neil greeted many old friends and caught up on everyone's news. To Ellie's surprise and relief, not one person mentioned her handling of the suit against Memorial Hospital. Nor did Neil bring the subject up. As Neil had told her earlier, everyone at the Medical Center where he worked seemed to have heard about Ellie's pregnancy via the grapevine. Together they accepted congratulations and advice, through every course of the meal.

"I figured the only way to get away from all the discussion was to start circling the dance floor," Neil teased several hours later.

"How gallant," Ellie murmured wryly against his shoulder.

"Not really." He gave her a direct, very sensual look. "As you well know, I'll take any excuse offered to be able to hold you in my arms. And especially tonight." They stared at each other a long time.

"Because of the baby?" she whispered finally.

He nodded, his look turning solemn. "And the fact that I love you very much."

Hope rose within her that everything would work out after all. The anger she'd built up against him was crumbling bit by bit, leaving her aching and far too vulnerable to his quiet, assessing gaze. When the song ended, Neil left her only long enough to approach the bandstand. She understood why when the next song began.

"Recognize the tune?" Neil asked as the jazz band played the sexy Count Basie notes and chords.

Ellie couldn't quite suppress an involuntary smile or her musical expertise. "It's 'Li'l Darlin'.'"

"Take me farther down memory lane," Neil urged quietly. He shifted closer, unnecessarily alerting her to the corded masculinity of his long limbs. She closed her eyes briefly, hoping that would dull the sensations flooding her brain. It only intensified his effect on her. His hands on her bare back held her close. She was wearing a glittery white-knit dress that clung in all the right places and fell to midcalf. The bodice edges were held together in back by a single cloth-covered button at the nape of her neck. The V neck perfectly outlined her breasts. Judging by the attentive looks he'd been doling out generously all evening, Ellie thought that he liked the way she looked in the gown. She tried to tell herself it didn't matter anymore, that they were finished, but it didn't work. She was still drawn to him immeasurably.

"Remember the first time we heard the song?" Neil asked.

Ellie nodded, content for the moment to let herself float around the dance floor, locked in his sensual hold. "It was played the night of our first official date, at the concert given by the Southwest Missouri State University jazz band." Her words were muffled against his shoulder.

"I never hear it without thinking of you."

The truth was that the song always brought a smile to her face, too. Glancing up at him, she was disconcerted because he kept wanting to look directly into her eyes. *Admit it*, she thought. *You still love the man.* She also loved the sexy laid-back foxtrot and Neil's superb skill on the dance floor. He always knew just how to hold her, not too tight, not too loosely. He could look so proper...and the feel of him moving just inches away to the same rhythmic beat was so erotic.

"You know what I'd like to do after this?" he whispered, not waiting for her to reply. "Go home. Put some records on the stereo, turn the lights down low." He grinned teasingly, giving her an affectionate squeeze. "Heat you up some nice warm milk...."

"Very funny." But she couldn't deny his romantic attitude was becoming contagious. She wanted to be alone with him, too.

He shrugged, deciding with exaggerated finality, "I suppose you could have a tiny glass of wine."

"Thank you, Doctor," Ellie returned in a prim, censuring tone.

Neil responded by holding her closer, his hand warmly clasping hers.

It was only when the band took a break that Neil and Ellie rejoined their group. Wanting to freshen up, Ellie excused herself and headed for the powder room.

And it was when she was returning to join Neil that she saw the senior physician named in the malpractice suit. Up until that point, Ellie had been able to regard the primary defendant, aside from the hospital, with professional distance, verifying medical facts by telephone, listening to the tapes of the radio contact made with the intern in the ambulance. But seeing the senior physician in a social setting, with his wife at his side, suddenly brought home to her what she was doing in more personal, human terms. Whether or not Dr. Talbot and Neil worked at the same hospital seemed a moot point. She was suing one of Neil's colleagues, a man who moved in the same professional and social circles as they did. It wouldn't be easy to avoid him. Nor could she blame the Talbots if they went out of their way to be unpleasant to her.

Glancing up and seeing Ellie there, Dr. Talbot met and held her gaze. He was of medium height, with sparse, neatly combed white hair—a very distinguished-looking man. He looked as if he were feeling a great deal of stress, as did his wife. Ellie knew from an introduction several years previously, at a similar medical society function, that the couple had several children, all of whom were married, with children of their own. He was nearing sixty, she guessed. And as far as she knew, this one mistake was the only error on an otherwise spotless record of community service.

Ellie realized then why Neil was so upset with her. And for the first time she considered the possibility that she had made a huge mistake. Getting a grip on herself, she forced herself to think only in professional terms once again, not as Neil's wife, but only as an attorney. The fact remained that Dr. Talbot had made a mistake in judgment that had nearly cost Audrey Middleton her life. It was a simple error, one that could have been avoided if only proper attention had been paid to the allergies of the patient before the medication had been prescribed. Ellie wasn't out to destroy the man, only to arrange related financial relief for the young couple. And had the hospital or Dr. Talbot acted more responsibly in the first place, by reporting the error to the insurance company themselves, even that step wouldn't have been necessary. But they hadn't. And the Middletons had placed the conflict in her capable hands. She had to continue with the lawsuit. But for the first time Ellie realized how difficult it was going to be for her and for Neil. Not just that evening, but for months and years to come. Would he be able to stand the pressure? she wondered. Would she?

Refusing to acknowledge her, the Talbots moved away. Ellie sagged with relief, and it was only then that she realized just how tense she had been during the few moments of wordless confrontation. She decided that she had endured more than enough socializing for one night. She fully intended to quit while she was still in one piece.

With a forced languor that was in direct contrast to the nausea abruptly churning in her stomach, she located Neil and set about joining him. He was standing at the bar talking to Jim Raynor and several other physicians, male and female, all of them her friends. Her hand lightly touched his arm and she drew him aside. "Neil, can we go home now?"

"What's the matter?" His eyes searched her evasive ones.

Everything, she thought. "I'm not feeling well." Ellie took a tremulous breath.

He was suddenly all action. "I'll get your wrap."

Twenty minutes later they were home again. Blessedly, Neil had asked no questions on the journey; instead, had concentrated on the driving while Ellie huddled miserably in her bucket seat.

"Are you sick, nauseated?" Neil asked specifically, once they were home and he was walking around, methodically turning on lights.

"Yes...no." Ellie sat down on the couch. She wanted to go to bed, but she knew she wouldn't sleep. "It's not morning sickness."

"Something someone said?" His tone was crisp, angry—but not at her.

"Or didn't say." Ellie glanced up. "I saw Dr. Talbot and his wife this evening. Neither of them spoke to me."

"It didn't occur to you they'd attend the function?" Neil's tone was harsh, impatient.

Ellie shook her head.

Neil remained silent. After a moment, he walked over to pour himself a drink.

Her hands tightened into fists as she finally found the courage to voice her worst fears, fears that had been haunting her all day, undermining her happiness about the baby. "Neil, what would have happened if I hadn't been pregnant? Would we ever have mended the rift between us?"

Again, Neil was silent for a long time, as if that was a question he was asking himself and, unhappily, had no real answers for. Finally he expelled a breath and said calmly, "Ellie, we love each other. Regardless of everything else, that much hasn't changed. You're going to have a baby. Of course we would have worked it out." He sat down next to her and took her hands, rubbing them between both of his, as if to warm them. The effort failed dismally; her skin remained cold as ice. "It might have taken a little longer," he said finally, as if needing to convince himself as much as her. "But we would have worked it out."

"How much longer?" Ellie asked. She wanted reassurances that the lawsuit didn't matter. That, he couldn't give.

"I don't know." Neil shrugged. "Maybe until the malpractice business had come to an end. I just don't know. I'm not very good with what-if's, Ellie. I can only deal with what is. And the fact is, you're going to have a baby. My baby."

My baby, she thought, not *our* baby, but his.

Neil continued distractedly, "So, no matter what happens, we have to work this out." He stared off into the distance, then took a calming swallow of bourbon.

"What if you don't get the position?" Ellie turned toward him slightly, her thigh brushing his.

There was another silence. Again he seemed almost to have to force himself to respond in a positive manner. With effort he smiled. "Then there's always next time," he said firmly. Yet even as he spoke, he looked decidedly uncomfortable. As if he didn't want to face the prospect of his losing that honor any more than she did.

Ellie removed her hands from his and stood restlessly. She pushed the hair from her face and fluffed the ends out, away from her neck. "I know what you're thinking, that all our problems would end if I'd just resign now, but I can't drop the Middleton case, Neil. It's too important to me professionally. My whole reputation is at stake."

For just as there was pressure in Neil's professional arena, so was there pressure in hers. Her peers would be watching to see if she were wife first, or attorney. She couldn't afford to let her personal feelings get in the way of her success—not without damaging her reputation and her financial future.

"I've accepted that." He stood. His jacket was open. He placed his hands in his pockets, jingling his keys.

Had he? Or was he just saying that because they were expecting a child together now? She knew he desired her, even loved her. But was it enough? Were they going to be able to manage for the long haul, or were they going to end up like so many others she had seen and, yes, even represented professionally, facing divorce, irreconcilable differences? She didn't want to bring a child into that kind of upheaval.

Feeling pressured, she moved to step past him. His arm shot out in front of her, halting her pace. His other came up to hold her. She turned and collided with him head-on.

"Don't walk away from me, Ellie," he said softly. "Don't put up any more barriers between us than there already have been this week." His hand was suddenly on the bare skin of her back.

What happened next was swift, instantaneous and, later she was to think, unavoidable. At the electric contact of skin against skin, his eyes darkened with need too long suppressed, and yearning. She knew how he felt; each and every emotion was echoed a thousand times in her soul. She had time for a quick intake of breath, the slightest shiver of anticipation, and then he was whispering her name reverently, lovingly, his mouth lowering, searching out hers. It was a gentle kiss, tender and seeking, persuasive and coaxing. She yearned to give in to everything he asked of her, yet even as she leaned into his embrace, her breasts brushing against the hard, indomitable wall of his chest, she was doubting the wisdom of her actions. For in the long run, wouldn't giving in now, so easily and unquestioningly, only complicate the difficulties in their relationship? Her hands splayed against his chest.

"Neil, no." She could hardly believe she'd said the words out loud. In the history of their time together, she'd never refused him before. She'd never felt the need, or the uncertainties haunting her now.

His head lifted in shocked surprise. There was no masking the hurt that he felt. Yet he retained a gentle grip on her. When she moved as if to resist him again, he held firm. "Ellie, we have to mend this rift between us sometime."

She shook her head, took a deep, halting breath. "Not this way. Not with something as impermanent as sex." Sex wouldn't hold them together. No. They needed a deep and abiding respect for each other's careers and the job responsibilities and opportunities that went with each. Without that first, they wouldn't have much of a marriage.

He moved back, looking as if she'd struck him. "If not for our sake, Ellie, then the baby's—"

"I don't want a marriage for the sake of a child, either." Her parents had tried that for several unhappy years. She wouldn't put her child through the same heinous turmoil.

"I guess the next question is, do you want a marriage at all, then?" Bitterness laced his voice.

She wet her lips, saying finally, "I want a partnership."

"One that won't demand anything of you that you're not prepared to give. Right?"

"Neil, please..." She was confused, tired. Tears misted her

vision. She'd thought earlier that she had wanted to discuss this. She realized she'd been wrong.

He must have realized the depth of her exhaustion, for he suppressed what he'd been about to say and instead counseled gently, "Go on to bed. I'll lock up and be up in a while. I've some reading to do."

Ellie paused, sent him an apprehensive look.

He read her reservations correctly. "I'll sleep in the spare room." Turning on his heel, he strode toward the den.

Chapter Four

Neil waited until he heard Ellie go quietly upstairs before venturing back to the kitchen. He was exhausted emotionally by the travails of the past week and yet keyed up, too, so much so that he knew sleep would be impossible.

Holding open the refrigerator door, he glanced at the contents. Normally a haphazardous shopper, prone more often than not to junk food and frozen TV dinners, Ellie had stocked the refrigerator that very morning with only wholesome, nutritious foods. That fact alone was an indication of how much she cared about their baby. And he knew from Jim Raynor that when she first heard the news, she'd been initially stunned and then ecstatic. Unfortunately, by the time Neil had arrived to share the happy tidings with her, she had turned introspective again—pleased yet guarded, wary of being hurt again. And what was worse, he knew he was responsible for the rebirth of her insecurity.

With an oath at his own shortsightedness, Neil rummaged through the refrigerator, finally deciding on a glass of juice. Walking back to the den, he settled himself in an overstuffed chair, determined to rehash their problems.

The trouble had started only when Ellie had taken the Middleton case, he decided. She'd known from the outset that he would be furious and had deliberately kept the news from him. If only she'd agreed to drop the case then, he thought woefully, or better yet, had bowed out from the beginning because of her personal conflict of interest. But she hadn't. And he'd only made matters worse, first by storming in demanding she drop it for his sake, then by storming out again. If he'd gone home that first night instead of spending it at the hospital, they might have been able to resolve the issue. He might have been able to coax or persuade her to give in, just this once, because it was a medical matter.

He hadn't even tried to discuss the matter with her again though. He'd hoped—stupidly—that his continuing coldness and disapproval would show her how deeply he'd been hurt by her disregard of his feelings. Instead, she seemed to have taken his anger as equal to desertion. And desertion wasn't something Ellie could deal with.

The real dilemma now was figuring out how to win back her trust, Neil concluded. Standing, he finished his drink in a single gulp, set the glass aside, stripped down to his briefs and turned out the light. He walked over to the sofa and stretched out on it, reaching for the afghan on its back and cushioning his head with several throw pillows. If the truth be known, now that he'd had a few days to reflect and cool down, her handling of the Middleton case was nothing more than an inconsequential nuisance. True, it still hurt that she hadn't consulted him or cared about his feelings or what happened to his career as a result of what she did with hers. But he could live with that. What he couldn't live with was the hurt he'd seen in her eyes when he had reached for her that evening. He wanted to make love with her, now more than ever. But he wanted it to be because it was what she wanted, too, and because she was carrying their child. In the meantime he could wait. And he would tell her first thing in the morning that he didn't give a damn about their jobs anymore. He only wanted what was best for them as a family. He only wanted to renew their love.

NEIL AWOKE to the soft sound of footsteps moving across the kitchen floor. He heard the refrigerator open, shut—open swiftly and shut just as quickly again. Then Ellie's low mutter, indistinguishable except for the emotion—foul-tempered self-contempt.

Morning sickness? His Ellie? With a perplexed frown on his face, Neil tossed the afghan aside and strode sleepily out to the kitchen. Ellie was leaning against the counter, her arms folded across her waist, her head tipped back. Though it was still quite early on a Sunday morning, she was dressed in linen slacks and a silk shirt. Her face was already made up, but beneath the light pink blush, Neil noticed her skin was unusually pale. "Want some eggs?" He stretched lazily, lifting his arms above his head.

She started. Immediately her right fist closed around the rope of pearls around her neck. "No—" she flushed slightly and with difficulty finished the sentence "—thanks."

"Milk? Orange juice? A saltine or piece of dry toast?"

"Maybe a Coke." Resolutely she opened the cupboard door behind her, extracted a glass from the shelf. He watched as she plunked ice into it, removed a can of Coke from the refrigerator and poured a glassful. When the liquid had settled down, she took several small, slow sips, confirming his original diagnosis. Knowing that she would perish before admitting any nausea to him, at least at that point, Neil said nothing.

He knew from her sharp, responsive glance that she knew he knew.

He couldn't help it; he grinned just a little. He was happy at any reminder of her pregnancy.

Ellie's jaw was set. Putting the drink aside, she reached for her handbag. For the first time he focused on the briefcase beside her purse. His brows narrowed. "You're working today?" Without meaning to, he let some of his resentment show. He'd thought—hoped—they could spend the whole day together, making up.

"Yes. I've got to go to the law library. I've got some articles to look up in the *Missouri Reports*." She slid her eyes away from his, refusing to meet his look head-on.

"The Middleton case?" This time he succeeded in keeping his tone mild, noncommittal.

Surprised, Ellie looked up, nodded wordlessly. "I've been so busy just doing the initial research, gathering facts that I haven't had much time for precedent-searching. I want to be prepared in case the worst does happen and it goes to trial."

She was only doing her job, he schooled himself sternly, fighting down his own dislike for anything to do with malpractice.

"You ought to hire a clerk to research for you, if only part-time."

"When I'm wealthy enough, I will."

He said nothing. He knew that her reasons for taking this case or any others had nothing to do with money, but with principle, with injustices she felt had been done. "I thought we could spend the day together." He moved toward her slowly, hoping against hope that she would somehow see her way clear to change her plans.

Her glance raked his hair-roughened form but moved away when it came to the low-slung briefs. She swallowed her unease and shook her head. "I can't."

"Ellie?"

"I'll...see you tonight." She moved around him to the door.

He resisted the urge to reach out and grab her arm only because he knew she'd resent it if he did. His hands curled around the countertop behind him. He glanced to the side, warning, "I'm only off until seven this evening. After that, I'll be taking calls."

She didn't respond visibly either way, except maybe to grow the slightest bit paler. "I don't know what time I'll be home," she said finally.

The upshot of it was that she didn't want to spend any time alone with him. And the hell of it was that after the way he had behaved earlier that week, Neil could hardly blame her. So, she needed to make him suffer a bit, he thought, as he had made her suffer. Well, he could wait it out. He would wait it out.

"Fine." He made no effort to drop his gaze.

She pivoted and stalked out of the house.

ELLIE'S HANDS were still trembling when she slid the car keys into the ignition. The problems with Neil were tearing her apart. She hadn't slept all night, only tossed and turned. And this morning it had been all she could do not to throw herself into his arms and beg his forgiveness and wish the whole outside world away. But, Ellie thought with a self-derisive twist to her mouth, that would have been pleasant only for a short time. Soon enough, their time-out would have ended and she still would have been duty bound to represent the Middletons and Neil still would have been diametrically opposed to any legal intervention in the medical profession. *Stalemate,* she thought, *again.*

Contrary to her expectations, once she arrived at the law library, the hours went quickly. Because she wished to get her mind off her own troubles, she was able to concentrate completely on her work. She took one break for lunch, another for dinner. By eight-thirty she had finished. Now the evening loomed ahead of her. She didn't want to go home, to find out Neil wasn't there. She didn't want to go home to find out he was. So, instead, she drove the short distance to her mother's town home, on the chance that Viv would be home and available for the mother-daughter talk Ellie felt she desperately needed.

"Ellie, darling, what are you doing here this time of night?" her mother asked, opening her door.

"I hope you don't mind my just dropping in." Ellie glanced behind Viv for any sign of other company. Blessedly, she was alone.

"What a thing to say! Of course I don't mind. Come in. Don't you have a jacket?"

"I forgot to take one with me this morning."

Viv's gaze narrowed assessingly. "Have you been out all day?"

"I've been at the law library, working."

"I see."

"The case is important to me."

Viv hesitated. Normally she didn't get involved in Ellie's life. She offered plenty of advice about inconsequential items, but not about her daughter's marriage. "I would have thought that with the news of the baby, you and Neil would spend the day together."

"We were out together last night. He's on call this evening." Ellie avoided discussing the hours in between.

"You look exhausted. Sit down. I'm just catching up on a little paperwork myself. Can I get you some milk?"

"To be truthful, Mom, I had three glasses from the vending machine at the law library. I'd much prefer juice."

"Not grapefruit, and that's all I have. It's too acidic. Whoops. Wait a minute. How about some tomato?"

Ellie didn't think she could stomach anything red. No reason; it just didn't appeal to her. "How about ice water, Mom, if it's not too much trouble?"

"No trouble." Viv came back minutes later, glass in hand. "Now, tell me why you came over so late. Neil is happy about the baby, isn't he? Last night he sounded simply thrilled."

"He is thrilled, Mom. But all this...it's started me thinking about my own father," she confessed in a troubled voice. Taking a deep breath, she went on. "Was he ever happy about having me, Mom? Did he ever want me, even before I was born?"

"Oh, honey." Viv's breath seemed to leave her in one quiet exhalation. She stood up and began to pace the living room restlessly. Finally she looked at Ellie honestly. "No, honey, he wasn't happy. He didn't want children."

"Then why did you get pregnant?"

Viv lifted her hands in a gesture of futility. "I hoped having a baby together would make him love me. And I thought he'd change his mind about having a child once you were born. Unfortunately, he...didn't."

"I see." Ellie felt tears well up behind her lashes. She hadn't thought about any of this for so long. But news of the baby she was expecting had brought all sorts of crazy musings to the fore. Though her parents hadn't divorced until she was seven, she could never recall any happy memories of the three of them. Nor had there been any violence or much angry shouting that she could recall, only cold impersonalism, a glacial chill, much akin to what she had felt with Neil earlier in the week. The silent disapproval, the unhappiness emanating from the man, her mother's hurt.

"And yet he stayed with us until I was almost seven," she thought aloud finally, picking up the threads of the conversation. "Why, Mom? If he felt that way, why didn't he leave right away?" He would have spared Ellie and Viv all that pain.

Viv shook her head in helpless reflection. "It was a combination of things," she said finally. "Societal pressures—he didn't want to face recrimination from his friends for leaving a wife and child. It was easier to stay married. And, too, it wasn't nearly as easy to get a divorce then. One had to have grounds, prove to the court that a real attempt had been made to save the marriage. In addition, we were both mature enough to realize that marriage was no picnic in real life, that we weren't to expect joy all the time. I guess we both deluded ourselves into thinking it would get better between us with time and that we would have more in common with an older child. I kept hoping that as you grew up and started school, he would be able to take pride in your achievements. You were such a gifted child, Ellie, so bright, always at the head of your class.''

"But none of that made an impression on my father, did it?'' Ellie had forgotten what a sense of failure she'd had then. Normally she was too busy to reflect on such matters, but this trouble with Neil had brought all the old self-derisive feelings into play again.

Sadly, Viv reflected, "No, nothing you did made an impact on your father.'' She paused, as if searching for some way to console her daughter. "Look, Ellie, I know our divorce hurt you. Divorce hurts everyone, but sometimes in the long run it's for the best. I know your father disappointed you by never being the kind of man you wanted him to be, but he was never deliberately unkind to you.''

"Just...uninterested,'' Ellie said numbly. And so cold to her emotionally. As Neil had been the past week. She'd never been able to hug her father. He'd never once hugged her, not even on the night he'd left for good.

Ellie lifted the ice water to her mouth, took a tiny sip. It helped only slightly to quell the fears building inside her. "When did you first know things weren't going to work out with my father?''

Viv was lost in her own thoughts. "There was no specific instance. Oh, there were lots of little signs, most of which I ignored. I never should have married him, Ellie. We were simply too different.''

Different...like Neil and me? Ellie wondered.

"Darling, what's wrong? You can tell me about it.''

Ellie forced a smile, swept the hair back away from her face. "It's just the pregnancy. It started me thinking.... I just realized how little I really knew about the past, that's all.''

Viv watched her carefully. "Were you thinking of contacting your father?" Her voice offered no judgment either way, only concern for her daughter's welfare.

"No." Ellie stood. Her voice became brisk. "He's out of my life, has been since I was seven. I just...wanted to know." Quickly, Ellie glanced at her watch. "I'd better be heading home." She gave her mother a hug. "Thanks for listening to me."

"Anytime, darling."

When Ellie arrived home minutes later, the house was quiet, silent. As she had half feared, half hoped, Neil was nowhere around. There was a note on the counter for her. It read:

Ellie, had to go to the hospital again. Emergency. Don't wait up.
Love, Neil

"Love, Neil," Ellie mused, repeating his signature and closing out loud. "That must mean something. That he still loves me."

Then, again, he wasn't there with her, was he? But given time, his schedule would slack off again. It always did. There'd be a couple of weeks of craziness, with deliveries every hour of the day and night, then a couple of quiet weeks or days, when no one, even women ten days overdue, went into labor. The obstetrics nurses at the hospital claimed that it was linked to whether or not there was a full moon. Ellie figured it was just dumb luck. And maybe an occasional kindness to obstetricians from Mother Nature.

When Neil did come home, it was at 4:00 A.M. Wearily he tossed off his clothes and crawled in beside her, cuddling up to her warmth. She was about to protest his presence—after all, they hadn't called a real truce yet or even solved any of their grievances—when she noticed he was already fast asleep. Exhausted herself and comforted by his presence nonetheless, she drifted back to sleep. When her alarm went off at six-thirty, he didn't even budge. She noticed he'd set the alarm clock on his side of the bed for eight. She rose and showered and dressed for work quietly, leaving the house a scant forty-five minutes later.

The first few appointments of her morning were uneventful. She handled a divorce that appeared to be amiable, at least on the surface. It was hard to say what would happen when the case got to court. And there was a less pleasant custody case, one where the mother was battling her deceased husband's parents. At ten Herb Cavanaugh dropped by.

"What brings you out of your insurance office this morning?" Ellie greeted him pleasantly. Although Neil's father was kind and gracious, she'd never felt quite comfortable with him when alone, or with any of Neil's family, as a matter of fact.

"I wanted to talk to you." Herb glanced hesitantly behind him, toward her open office door. In the outer reception area Hazel was typing away rapidly on a brief. "Mind if I shut this?" he asked, indicating the door.

"Go ahead," Ellie said, though in the pit of her stomach she had a sinking feeling of dread. She had a horrible feeling that she knew what was coming, and the wordless disapproval emanating now from Neil's father was reminiscent of the silent, continuous rejection she'd suffered from her own father years before. The door was shut, and the room was bathed in silence. Neil's father looked at her with weary, brooding eyes. She felt trapped and more inadequate than she could remember feeling in years.

Nonetheless, she sat down behind her desk, gesturing for Herb to have a seat. Herb glanced at her, shook his head and leaned against the wall, his palms flattened out behind him. At fifty-four he stood six feet two; his hair was still more black than gray. He had a perennially tanned complexion and a trim form that declared him an avid golfer and tennis player. "I wanted to talk to you about the Middleton case."

Ellie's chin rose several inches.

Herb held up a cautioning palm, continuing before she had a chance to speak. "I know you think this is none of my business. And I guess it isn't. But I have an inkling of how important this position of chief of obstetrics is to Neil." He paused, for the first time looking reluctant to say what it was he'd come to convey. "Ellie, I think I have an idea how much your career means to you, and that's all well and fine, but you can't let your own considerable ambition ruin his chances to get ahead in this

world.'' Ellie couldn't help it; her spine went rigid. Herb continued, still assessing her from head to toe, ''And especially now
that you're pregnant—''

''Now that I'm pregnant, what?'' she asked coolly, tossing
down the pen she'd been idly cradling in her hand. She knew
Herb meant well. The problem was that he was still living in the
Dark Ages when men worked outside the home and married
women—mothers—didn't. She knew he wasn't trying to be unkind, only practical. Yet almost unerringly, her temper was soaring out of control. ''Now that I'm pregnant, am I supposed to
quit working?'' she countered civilly.

''All things considered, that wouldn't be such a bad idea,
would it?'' Herb shifted from foot to foot, looked as if he were
standing on a bed of hot coals.

He had no idea what a bad idea that was. Ellie's independence,
financial and otherwise, was her major source of security, aside
from Neil. Now that she'd apparently lost Neil, at least temporarily in an emotional sense, she had to work at her job harder
than ever. She had to be prepared for whatever the future
brought. Knowing that her father-in-law meant well, however,
made his interference somewhat easier to bear. Gently, she said,
''Herb, what I do or don't do with my career is not open to
family discussion. I'm sorry you're concerned. But I really am
not going to talk about this with you.''

Her rejection of that much he'd apparently expected. ''I'm the
baby's grandparent,'' he pointed out steadily.

''And I'm the baby's mother.'' There was a potent silence in
which neither gave ground nor said any more. ''I don't intend
to stop working,'' she said quietly at last. ''Either before or after
the baby is born.''

For a second she thought he would argue the point. He didn't.
His gaze softened compassionately, persuasively. He spoke in a
soothing tone that very much reminded her of Neil's bedside
manner. ''All right. I respect that. I don't agree with the decision
and I expect you know that, but I respect it.'' He paused and
noisily cleared his throat. His gaze was level, searing. ''I still
wish you'd think about what your actions are doing to Neil's
chances for advancement. He's worked damn hard to get where

he is.'' Herb's voice radiated a father's pride and concern for his son.

"And I haven't?"

"Of course you have. But you're going to be a mother now."

"And Neil's going to be a father."

A corner of Herb's mouth crooked ruefully. He rubbed his jaw. "We're never going to agree on this, are we?"

"It wouldn't appear so, no." Outwardly, Ellie's voice was calm, but inside she was quickly crumbling. Although she'd tried hard to become close to Neil's family, she had never quite succeeded. Part of it was owing simply to a lack of time, she knew. They were never able to spend much time at all together, generally because of conflicts in her schedule or Neil's. But there were other barriers, too. Barriers she had no idea how to break down, get across. But in an effort to keep peace within the extended family, she said nothing more to counter Herb's outlandishly chauvinistic thinking.

Herb sighed deeply, as if abruptly questioning the wisdom of what he had done. "Look, I know what you're thinking. And you're right. I shouldn't have said anything. I know this is none of my business. It's just...when you have a son and you watch him grow up, you kind of know, in here—" Herb pointed to his chest "—what your son needs. Marriage to an obstetrician would be tough enough with your not working."

It would be impossible, Ellie thought. What would she do, sit around waiting for him to come home, then wait again while he dashed off to the hospital to deliver another baby? No, thanks.

"Neil needs a wife who'll support him one hundred percent."

And I need a husband who'll support me one hundred percent, Ellie thought.

"I know it's tough, having to give up your work—or even part of it," Herb hastily amended, "especially after working so long and so hard to earn your law degree, pass the bar and set up practice, but you have to think of the marriage, Ellie. You have to think of the baby."

She was. And the only way she could provide security for her infant was by continuing to work, to ensure that she alone would always be able to make a home for her child.

Herb rambled on for several more minutes. A salesman by profession, he could speak quite eloquently once he got started. But this time it was more what he didn't say than what he did. She gathered he didn't know about the recent trouble between her and Neil, had only guessed at it, much as her mother had suspected. He was alarmed about her handling a malpractice lawsuit for the same reasons as Neil, as well as for fear it would break up the marriage. More important still, though, he seemed silently to be imploring Ellie to be the kind of wife he wanted for Neil now that they were expecting their first child. He wanted her to be acquiescent, a live-in-the-shadow-of-her-man woman Ellie would never and could never be. What he failed to realize was that in the end it wouldn't matter whether she held down a paying job or not, Ellie thought. She would always have her own ideas, her own beliefs, separate from those of Neil.

"Enough of this philosophical discussion," Herb said finally, winding down at last. "As strongly as I feel about what's best for Neil and for you, telling you my theories wasn't the only reason I came over here this morning. I wanted to congratulate you, too." Herb looked bashful, nonplussed, as if inwardly surprised that he had actually spoken so freely to her. In the past he and Ellie had conversed of nothing more pressing or intimate than the evening headlines or sports scores. "Adele and I, Mimi, too—we're all damn happy about your pregnancy."

"Thank you." She accepted his hug of congratulations. They talked briefly, impersonally. He left seconds later. Ellie couldn't help but see that he was sorry he'd come, sorry he'd spoken so freely and maybe—worst of all—sorry it was she who had married his son. Her sense of inadequacy and failure where Neil and marriage were concerned deepened. Both were feelings she hated.

The morning dragged on interminably. As much as Ellie tried, she couldn't put the meeting with Neil's father out of her mind. She decided finally that she had to talk to Neil, to see if perhaps there wasn't some way they could slowly begin to make amends. She knew she wasn't going to change her mind about handling the Middleton case. Nor would he forgive her easily. But maybe, slowly, step-by-step, they could work their way toward each other again. At the very least, it was worth a try.

Resolutely she buzzed Hazel on the intercom. "I'm going to the hospital to try and catch Neil."

There was a pause, in which Ellie imagined her secretary's knowing grin. "Any idea when you'll be back?"

"Probably not until one or two-thirty."

"Have fun."

I'll try, Ellie thought. But it wasn't a likely prospect. Still, nothing worth having had ever come easily. Satisfied that she was finally taking a positive step again she hummed softly, happily, to herself as she left the office and strode out to her car.

Chapter Five

"I'm sorry, Mrs. Cavanaugh, but Dr. Cavanaugh's in surgery," Neil's receptionist reported. "He'll only be another half an hour, though. Would you like to wait?"

"Yes." She knew she should have called to find out what his schedule was first, to let him know she was coming, to arrange a time that would have been good for both of them, without all this waiting around. But she had been afraid that he wouldn't want to see her. And so, rather than face rejection or give herself time to lose her nerve, she'd chanced it.

"Would you like to wait in his private office?" the receptionist asked.

"I think I'll walk downstairs and have some lunch first." Her stomach was rumbling emptily. She had to think of the baby, their baby.

"All right." The receptionist smiled. "I'll have someone let Dr. Cavanaugh know you're here the moment he comes out of surgery."

"Thanks."

Ellie went through the cafeteria line, selecting items solely for their nutritional value. Her mind still on Neil and possible solutions to their problems, she seated herself in a far corner booth next to the windows. As the noon hour progressed, the cafeteria became more crowded and noisy. Nearly every table was occupied. And that's when Ellie picked up the threads of a conversation at a nearby table. The voices were low, female, and spoke in gossipy tones.

"Look, what else can he do? The woman's pregnant, for God's sake! Of course he'll stay with her. Then, once he's established in the eyes of the court that he's a good husband, despite *her* actions, he'll be able to sue for custody."

"Why doesn't Dr. Cavanaugh just leave his wife now?" the other asked in a bored tone. Icy sweat ran down Ellie's back and she felt more moisture between her breasts.

"Because if he left before the baby's born, his wife might be able to claim desertion."

Ellie put down her spoon and pushed her soup aside. She wanted to leave. But she didn't want to face the two witches behind her. So, instead, she did nothing, detesting herself all the while for her lack of action. Yet she was unable to shut them out entirely and listened with a sort of morbid curiosity to the vicious chatter that went on incessantly.

"Do you really think he'd want her baby after what she did to him?"

"You've seen the way he looks at kids in pediatrics." The first woman laughed raucously. "Like a kid in a candy store with only a nickel to spend. He's always stopping in to say hello to the older kids. And when they lose one of the premies—" her voice lowered more reverently, proving, Ellie thought bitterly, that the woman did have a heart somewhere "—well, you know how broken up he is."

Ellie knew, too. At home, Neil would anguish for hours over whether there was something, anything, more they could have done. He'd go over and over the case.

"Yeah, but still..." The conversation behind Ellie continued, making her very glad that the two women couldn't see her face. From the free way they were talking, she was sure they didn't know they were sitting within earshot of Neil's wife. "Do you really think Dr. Cavanaugh's going to leave his wife?"

"Yeah, I do. Oh, he'll stay with her until after the baby is born. But after that, well, let's just say I wouldn't be surprised if he found someone who would help him build a career and not be a hindrance to him, someone who would have as many kids as he wanted, without worrying about how it's going to affect her career. Someone who wouldn't tangle his name up in the dirty business of malpractice. And there are plenty of women around here who'd be willing to put their name on a waiting list.''

The second woman laughed lightly, attesting to the truth of the statement. After a moment she continued more somberly, in a naive tone, ''But Dr. Cavanaugh's never even looked at anyone else. At least not since I've been working here.''

''And how long has that been? For a year? Sure, since he's been married, he's been true blue and all that. But that was before this malpractice business came up. Let me tell you, he's plenty ticked off about that. Just mention the name Middleton around him and he gets a murderous look in his eyes.''

Ellie heard a quick intake of breath.

''You didn't—''

''No. But some of the other doctors haven't been so considerate. Dr. Cavanaugh almost punched one of them out in the hall the other day.''

''You're kidding.''

''Well, that's what I heard. Anyway, there are plenty of women here willing to take advantage of the—shall we say?— rift in Dr. Cavanaugh's marriage.''

''He wouldn't—'' the second breathed, with such rapt attention that Ellie thought she'd be sick.

''He had one hell of a reputation as a womanizer before he started seeing her.''

That much was true, Ellie knew. She'd heard of the legendary Dr. Cavanaugh long before they'd ever met. She'd only come to Joplin after law school to set up practice, to help her mother start up her temporary-employment business. Before that they'd always lived in St. Louis. And Neil, Neil with his good looks and gallant charm, had always lived here. He'd had quite a reputation, her Neil. So much so that she'd been half afraid to go out with him for fear of being hurt. Maybe she should have heeded that inner warning, Ellie thought, tears blurring her eyes. Maybe she should listen to his father now. Because she wasn't right for Neil, not really. Oh, she loved him. She loved him more than life. But she had hurt him, and he had hurt her. So much so that had it not been for the pregnancy...

Unwillingly she recalled his hesitation when he'd tried—and failed—to assure her that they would have worked their problems out even if she hadn't become pregnant. She thought of the nights he'd spent at the hospital, away from her, his silences, the fact that he'd walked out on her in anger and would still undoubtedly be away from her had it not been for the news of her pregnancy.

And last she thought of the pain she had suffered when her father walked out on her. Could she put her own child through that? Could she risk Neil's taking her baby from her? The answer was no. Calm stole over Ellie. She knew now what she had to do.

The two women behind her went on to converse about someone else. She turned them out with effort. No longer hungry, she nonetheless forced herself to sit there and sip her milk slowly. The gossip mongers left. A half hour passed. Ellie went up to talk to Neil.

HE'D JUST WALKED into his office in rumpled sweat-stained clothes to return his calls when Ellie entered. She sat quietly while he finished, not really listening as he soothed and advised one patient after another and confirmed another doctor's original diagnosis on a consultation. Ellie sat twisting her hands in her lap, tighter and tighter. She knew what she had to do, she told herself firmly. She knew what she had to do.

Finally he hung up. He looked at her across the softly lighted private office. His receptionist knocked, entered with a carafe of coffee and several cafeteria sandwiches on a tray. Neil shot her a grateful look, thanked her; the receptionist left as soundlessly as she'd come and closed the door behind her. Silence reigned. Neil seemed to have picked up on her dark mood. He reached for a sandwich and calmly poured himself some coffee. Wordlessly he offered to share his lunch.

She shook her head. "I've already eaten."

This was ludicrous, she thought. Absolutely ludicrous. But there was no denying the tension between her and Neil, where weeks before there had been only happiness. Or the wary distrust in his eyes. He looked exhausted. And suddenly she knew they couldn't go on as they had. Something had to change. They had to know, both of them, that there was a way out, a way that would salvage what precious little friendship they had left. It was important for the baby's sake that they be friends, she thought. In her work she'd seen too many couples use their children as weapons, slowly destroying the children as they destroyed each other. She didn't want that to happen to her. She wanted a clean, quick break. And most of all, she wanted the hurting to stop.

"I want a divorce." Ellie said finally. She'd expected her voice to break; instead, it remained inordinately calm, so deceptively casual compared to the anguish she was feeling. But that was good, she told herself firmly. She needed Neil to think that she was in control, that she could handle this, that she could handle raising a child alone.

For a second Neil didn't react at all, his lack of response confirming Ellie's worst fears. He shook his head as if that would clear it, as if he were sure there was some mistake, that she couldn't, wouldn't, leave him. And considering the droves of women waiting in line for him, Ellie thought a trifle jealously, why not? Why shouldn't he think that way?

Neil put down the coffee he'd held without sipping it. "What did you say?" he asked quietly. His stare was both enraged and incredulous. With effort Ellie repeated herself.

Not surprisingly, considering what had been going on between them, he didn't argue about what she wanted. Rather he focused on how and why she had come to that decision.

"What's going on? Who's been talking to you?" He stood up restlessly and put his hands on his hips. His eyes narrowed.

There was no way she was going to repeat what she had overheard in the hospital cafeteria. She had lost a lot, but she still had her pride. No way was she sacrificing that. She thought about conveniently forgetting to mention his father's visit, then decided against it. Knowing Herb, she figured he'd tell Neil himself before the day was over.

"It's a lot of things combined, Neil. The way we've been arguing lately, your absences, the baby. Apparently, I'm not the only one who sees there is trouble in our marriage, though." She took no pleasure in telling him. "Your dad came to see me. He wanted me to drop the case, to be the kind of wife a dynamic man like you needs." She still felt humiliated, remembering. Because she had known, in a sense, that Neil's father was right, as were the women in the cafeteria. Neil did need someone different—someone who could concentrate only on him, someone who wouldn't need a career to make her feel safe and secure, to give her the knowledge that she could always take care of herself and needn't fear being left, abandoned.

"He said that?" Neil looked furious at his father's interference.

"More or less." Momentarily, her conscience was pricked. She knew she was paraphrasing Herb's actual words, but she felt the essence of his message, however awkwardly it had been delivered, was right on target. It was exactly what he would have said if he hadn't been trying so hard not to cause trouble or hurt her feelings. "He's also upset about the fact that I plan to continue to work after the baby is born."

"I hope you set him straight about that much. That I support you in the continuing of your career. That I think it would be a mistake for you to give it up, even briefly, for my sake or the child's."

She took a deep breath and regarded her husband with suspicion. Why was he suddenly being so reasonable? Why couldn't he be as cold and unforgiving as he had been the previous week? Was he trying to ensure that she would have something to sustain her after he left her? Was he, as the women had asserted, preparing to sue her for custody of the baby? She knew Neil, knew in her heart that he would never willingly give up his own child. Oh, God, she felt she was going to be sick.

Waves of dizziness engulfing her, Ellie gripped the sides of her chair to retain her balance. Neil reached backward to his desk. She heard a faint hissing noise, then the acrid smell of ammonia assaulted her nostrils. She coughed and sputtered and, swearing, pushed it away.

"I think you should go home and rest," Neil said in a soothing doctor-patient tone that carried an added dimension of intimacy—an intimacy she was struggling to forget, for fear she'd come to rely on the closeness and him far too much. His hand brushed her shoulder, stayed momentarily, then withdrew as she stiffened. His voice became harder, more penitent, yet carried with it a faint note of aggravation. "I'm sorry about the visit from my father. I had no idea when I talked to him Saturday he'd—" Neil stopped, swore, promised evenly, "It won't happen again."

She caught the glimmering mixture of guilt and anguish in Neil's eyes. She knew he lamented the lack of closeness between Ellie and his family. She was mystified about why he'd gone to his father. To her knowledge, he'd never been motivated to seek advice or comfort before. Another indication of how serious the problem was? she wondered. Had Neil's father urged him to stay and work things out? No. She had to believe that Neil hadn't told his father how fragile their relationship had become. Neil had simply needed solace and had gone home to see his folks, much as she had gone to see Viv Sunday evening. Since they knew about the position at the hospital and Neil's interest, it was logical that the subject would have come up, along with the news of Ellie's involvement in the malpractice case, now in the media. Herb had just been acting on instinct when he came to see her.

Ellie studied her husband wordlessly. There were lines of fatigue and strain around Neil's eyes. The set of his mouth when she'd entered his office had been unerringly grim. It was still that way now.

"Then your father was right. You do still wish I'd drop the case?"

About that Neil couldn't, wouldn't, lie to her. "Yes," he said simply. "I do wish you'd at least refer them to someone else." His direct, honest look was more than she could bear. "I don't want a divorce."

"You may feel differently later." She set him up passionately, hoping he'd give her some clue as to how he was really feeling.

"Maybe I will," he returned in a controlled voice.

Numbly, she watched as he walked to the waste can and threw the smelling salts into it. She saw then that he really wasn't upset at all that his father had come to see her. Was it possible he'd asked Herb to talk to her, on the off chance he would get through to her where Neil had failed? Whatever the reason, she didn't want in-law interference to continue. In a voice that was low and shaking, she accused, "You wanted him to come and talk to me." Part of her knew, even as she spoke, that she was being irrational. She couldn't help it. Neil's treatment of her had been highly upsetting. She no longer knew where she stood with him. She wasn't sure he knew, either.

He retrieved the coffee he'd neglected earlier and took a deep draft. "You're talking nonsense, Ellie. And I suspect that if you weren't pregnant, and hence highly emotional, you'd know that." Deliberately he emphasized his words, taking perverse pleasure in her annoyance.

So, he thought inadvertently he'd been given the upper hand, did he? "Pressure tactics from your family won't work to get me to give up the Middleton case, Neil." She began pacing his office like a football player psyching himself up for the game. She turned and issued a warning stoically, "Make sure your father and everyone else in your family knows that."

Neil flinched as if she'd struck him. His mouth tightened into a thin, unrelenting line. "I'm sure I won't have to," he responded placidly at last. "I'm sure you made it abundantly clear. You've pushed them away from the start. You won't get close to anyone or let them get close to you."

His assessment hit her like a slap in the face. His next words followed like a double blow, stunning her into a silence fraught with hurt. "Frankly, I'm not sure I can take it anymore."

She tried but was unable to get a breath. When she managed to speak again, her voice was thready, barely more than a whisper. She was trying desperately not to cry. "Then make it easy on yourself. Give me a divorce now. Let's end it while we can still be friends."

His face lost all color as she repeated her earlier demand. For long seconds he didn't move. Neither did he immediately refuse or try to dissuade her. The pause seemed to extend forever. "You're sure that's what you want?" His voice was unerringly collected when at last he spoke.

Ellie nodded distraughtly.

The set of his lips tightened implacably. "Fine. But nothing legal can be started until our baby is born and settled comfortably in his or her home. I want no more in-law interference during your pregnancy than we've already had, for your sake and the baby's.''

Ellie wanted to sit down again. She wouldn't give him the satisfaction of seeing her upset to the fainting point once again. She moved past him, toward his desk. ''And you're willing to put this in writing?'' She focused on the specifics, knowing it was the only way she could continue to get through the ugly scene.

Neil shrugged. ''If you think it's necessary.''

Ellie reached for a piece of stationery and a pen. Quickly she drew up a simple contract, trying to reassure herself all the while that everything would be all right, that she and the baby would manage just fine without him. ''I suppose this is really for the best,'' she said, finishing minutes later. She glanced up at him impersonally, with the same interested but professionally remote attention she would give a client. ''It'll be simpler, knowing where we stand with each other.'' The divorce would be final. Then she could go on with her life, without waiting forever and indefinitely for him to get angry and walk out again, for him to realize, as his father apparently already had, that he needed a very different kind of wife. Not a crusading lawyer-partner, but a helpmate, a morale booster. Someone willing to step back and give up her own independence and entrust her life completely to him, something Ellie knew she could never do—not for Neil or any other man.

''Sign here.'' Ellie indicated the bottom line she'd drawn.

Neil picked up the pen. His jaw looking hard as granite, he signed. When he glanced over at her, his eyes were glittering, full of suppressed emotions and thoughts Ellie didn't trust. He seemed abruptly almost as relieved as she and twice as far-sighted, as if he had already decided for himself how their last scene together would be played.

Ellie signed the document herself, aware that her hand was trembling slightly as she did so and that she had a sinking feeling in the pit of her stomach, as if she had just signed away her entire life. What should have been a very freeing moment for her actually felt like an imprisoning one. "I suppose we should have two witnesses," Ellie said.

"We don't need witnesses," Neil said tightly, looking angry again, very angry. "Trust me. If you want a divorce at the end of this time, you'll get one. So damn fast it'll make your head spin."

She didn't doubt him, not for a minute. Suddenly, Ellie couldn't get out of there fast enough. She grabbed her purse and the agreement and bolted for the door. Neil watched her steadily but said nothing more as she left. It was only later that she realized they had left out the most important factor of all, custody of their only child.

SEVERAL HOURS LATER, Neil thought despondently, *I never should have let her goad me into signing that divorce agreement.* But what choice had he been given? To fight her at that point would have made her all the more determined. Besides, they'd been at the hospital, his work arena. She'd come there, knowing the discussion would have to stay calm, simply because of where it was taking place. Well, he'd remained relatively unemotional, all things considered. But he didn't feel the least bit stoic now. He felt angry and hurt. But he also wanted the fighting between them to end once and for all. And he wanted to make love to her. Not simply because of desire, although passion was there as always, but because he wanted to feel close to her again. He wanted her to know he loved her. He wanted her to love him back. He knew, as a man, that there were barriers touch could break down that words couldn't begin to penetrate. So maybe, just maybe, if he could be with her again, sleep with her, wake holding her in his arms, maybe in that way, piece by piece, the tensions between them would disintegrate. He only knew he had to do something. At this point, anything was worth a try.

He phoned her office, only to find she had already left for the day.

Ignoring the stacks of paperwork on his desk, Neil left the hospital and drove home to have a talk with his wife, one that would occur in private.

Ellie's car was parked in the driveway. Neil pulled up beside

it and got out of his car. As he strode down the walk toward the
front door of their slate-gray-and-white Cape Cod, he thought he
saw the curtains draping a second-floor window move slightly.
Once inside, he headed straight upstairs. He found Ellie tossing
his shoes in madcap style into a box just outside the closet floor.

"You're not supposed to be home yet," she decreed inflexibly. Shoes continued to fall from her hands.

Neil clamped his teeth together. He'd known she was angry,
but this? The single-handed clearing out of all his personal belongings? He stared at her in agitation. Loosening the knot of
his tie with one hand, he demanded, "What in blazes is going
on here?" Clearly, she wasn't wasting any time getting rid of
him, he thought irately.

Ellie tossed him a cold-blooded look over her shoulder. She
was still wearing her glasses. Looking slightly disheveled, her
blond hair flying every which way, she nonetheless had an aura
of cool elegance and sophistication. "What does it look like?
You're moving out."

He gave a harsh laugh. Pushing his suit coat back, he let his
hands rest against his waist. He stood watching her with a hunger
that surprised him. "The hell I am, Ellie." She turned to him
with a mocking sweetness that made him want to kiss her until
she swooned.

"All right. Then I will." Her palm flat on his chest, she
pushed him aside as she moved past.

He caught her, one arm easily encircling her still-slender waist,
and spun her around until she was drawn up against him, length
to length. He could feel the jackhammer beat of her heart against
his chest, knew a brief moment's satisfaction before she pushed
away from him resolutely, her eyes glacial and indifferent to him
and full of her own private pain. The triumph faded.

"I can't continue on like this, Neil." Her whisper was harsh,
pleading. She pushed away from him again and glided a safe
distance away.

It would have taken a man of stone to deny her anything. He
wasn't made of granite. Neither could he face losing her. Not
when he still loved her the way he did. Yes, he'd made mistakes,
a lifetime of them in the past week, but he also knew that he

wasn't totally out of line, that she was wrong, too. Even so, he wasn't ready to let her go. Not now, not ever. "Then, let's stop fighting," he suggested implacably.

"I want you out."

Her stony insistence made it easier for him to stay his ground. "Oh, no, Ellie." It might have been his imagination, but he thought he saw a brief flicker of relief register in her face. It was swiftly replaced by her most stubborn look, one that caused him to further bolster his position. He advanced on her, moving beside her and reaching into the carton of shoes. He tossed them like a juggler back into the closet. Dusting off his hands, he straightened up. "And as for the packing, you can forget this. I'm staying right here. And so are you. Think of it this way," he continued when she made a moue of extreme distaste. "You'll have your own in-house physician."

"I don't want my own in-house physician."

Neil was willing to bet she would, if it took every ounce of negotiating and peacemaking skill he had. "There is no other way," he stressed tranquilly. The first item of business was to keep them together physically as much as possible, he decided. The rest would come in time. With effort he offered up something concrete, "If I move out, people will talk."

She tilted her head in a disagreeing manner. "You didn't care about that the nights you slept at the hospital."

"And look where that got us," he countered dryly. "Besides, that was different. I had patients in labor, not a whole wardrobe in residence with me. No, I'm staying, Ellie." When she opened her mouth as if to argue again, he looked at her in such a way that let her know once and for all that it would be useless for her to fight him on the matter.

As he had hoped, she gave in slightly. "All right, then we'll have to find a way to divide up the house."

"Don't you think you're being ridiculous?" Neil's patience was waning.

"I'd call it sensible." This time she cut him off. "I don't want to be hurt, Neil."

He shook his head in wonderment, mutely marveling at the lengths she would go to to protect herself from being hurt—or abandoned, fears he had unwittingly fostered into being again. "And you think this will prevent it?" he asked gently.

Avoiding his eyes and scowling, she surveyed the mess she had made of the master bedroom closet. "If we can stay out of each other's way, yes."

So, she wanted him out of her life. Part of her may have even always wanted that, he realized. The notion stung. With the hurt came the temptation to let her see and feel firsthand just what she would be missing without him. And maybe the best way to do that was for him to be there—and yet not be there for her. To be within her reach and her sight, but not exactly available to minister to her every whim, either. "Go ahead, then." He folded his arms against his sternum and waited, curious as to what she would propose.

She swallowed hard and turned back to him with obvious reluctance, as if she knew instinctively to win that point she would have to look at him directly and mean what she said. "First, I want you to sleep in the den downstairs." There were two extra bedrooms upstairs, but neither had yet been finished.

Neil decided to give her that point, temporarily. "All right. But I'll have to shower up here. And I'm leaving the majority of my clothes in this closet." *Just in case you change your mind, Ellie,* he thought. *If you want me, all you have to do is ask.*

She opened her mouth as if to object, then shut it tightly. "I want you to fix your own meals."

He raised and lowered his brows once to signal his exasperation. "I thought we did that now."

"If I cook, I'll be cooking for one, not two."

"Even if I'm here?" He looked at her in exaggerated consternation, as if scandalized by her sudden lack of manners. Did she really think this ridiculous charade would make him love her any less? Or lessen the tension they were now operating under? Apparently she did.

"We'll be roommates, Neil. Nothing more. Nothing less."

He decided he would give back as good as he got. Evenly he pointed out, "Roommates would cook for one another."

"Not this one. Not all the time."

He shrugged carelessly. "As I'm rarely here for meals lately,

I think that's wise. I want you to know, though, that if I'm home and cooking, I'll make something for you." His tone dripped with generosity.

"I don't want you to do that for me." Angry color flooded her cheeks. Her eyes were glowing. Abruptly he had the feeling that it was all she could do at the moment not to stamp her foot, and he grinned.

"Now who's being ridiculous? Why not?"

She exhaled wearily. "Because then I'll be obligated to do the same for you."

"And we might start sharing?" In his mind there were far worse fates, such as that divorce he had stupidly agreed to.

She nodded dispassionately. "Or fighting again, even worse than before."

Again, Neil was consumed by the urge to take her into his arms and just kiss her until she forgot everything but the forces that had drawn her to him and him to her in the first place. Knowing the resistance an action like that would meet, he relented, "All right, so we won't cook for each other. We'll share a bath, but not a bed. Anything else?" he asked in a deliberately relaxed manner, just as the beeper in his pocket began to sound.

She looked at the beeper appreciatively. He knew what she was thinking: *Saved by the bell.* She shook her head silently.

"We'll talk about this some more when I get back from the hospital," he warned.

Without preface, she looked panic-stricken again. "Neil, we signed an agreement this afternoon. It's legal. I intend to hold you to those terms. I want a divorce the moment the baby is born and, as you stipulated, settled into a schedule at home."

Ellie might have been angry with him, Neil concluded, but she wasn't indifferent, no matter how much she tried to pretend.

"Is that what you really want for your child?" he probed. "Parents who are divorced?"

She flinched momentarily, then recovered. "It's better than parents who fight every second they're together or, worse yet, have nothing to say to each other, ever."

Neil knew things had been bad between them, but he had no idea until that moment how far the depth of her hurt, her insecurity, reached. It would be damned difficult, if not nigh impossible, to reach her again, to gain her trust in more than just a superficial sense. But he was going to try. And keep trying. Unfortunately, at the moment his work beckoned.

The situation with Ellie could only be resolved by lengthy, continual efforts. Maybe his first instincts had been right. Maybe he needed to give her exactly what she had asked for—time and space, alone. By living there he could still see her daily and slowly win her trust and her love again. In the meantime he could bury his frustration in his job, devote his personal energies to the patients who needed him.

But it was a move on his part that needed to be done out of love, not revenge. If their arrangement were to work, he would have to accept her terms for now. And hope that, sooner or later, she would miss him enough to realize she really did love him after all. He hoped that under those conditions she would realize how much they had shared the first two years of their marriage. He had to believe that she would eventually want to talk, to work things out for both of them and especially for the baby. At least, for now, this way he had them still living in the same house. That was a start. "All right, Ellie, you win."

ELLIE WAITED until she heard him leave before collapsing on the center of the king-size bed. Pausing only to kick off her shoes, she drew the coverlet up around her. Without a doubt it had been the worst day of her life: first, Herb Cavanaugh telling her that she wasn't the right woman for his son; then the ordeal in the hospital cafeteria as she'd listened to total strangers analyze the problems in her marriage; then Neil's agreeing to the divorce without batting an eye, so long as his baby and Ellie were under his continued supervision and scandal was kept at a minimum. How could he have been so cold-blooded? she wondered. So calculating? If he'd really loved her, wouldn't he have fought for her? Wouldn't he have demanded they work their problems out? Wouldn't he have refused even to talk of divorce?

She had to face facts. Neil no longer loved her. Whatever they'd had she'd somehow destroyed as she'd pursued her own career. Now all that was left to her personally was her baby. She wouldn't let Neil take that from her.

Moaning her dismay, Ellie buried her head in her pillow. She'd never make it, not for nine whole months. She fell asleep curled up on the bed.

Ellie woke at 5:00 A.M. The coverlet was wrapped around her, topped by a second. She was still dressed. Neil was nowhere in sight. With a groan she recalled their fight, the tempestuous previous day.

Before she could do much more than take a breath, the nausea hit her full force. Not the tiny queasy feeling she'd had previous days, but raging morning sickness—an ailment she'd resolved never to let get the better of her. Yet here it was, holding her entire body hostage before she'd had time even to get fully awake. Tossing off the covers, Ellie made a mad dash for the bathroom.

Morning sickness wasn't the proper name for it, Ellie decided long minutes later as she moved a cool, damp cloth over her face. It was like morning death.

"Ellie?" Neil moved sleepily beside her. Embarrassed, and still struggling valiantly to exercise some control over the flulike symptoms ravaging her body, Ellie made no response to his inquiry. Rather, she finished rinsing her mouth with water and, when she was able, sat on the edge of the bathtub, cradling her head in her hands. She'd never felt more miserable in her life. Worse, she was mortified to have Neil witness to such an awful scene. She knew she must look ghastly in the bright fluorescent lights. Like a figure out of a horror movie.

Without warning, another bout of nausea hit her full force. When she'd finished being sick, Neil knelt beside her and asked, his concern for her apparent, "How long have you been up?"

"I don't know." Ellie's eyes were filling with tears. Was he beginning to suspect, as was she, that this was no ordinary bout of morning sickness? Nor did the disabling nausea seem to be tapering off. "Half an hour maybe..." She pressed the damp washcloth to her mouth and then prepared again to be sick.

Her retching went on interminably. When the cramps had subsided, enough for her to talk, Neil asked her several more questions, about what she had eaten and when, whether or not she had any other symptoms. "Is it this bad every day?" Although his demeanor was calm, his expression was worried. He touched a hand lightly to her forehead, as if checking for fever.

"Never this bad." Ellie moaned, doubling over as the spasms racked her middle yet again.

"I'm calling your obstetrician." He walked into the bedroom.

Neil's voice was low but worried. Ellie dimly heard Neil discussing hyperemesis, the potential loss of body liquids and chemicals, the harm to Ellie's general health and that of her baby, should the vomiting continue. Neil confirmed Ellie had been under an enormous amount of stress.... He, too, hoped hospitalization would not be necessary. He finished by promising to call Jim back to report on Ellie's condition in an hour.

When Neil returned to the bathroom, Ellie wasn't surprised to see that he was carrying his medical bag. The advantages of being married to a doctor, she thought. Being treated at home rather than in the hospital emergency room. Although how she would have managed any trip in a motor vehicle at that point, she didn't know. Just thinking about walking two steps gave her acute motion sickness.

Still looking grim, Neil rolled up her sleeve and began swabbing her arm with alcohol. "Jim wants you to have a shot of dicyclomine hydrochloride to stop the spasms."

Ellie nodded her understanding through a blurry film of tears. She felt barely able to breathe and was mortally afraid of being sick again.

She was glad Neil was there with her, glad she wasn't alone.

Fortunately, the shot he gave her helped. Within minutes after receiving it, Ellie was able to return to bed, with Neil's assistance. Although she tried halfheartedly to dismiss him several times in the half hour that followed, he insisted upon staying with her. With effort, she tried not to make too much of his tender concern for her. After all, she told herself sternly, Neil would have done the same for anyone. A roommate, friend, patient...

She closed her eyes. Moments later, her drowsiness returned. Sleep soon followed.

When Ellie awoke again, sunlight was flooding the bedroom. Neil was standing in front of the mirror, routinely knotting his tie. Remembering what he'd witnessed in the hour before dawn, Ellie barely restrained herself from pulling a pillow over her face. What a time to have him around, she thought morosely, when she was at her worst.

Neil turned a sympathetic glance her way. "Feeling better?"

"Yes...I think." She sat up in bed and was relieved to find no repeat of the earlier abdominal spasms. She ran a hand self-consciously through her hair. "Was that...simple morning sickness that I had?" she asked. Now that she was better, she wanted to know every specific of the diagnosis and treatment.

"Compounded by a combination of fatigue and the extreme amount of stress you've been under, both personal and professional." His brows rose archly as he expertly centered his tie and turned to face her. "As well as the fact that you hadn't eaten any supper, but went to bed with an empty stomach. Didn't Jim caution you about the need to eat regularly, never to let your stomach get too empty during the first trimester?"

"He said something about it, yes."

"And?" Neil was watching her contemplatively.

"And I didn't pay much attention to what he was saying about either the reasons for the malady or the ways to prevent it." She blushed, thoroughly embarrassed by her lack of foresight.

"Why not?"

"I didn't think I'd get it. I thought—then, anyway—that morning sickness was at least in part psychosomatic. I was determined not to get it." To her chagrin, the blush staining her cheeks grew warmer. She gestured effusively and pulled the covers up tighter around her. "As for last night, I didn't mean to fall asleep when I did. Had I awakened, I would've eaten a proper dinner."

Neil admitted in a subdued tone, "I forgot all about dinner, too."

Ellie was silent. They'd both been upset, exhausted.

The tantalizing smell of his after-shave pleasurably flooded her senses as he strolled closer. "I'm sorry you've been under so much stress," he said softly. "I take full blame for that."

"It's not your fault I was sick."

"I could have been easier on you. I will be in future." Casually, he seated himself at the foot of the bed. "In the meantime, since you didn't pay much attention to Jim's talk on morning sickness, I'll go over it with you again. First and most important, despite what some so-called experts would have you believe, there is a very good reason and simple medical explanation for morning sickness." He sat next to her on the bed, making no move to touch her. "When a woman becomes pregnant, muscles in both the diaphragm and at the junction of the esophagus relax. Add the reflux, or backward flow, of gastric fluids and a delay in gastric emptying time and—"

Ellie held up her hand. "Enough, Neil. I get the picture."

He nodded, apparently glad that she had accepted the affliction as a valid illness. "Stress and fatigue both make the malady worse. So it's important that you try to take it easy now as much as possible. In addition, there are a few steps you can take to alleviate or lessen recurring nausea."

"Such as?" Although he'd been careful not to touch her, or crowd her in any way, his steady perusal was getting to her. Walking into the bathroom, she washed her face and brushed her teeth.

"Eat or drink only small amounts of food frequently. Avoid hunger whenever possible and give those fluids something to mix with. Limit your diet to bland foods only. Soda crackers and a soft drink will usually help relieve nausea. You can also eat before rising. Just keep a container of saltines beside the bed. Munch on one or two before you get up. It'll help. And you'll feel even better after that, once you can manage to eat some breakfast." He leaned against the door frame, watching her movements with interest.

After the bout of morning sickness she had just suffered, Ellie didn't think anything so mundane as munching on a saltine would halt the nausea once it had started. "What happened to me last night wasn't typical?" She pivoted toward Neil.

"No, it wasn't. The episode you suffered was unusually severe. So it's important that you take steps to prevent it from happening again.''

"Didn't they used to give women medication to take nightly to prevent morning sickness?" Ellie asked, vaguely recalling Hazel's mentioning something about doing so, years before, when she had been pregnant, to good result.

"Yes, but that's no longer done. We physicians are all very conscious of the potential side effects to the developing fetus. No medication of any kind is given unless it's absolutely necessary. In most cases, morning sickness has proved to be controllable by the methods I've just recommended to you.''

"So...soda crackers it will be.''

Neil grinned. "Looks that way, doesn't it? At least for a couple of months. Generally, after the first trimester, nausea is no longer a problem.''

"I'll look forward to that time," Ellie said dryly. She paused to run a brush through her hair, then turned, to find Neil watching her intensely.

He straightened, braced one loosely knotted fist on his waist. "I left some oatmeal in a casserole in the microwave for you. I figured you'd want to eat something. I didn't know if you'd feel up to cooking. Anyway, the cereal is all ready to go. All you have to do is turn the oven on for a few minutes before you're ready to eat.'' He glanced at his watch and frowned, as if realizing he was late. "I've got to go.''

He'd done so much for her, Ellie thought. Unbidden, tenderness flowed through her. In that instant, she could almost forget all the rotten things they'd said to each other lately. With effort she gathered her composure. "Neil? Thanks for coming to my rescue this morning. And for breakfast, too.'' Despite her efforts to retain a casual facade, her tone was unaccountably soft, almost soggy with repressed emotion. It's the pregnancy, she thought. It's doing strange things to my hormones.

Neil reached up, almost involuntarily it seemed, until the palm of his hand lightly cupped her chin. For a moment there seemed much he wanted to say. He let it pass without voicing his thoughts.

"Have a good day,'' he urged softly, tenderly.

"You, too.''

Chapter Six

"Ellie, how nice to see you!" Adele Cavanaugh exclaimed from the adjacent department store aisle. "You're looking wonderful."

The tall woman neared, looking fine as usual, with a chic but casual flair. Although summer had officially started just a few days previously, Adele already had a nice tan. Ellie envied her the time in the sun. Lately it seemed the only sunshine she'd seen was coming in through her office windows.

"Thank you, Adele." Ellie smiled at her mother-in-law, moving so that the rack of maternity dresses was behind her instead of shrouding her. She tucked the overflowing sack of slacks, shirts and casual dresses beneath her arm, put another of undergarments at her feet.

"Getting into maternity clothes now?" Adele questioned gently. Using the tips of her fingers, she tidied her soft gray curls. At fifty-four, the vivacious, outgoing homemaker was fit enough to lead an aerobics class.

"Yes." Ellie smiled, self-consciously patting her ever-expanding waist. She might be only three months pregnant by the calendar, but it seemed to her that the child she was carrying had been a part of her forever. "I can't seem to fit into any of my slacks anymore, and even the largest of my skirts is too tight." Uncomfortable with the subject of her weight, Ellie glanced behind Adele, seeing Neil's sister Mimi in the distance. "What are you up to?" Although, typically, she and Neil tried to keep in touch with their respective families by phone on a regular basis, neither Ellie nor Neil had been by his folks' house much the past month. Except for the occasion of Herb's visit to her office, she hadn't seen or spoken to them at all.

"Mimi has been baby-sitting this summer. She's saved her money and for reasons related to weight as well as style—she's just lost five pounds—intends to update her wardrobe."

"She's starting high school in the fall, isn't she?"

"Uh-huh. And she's nervous about it to boot."

"I'm sure she'll do fine," Ellie encouraged, smiling over at the teen.

"I hope so." Adele frowned worriedly for a moment, all maternal concern for her youngest—a change-of-life baby she'd had when she was forty. For a moment Ellie thought Adele would ask her to say something reassuring to Mimi, but she didn't. Despite the fact that she and Neil had been married for two years, the bonds between Ellie and Neil's family were fragile at best. Not because there had been any dissension between her and the Cavanaughs; rather, because they were still at the stage of carefulness with one another, of trying to please. "So, what's new with you?" Adele continued, not skipping a beat. "Neil's been busy, hasn't he?"

"Busy" wasn't the word for it, Ellie thought to herself. More like driven. Since moving permanently into the den the month before, he had been cordial but distant. "Yes, he has. But that's not unusual. All obstetricians lead work-oriented lives." Ellie tried to make light of his absences.

Adele's gaze narrowed contemplatively. "Yes, but when I drive by the Medical Center, I notice his car there more and more. Have you talked to him about cutting back on his patient load, now that you're expecting?"

Ellie wasn't surprised that Adele had zeroed in on one of her primary concerns from the early days of her marriage. Neil's mother always had been intuitive where both her children were concerned. "No." Ellie nudged the floor with the toe of her shoe. "I really don't think that's any of my concern."

Adele gave her a look that brimmed with curiosity. "Of course it's your concern. Ellie, you're his wife."

"That doesn't give me the right to dictate to him how to run his career.'' Though, before the rift between them, she had wished for more time alone. Since then, she was glad when he wasn't there, glad she didn't have to deal with the tension or work so hard at not having another fight. And in the interim he'd been preoccupied with his work, she with hers. They had finally become accustomed to living as roommates, not as man and wife. The handwritten agreement to divorce was in her office vault. No, the marriage was over—unofficially, at least—and the sooner Ellie faced that, the better.

''When does the staff vote on the new chief of obstetrics?'' Adele asked.

''Sometime next week, I think,'' Ellie said. Another reason Neil had been working around the clock, to prove himself ready and capable for the job, no matter what his wife did.

There was an awkward pause. Adele took a deep breath. ''Listen, Ellie, Herb told me what he did. I want you to know he meant no harm, coming to your office that way. But he's always been so proud of Neil.''

''Yes, I know.'' Father and son were close. Ellie asked impulsively, ''What do you think? Should I have given up that case for Neil's sake?''

Adele hesitated. ''Ellie, I don't want to get into that with you. I know Neil's been upset about it, as has Herb, but, really, I think the matter should stay between you and Neil and end there, too. Whatever happens, the two of you will have to work it out.''

A smart lady, her mother-in-law, Ellie thought.

Before they could go on, Neil's fourteen-year-old sister, Mimi, walked up to join them. Lively and pretty, she was slightly overweight, a fact that Adele worried about constantly. Mimi held up a vibrant Hawaiian-print dress. Aside from a high hemline and plunging neckline, the dress featured a cutout back that in no way would have permitted Mimi to wear any sort of undergarment. ''Hey, Mom, what do you think?'' Mimi asked in a teasing tone.

Adele smoothed her pullover over her slacks, trying hard to suppress an amused grin. ''Do you really think your father would let you out of the house in that?''

Mimi's grin widened as she contemplated her father's reaction. "Maybe if I wore a sweater?"

"Try a sweater and galoshes and a raincoat and hat. And he'd probably still want to know what you had on underneath. No, Mimi."

Mimi exhaled dramatically, then shrugged. "Wouldn't have fit anyway. It's a size three!"

The three of them walked toward the teen department so Mimi could return the outrageous dress to the rack. The women browsed languidly, each selecting items they thought might work. Excitedly, Mimi dashed into the dressing room, only to return ten minutes later with a forced smile of casual indifference.

"None of them fit?" Adele asked.

Mimi shook her head. "Not a one."

"Maybe we have the wrong sizes. Perhaps if we got a saleswoman to help."

"No." Mimi's decision was quick, brutal. More quietly she continued, "The saleswoman would only suggest I go to the Adorable Plus department, where I bought all my clothes last year. Mom, I'm tired of wearing fat clothes. I'll just wait until I've lost another five or ten or fifteen pounds, or whatever it is I need to get rid of, so all this baby fat will disappear."

Adele nodded, then suggested brightly, "Ellie, have you eaten?" Seeing that the answer was no, she continued, "Well, why not come over to our house and have lunch with Mimi and me? Herb's off playing tennis today, so we'll have the house to ourselves."

"I'd like that very much."

Twenty minutes later they were sitting in the Cavanaugh kitchen. The room was spacious, equipped with every modern convenience imaginable. Ellie set the table while Mimi cleaned greens for a salad. At the butcher-block counter, Adele chopped lean meats and cheese into bite-size pieces. Mimi was still looking dejected after the disastrous turn of the shopping trip, and Ellie felt her heart go out to her.

In the past, Ellie had always tried to mind her own business and stay out of what clearly was Cavanaugh family business.

She'd assumed that was what they would have wanted from her. But Neil's comments about her not letting anyone close to her had also struck a chord. She knew she'd kept her distance for other reasons, too, the primary one her fear of getting hurt. To have welcomed Neil's whole family into her heart as family would have been to have risked losing even more should the marriage break up. In the past, if she were truthful with herself, she realized she hadn't really wanted to chance it. But seeing Mimi in the store today looking so obviously unhappy with her appearance had prompted a fierce protective urge. Ellie didn't know whether it was the pregnancy that made her want to take Mimi under her wing or her own distance from Neil and the knowledge that she had been lonely recently, far too lonely. She only knew she wanted to help. And with high school just around the corner for Mimi...well, Ellie could remember only too well how grueling that could be, even for girls who were slender. Teenage boys approaching the dating age could be very cruel indeed.

"I heard you've been baby-sitting this summer," Ellie said.

Mimi nodded, her expression remaining downcast. "Uh-huh."

"She plans to buy her own fall wardrobe," Adele related proudly when no other information was forthcoming from her daughter. Above Mimi's head, Adele shot Ellie an anguished look.

"Good for you," Ellie said encouragingly to Mimi, resting her chin on her clasped hands. "Any idea what you want to get?"

Mimi scowled, finishing up the table. "All depends on what I can fit into, I guess. Maybe I should just buy a tent from the local discount store and make do with that."

Adele started to comment, then stopped herself with effort.

"I know what you mean. I feel fat, too," Ellie complained.

"You!" Mimi scoffed, glancing harder at Ellie's expanding waistline.

"Yes. Look at this!"

"But you're pregnant."

"True, but it's not the first time I've had to be very careful about gaining."

Mimi's gaze was narrowing intently. She was listening to Neil's wife in a way she never would have listened to her own mother. "When have you ever had to watch your weight?" she demanded disbelievingly.

"When I was in college." Ellie smiled, recalling. "The first semester I was so homesick. I'd never been away from home. And the dorm had all this great high-calorie food, pastries and chocolate. All the meats were served with mashed potatoes and gravy. I found my refuge all right. I gained fifteen pounds within three months. Absolutely nothing I'd brought from home fit me. And I didn't have any money to buy new clothes, nor did I have anything at home I could have wiggled into or have altered."

Smiling, Adele brought the salad to the table.

"What did you do?" Mimi asked as they began to eat.

"Exactly what you've done, Mimi. I went on a diet. And, darn, was it ever hard! I've never been so miserable in all my life. Seemed like everywhere I looked, food was jumping out at me. On TV. In magazine ads. On billboards. Not to mention that every time I got nervous, I automatically reached for a chocolate bar as consolation."

"I know about that," Mimi said after a reflective moment. "My secret snack is chocolate-covered granola bars. I could eat them by the dozen." She traded affectionate glances with her mom. "Of course, when Mom discovered that, she stopped buying them. It helps not having them around all the time."

For the next half hour, they talked about all the current fad diets, some Ellie had tried in her prepregnancy days, some Adele had tried herself. All agreed that there was no easy way to lose weight, and that peer support was invaluable.

Eventually, though, talk turned to clothing again. Adele suggested, "Look, there's no reason for you to have to buy clothing from the Adorable Plus department if you don't want to, Mimi. If, by the time school starts, you haven't lost quite enough, we'll simply hire a seamstress or take sewing lessons and make some clothes for you in the current style. And if you really want a show-stopping dress, you can have that, too—provided you're able to wear the appropriate undergarments."

Mimi grinned. "Thanks, Mom—" her expression turned determined "—but I'm going to lose enough to buy my clothes from the regular teen department. I don't have too much further to go. Only about ten pounds. I should be able to do that before summer's end, or just about." Mimi looked appreciatively at Ellie. "Thanks for giving me that pep talk. It helped."

For the first time, Ellie sensed what it must be like to be a big sister. She liked the feeling. She looked at both Cavanaugh women. "Thanks for having me to lunch."

Adele looked pleased, too, with the way the afternoon had turned out. "Let's do it again sometime, Ellie. Without the men."

Ellie smiled. "I'd like that very much."

"WHAT'S THIS I HEAR about you and Mom and Mimi going on diets together?" Neil asked, coming in the back door of the sun porch after a tennis game with his dad. "My mom said you had lunch at her house last week and that the three of you had planned weekly support meetings that would continue for the rest of the summer." His voice clearly relayed his astonishment.

The truth was that Ellie was a bit astounded, too. She didn't really know how it had happened. One minute she had been trying to help Mimi snap out of her doldrums, and the next, the invisible barriers between the Cavanaugh women and herself were tumbling down and she was agreeing to continue to get closer to them. Having no explanation to give him, she watched wordlessly as Neil dropped his tennis racket next to the door. A hand towel had been slung around his neck. Still surveying her curiously, he used the edges of the terry cloth to wipe the perspiration beading his forehead. Finally she said, lowering her eyes to the hands knotted together nervously in her lap, "It's no big deal, Neil. Just women helping other women."

He seemed to think otherwise, but his tone was offhand. "I'm glad you're helping Mimi. She needs all the emotional support she can get in this. Everyone struggles to lose weight, but it's especially tough on a kid, I think. Mom is pleased, too, that she's finally getting to know you better, to feel that you're becoming part of the family. She feels it's because of the baby. I told her I didn't know what to think." Neil sank into a chair opposite her. He was dressed all in white and looked tanned, fit, healthily content. The sun porch at the rear of the house was filled with the fragrant scent of June flowers and fresh-mowed grass.

Ellie ignored his probing look and briefly explained what else she'd learned in subsequent meetings with his younger sister. "Mimi's very nervous about entering high school, about being accepted. Maybe it would help if you talked to her a little bit about your feelings when you entered high school."

"I already have," Neil said quietly, beating her to the punch. "She also told me you'd had a weight problem in college. I didn't know that."

There was a lot Neil didn't know about Ellie, as she'd carefully edited out all unflattering facts about herself. Embarrassed, Ellie flushed. "True," she said shortly.

Neil watched Ellie for a moment longer before turning the conversation back to his younger sister. "I'm proud of what you're doing for Mimi," he said gently at last. "It means a lot to me, my family."

"Well, she's doing very well," Ellie observed proudly, trying not to let herself get worked up about his praise. "She's started jogging every morning before she goes out to her summer babysitting job. And she either swims, or rides her bicycle at night. I've been walking as much as I can. And, of course, your mother plays golf and tennis every week for exercise."

Neil nodded, then, as moments passed, went right on watching her. Ellie tried repeatedly to block him out but failed. She had a fair idea of how she looked to him. She was wearing a soft pastel maternity dress that bared her shoulders and back, and lacy white sandals. Her ivory skin had acquired a faint tan. The glow in her cheeks matched the peach shade of her dress. Her golden-blond hair looked as windblown as usual. She hadn't had the time, energy or inclination to curl it earlier, and it hung in soft waves.

"Are you having trouble keeping your weight down?" Neil asked finally, his eyes drifting down her softly rounded form, with more masculine interest than medical.

"A little. The first two months I lost. The third month I recouped the loss. Now, at the beginning of my fourth month, I seem to be gaining almost too quickly. I don't want to turn into the Goodyear blimp, so I decided I had better do something about it.''

"But you are still following the basic food plans Jim Raynor gave you?" Neil asked seriously.

Ellie nodded. "But it's time-consuming to have not only to weigh and measure all that food but also plan ahead what I'm going to eat. Mimi has it a little easier, because they're all on a diet over there.''

"I know. My dad was complaining during tennis. Seems my mom didn't consult him before making the decision he could stand to lose five pounds, too. She's given away all his favorite junk food, and the refrigerator is now stocked with lots of low-calorie items like broccoli and cabbage.'' He paused. "If you like, I could set up a meeting with the hospital dietitian, to help you plan your menus.''

"Perhaps for your mother, since she's trying to cook for three different people. Not for me.''

"Afraid to face the people who work at the Medical Center?'' His tone carried a casual taunt, the first and only indication of his anger.

Ellie's head lifted at his warning tone. Yes, she thought. And not only that, but she didn't want to chance encountering any ugly gossip again about the state of their marriage or Neil's future plans or romantic inclinations. "No, of course not.'' His mouth curled as if she'd just confirmed his every suspicion. Feeling backed into a corner, she relented. "All right, if you insist, I'll talk to the dietitian.'' Knowing Mimi and Adele, she thought they probably would've insisted she go, anyway.

After a pause, Neil disappeared into the kitchen. She heard him call his service. Moments later he reappeared, bringing with him a pitcher of apple juice and two glasses filled with ice. It seemed a peace offering for his earlier curtness. She watched in silence as he filled her glass and handed it to her.

"What are you up to?" he asked. With a nod, he indicated the catalogs that lay open beside her on the cushioned glider.

"I was looking at cribs.'' *And daydreaming about our baby,* she thought. *Wondering if the child would be male or female.*

"Find anything you like?" Before she knew it, he had moved over to sit next to her on the glider.

She wanted to move away but refused to alert him to the knowledge that his closeness made her uncomfortable. Capriciously she handed him several open catalogs. "All the cribs are so cute. I don't know what style to choose. I could sit here and daydream all day."

"Looking at them makes it all real, doesn't it?" Neil murmured, a smile curving the corners of his mouth. She was close enough to see the beginnings of an evening beard.

"Yes, it does," she said softly. He settled more comfortably into the cushions of the glider and his thigh nudged hers inadvertently, then moved away. Turning toward him involuntarily in response, she caught a drift of his after-shave, the scent of his skin and hair. She knew a longing to be held again, touched, loved; the yearning was so deep and fierce that it hurt. Swallowing hard, she focused on the catalog pages.

"Let's decorate the nursery together," Neil surprised her by suggesting.

"I hate to do it too early."

"Bad luck?"

"I had a friend...she had everything ready by the time she was four months along, and she lost her child."

He nodded, understanding that her fears were overly superstitious, but real nonetheless. "Okay, in another month or so, then, we'll get started. We won't finish the room completely, until after the baby is born."

"Agreed." Ellie took a deep breath. She rose, moving idly to the row of windows along the back of the house. They were all open now, letting in the last warm summer breeze. The ceiling fan was whirring rhythmically, the lulling sound reminding her of the previous happier days—before the fertility pills, the pressure to conceive, the Middleton case. If none of that had come about, would they still be happy? she wondered. Or would something else have come along to drive them apart?

Abruptly, Neil shared her introspective mood. He glanced over at her, his jaw hardening stubbornly.

"Don't you think it's time we called a halt and tore up the

divorce agreement for the sake of the child?'' His persuasive tone surprised her and left her momentarily speechless. His words, obviously thought-out and well rehearsed, were no impetuous speech, but the result of much soul-searching.

"I know you've been upset," he continued in the same reasonable tone. "I've been short-tempered and overworked as well. But is that any reason for us to throw everything away? Ellie, we need to talk. And," he went on, less sure of himself, "we also need to take into consideration the possibility that the hormonal changes due to your pregnancy might be making you overemotional—"

"I can't believe you just said that," Ellie interrupted in amazement. She didn't know whether to laugh or cry.

His brows drew together dramatically. "You deny you've been moody—quick to laugh, shout or cry?" His tone was low and laced with husbandly amusement.

"No, I don't deny that." She blushed hotly, embarrassed despite her resolve not to be. "But to blame all our problems on either our hectic schedules or my hormones—"

"Maybe it is too easy," he interjected evenly.

"Neil, you were all too quick to agree to my request for a divorce."

The corners of his mouth turned down grimly. "Believe me, I've regretted losing my temper many times."

"But you did lose your temper. And I did ask for a divorce. The impact of those two actions alone shows just how upset we've been. Upset enough to consider ending the marriage."

"Then we overreacted." He was firm about that much.

Had they? Sometimes Ellie thought so. At other times, alone, she wondered. She knew Neil was the man for her, flaws and all, but was she the woman for him? Was simply loving each other enough? Why was marriage so damn complicated? Why, suddenly, did everything count for so much? There'd been a time, early on in their courtship, when just the simple act of being together, spending time together, had been enough, when it wouldn't have mattered what either of them had felt about any political or professional issue. How and when had they lost that?

"Just for a moment, forget what we said and did in the heat

of a very emotional battle," Neil said, not to be deterred from what he'd originally set out to do, convince her that an immediate reconciliation was for the best. "Realistically, you and I both know from our experiences with clients and patients that very often couples rush into a divorce without stopping to consider just how very much they're really giving up. And it's not wise for people to make major changes in their lives when they're under unusual amounts of stress. Not if they don't have to. Generally, it's better to wait. Sometimes, when the additional stress disappears, so do the problems."

"You think that's what we've done?" For not the first time, she allowed herself to hope he had been acting uncharacteristically, that his cold behavior wasn't an indicator of their future life together.

"Yes, I do."

"If I thought for one moment we could pick up where we left off, that you'd stop trying to interfere in my career—" Ellie's voice was laced with fervent longing.

At the mention of her career, his expression closed. He stood, turned away restlessly, shook his head in a way that let her know he thought she was asking for miracles.

"Even the baby doesn't change the disapproving way you feel, does it, Neil?" she said quietly, dismayed to find that his silent disavowal of her actions hurt as much if not more now than it had initially.

"How can I help but feel the way I do?" he countered honestly but inflexibly. He wanted to reconcile, to let the difficulties between them end. He wouldn't lie or misrepresent his feelings to achieve that. "When I see the surge of malpractice suits negatively affecting the practice of medicine every day?" Emotion permeated his low voice, revealing just how passionate were his beliefs.

"When surgeons have to pay upward of eighty thousand dollars a year in insurance premiums, just to practice medicine? When some doctors, pressed to hold down costs, are now prescribing fewer levels of diagnostic tests and prescribing lower levels of care so their patients can afford to come into the office and get treatment? As other doctors turn their offices into mass-production lines and hence foster less personal doctor-patient relationships? When still other physicians are prescribing unnecessary tests, just to protect themselves from later being sued? What's most distressing is the fact that the patients are ultimately the ones who suffer most. Ellie, it's gotten to the point where even I've been affected! I think twice now about taking a difficult or exceptionally quarrelsome patient because I'm not sure that at some point down the road she isn't going to turn around and try to sue me—for God only knows what!''

Ellie was silent, depressed. She was glad he had opened up to her. They needed to talk, to share their feelings. And yet, by doing so, he'd made it clear they were still miles apart in ideology.

"Look...maybe it's time we put all that aside and concentrated on the baby we're going to have—a baby we've both wanted for a very long time,'' he said judiciously, reading her discomfiture.

She swallowed hard. Part of her wanted that, but another part of her knew that to presume that would work was more naive than her assumption that Neil eventually would understand and approve of her professional decision to take the Middleton case. Nor did she want him to stay with her just for the sake of the child. Still, she tried to meet him halfway. After all their marriage had meant to them, she owed him that. "I'll agree to continue to live here with you platonically. To let you share in the baby's birth and keep up the appearance of being a couple. But anything more than that, Neil, we'd be pushing it. I don't want to risk losing what little peace we've recouped.''

"Ever the skillful negotiator, aren't you, Ellie?'' His tone was bitter. Abruptly, he seemed as frustrated as she had felt initially when she couldn't get through to him about why she'd taken the case. The difference was that she wouldn't overreact and walk out on him now.

She had at least learned not to act too hastily but, instead, to bide her time, to play it cool. "I'm very adept when it comes to getting what I want. And what I want is a marriage that works again, Neil. Unfortunately, to achieve that monumental task, we're going to have to work hard at it, not just mouth platitudes and theories we don't really believe with all our hearts. We can't just cross our fingers and hope to heaven it works! We can't just leave it to chance! I want a marriage that's solid, that will stand up to the stresses of both a two-career marriage and the demanding process of raising a child. A marriage that will stand up even to the pressures of my taking a malpractice case. I thought you did, too."

"I do. You know that." He was serious, intent.

Ellie lifted her face pleadingly to his. They had so much riding on this—their whole future! "Then give us time; give us the opportunity to work this out, step-by-step, no matter how time-consuming and arduous the process is. Love me enough to let us take it one day at a time for now." *Love me enough to let me know that my professional decisions are mine to make,* she finished in a silent prayer.

"And after the baby's born?" He was skeptical, but interested, just the same. As he waited for her answer he stood, legs braced apart, thighs girded, calves taut. His hands were thrust into his pockets. His eyes never left her face.

Ellie took a deep breath, mentally wishing for luck. "We can reassess our situation then." She hoped time would provide all the answers, but she wasn't going to make any promises that might prove impossible to keep. "Right now what we need is caution. Communication. Respect. A sense of sharing our lives again, as friends first, then as husband and wife. We need to work toward each other, toward achieving renewed intimacy one step at a time. Only then will the commitment last."

"All right," he allowed finally. "We'll do it your way for now. But I want us to spend time together, Ellie. As much as our schedules—and the difficulties of the situation at hand—allow." He was stern and uncompromising about his demands on her.

"Agreed," she said softly, very glad they had taken the first important step toward reconciliation. They still had a long way to go. But, with love, eventually everything would work out. They would see to it.

Silence fell between them once again, but it was a more companionable quiet now, less tense. They might have been alone in the world, she and Neil, Ellie thought. The backyard was fenced in for privacy and a circle of trees added to the tall wooden parameters. In the distance the sun was slowly sinking lower into the sky. The neighborhood was quiet.

"Have you had dinner?" Neil asked.

Ellie shook her head. She pivoted toward him.

"Anything in mind?" His eyes traced the faint rounded curves of her abdomen, visible beneath the smock of her dress. She felt her cheeks again heat.

"Just broiled chicken, a salad, baked potato. Maybe a tiny bit of fruit and cheese for dessert."

"Sounds good. Got enough for two?"

She nodded. There always was. Though in deference to the separate way they had been living their lives of late, everything was frozen in single portions. Somehow, she found her voice. "I'll have to take another chicken breast out of the freezer."

"Sit still. I'll get it. You look tired," he continued when she was about to protest.

Ellie was tired—exhausted, as a matter of fact.

Neil disappeared into the kitchen. Minutes later the sounds of Grover Washington, Jr.'s jazz album, *Winelight*, were filtering through the back of the house. Ellie could hear Neil banging around in the kitchen, whistling along with the record. She curled up on the cushioned chaise that matched the glider, watching the sunset for just a moment, listening to Neil, the music.

The next thing she knew, a leg was nudging her bare knee. "Hey, sleepyhead." Fingers touched her hair, curved down to her chin. "Ready for dinner, or are you going to sleep all night?"

Ellie woke with a start. Neil was staring down at her. Darkness had descended. The night was soft, warm. Fragrant smells wafted from the kitchen. Beyond her on the sun porch, their white wrought-iron table was set for two, complete with candles and champagne. "We never really did celebrate the baby," Neil said with a tender smile as he helped her to her feet. "I thought tonight was the night."

Ellie stared at him, still sleepily mute. He laughed, the sound low and tempting and reassuring in the darkness. His arm wound around her waist. He led her to the table.

Dinner was delicious.

Neil seemed in a very strange mood. He chatted incessantly, though he said nothing at all about his work or the hospital or any of his medical chums. He talked more about his family, about the latest movies, books, where he would like to vacation that he'd never been. It seemed almost as if he were trying to ward off some very great depression, Ellie thought, puzzled and perplexed.

"Is anything bothering you?" she asked as they cleared the table together.

For a sharp moment she thought he would say something about the divorce agreement. She could have kicked herself for ever asking if anything was wrong. But he let the opportunity to comment sardonically slide and, instead, said only, "I've missed you, Ellie. Missed being with you and talking with you."

For the first time in their marriage he was withholding ten times more than he was telling. But whatever it was that was plaguing him was not something easily discussed. They'd had so much trouble between them recently that she feared to pursue it.

"I'll finish up in here," she said quietly, gesturing toward the few dishes that were left. "Why don't you go out on the porch and relax?" Busily she began loading the last of the silverware and pots and pans into the dishwasher.

After a moment the door to the porch opened and shut.

Because it seemed the polite action to take, Ellie walked out on the sun porch after she had finished, intending to tell him she was going upstairs to read a bit, then retire. Neil was standing quietly, gazing out toward the darkened backyard. His legs were slightly girded; his hands loosely encircled his waist. There was a quarter-moon illuminating the backyard, but about all Ellie could make out was the shadows of trees and bushes and a faint sprinkling of stars overhead. Several candles, set in glass, were arranged at various places on the porch. Aside from the moonlight filtering onto the porch, the candles provided the only illumination. But it was enough to see the melancholy on Neil's face.

He turned toward her with a buoyancy that seemed forced. "The baby will need more than just a crib, you know. There are swing sets and bicycles, maybe even a sandbox."

"Neil, what is it?" He'd never shut her out that thoroughly before when he was so clearly upset about something. It was alarming. It hurt. She moved toward him imploringly, knowing she wanted desperately to help him, to be there for him about whatever was bothering him, if only because, despite everything that had passed between them, they had always been and would be friends first.

"What I said earlier." His voice was gruff, impatient, with himself and with her. "I've missed you. Damn it, Ellie, the frustration is tearing me apart." His arm encircled her waist, drawing her against his side. But as she half feared, he made no effort to caress her, just held her there against him, so close she could feel the steady pounding of his heart. He swallowed hard. "This living together and yet not..." He turned her toward him, his hands gripping her shoulders.

As if in a slow-motion dance, she extricated herself from his hold, backed around and away. Without warning, every bit of self-preserving instinct she possessed had come into play. The incredible tenderness he'd evidenced earlier had been replaced by a yearning that was stark and sensual in intent. She could feel the need pouring out of him, a frustration that echoed her own. But she didn't want to be involved again. What he was seemingly luring her toward was exactly what she was fighting against.

"I don't know how much longer I can go on sleeping on the sofa." As he spoke he moved toward her, taking slow, gliding steps, like a cat stalking its prey. She backed up against the wall, missing by inches the open French doors that led to the interior of the house.

"You want to move out?" Her breath was coming in short bursts, and no matter how much she tried, she couldn't seem to get any oxygen into her lungs.

"No, I don't want to move out." His voice was harsh, low, as he trapped her with his body against the wall. His fingers tangled in her hair, preventing her escape. Yet the motion was gentle, lulling, as he stroked the strands into order. "I want to move back into the bedroom with you."

"Neil." Ellie's throat was dry; her heart was racing. Every

nerve ending was alive with sensations, a mixture of anticipation and fear.

"Tell me you don't want me, Ellie," he said softly, roughly. His tongue parted her lips, touched, very gently, the edges of her teeth and then returned in a series of soft, drugging kisses that robbed her of her will, of the ability to think. Her knees were suddenly unsteady. Desire was flowing through her, more potent and mesmerizing than ever before. "Tell me you don't want this." His hands touched her breasts; his mouth lazily followed the trail his fingertips had blazed. Her head dropped back in abandonment. Hands pressing against his shoulders, she tried halfheartedly to step past. He caught her wrists and wouldn't let her; rather, moved closer until their bodies were intimately aligned, length to length. When she turned toward him to protest, his mouth lowered, touching hers, once, twice, then searingly in a contact she couldn't have broken if she tried. She moaned deep and low, and he responded even more fiercely, wrapping his arms around her. A flood of pent-up passion came pouring out of her, the result of weeks of need, of days spent alone. She returned his kisses almost mindlessly, needing, wanting so much the physical comfort he could give her. Yet even then she could feel the danger, the sensation that he knew exactly what he was doing and that she was all too willingly allowing herself to be swept away. And a one-night stand, a temporary liaison with her estranged husband, was not what she wanted. She needed patience, security and understanding, none of which he had been able to give lately.

"Neil!" With sanity returning, she turned sharply, breaking away.

He was breathing quickly as he surveyed her with heavy-lidded eyes. She expected him to say he was sorry, to promise it would never happen again as long as they shared the house. He did neither.

"I still want you," he said softly, unrepentantly, at last.

And, God help her, she still wanted him. But that didn't mean they could make their marriage work. And she was tired of being hurt. She folded her arms across her waist, paced away from him, as if that action alone would put an end to the tumultuous feelings of both love and unbearable hurt inside her. "Our marriage is over." She made her voice as cool and logical as possible. Yet, inside, a storm of yearning still raged.

"Is it?" His low murmur was a derisive challenge.

"It will be." Ellie twirled back to face him. She had to learn to get along without him now, much as her mother had learned, to raise a child on her own. Without help from anyone, even the child's father.

She wouldn't discount the magic of the time during which they had conceived. Numbly, she counseled, glad for the semidarkness that hid the tears sparkling in her eyes, "A baby doesn't magically fix problems in a marriage, Neil." She saw cases that documented that in her practice.

"Instead, he or she will learn right off that Mom and Dad no longer live together." Contempt underscored his every word.

"Better than suffering through the trauma of a divorce." But how well could Neil understand? His parents had a happy marriage. He'd had such a secure childhood.

"I don't agree." He sighed heavily, raked a hand through his hair. "But obviously this is nothing we'll settle tonight. We're both tired. It's been an exhausting day, an exhausting couple of weeks...." His voice trailed off dispiritedly.

Ellie felt the crushing disappointment displayed in his expression. Her hopes for them had been quite different from the reality of what they'd experienced, too. "I'm sorry, Neil," she said in a strangled voice, reaching out to him at last in the only way she could. She wanted desperately to maintain their friendship. Surely they could keep that much. She should have seen his physical attempt at persuading her coming; she should have fought harder, not allowed herself to return his kisses, even for a moment. But she had. And now they knew that passion still existed between them. And Neil was no monk, never had been.

"I'm turning in." He locked the back door, moved past her to the den.

She followed, turning off the lights, bypassing the den in favor of the bedroom suite upstairs. Desolation washed over her, more complete and haunting than ever before.

Chapter Seven

Neil woke feeling stiff and grumpy after another night spent on the sofa bed. In the distance he could hear the rustle of the newspaper and smell coffee and freshly baked croissants. Sunday morning—normally a time of relaxation and togetherness. Or at least in the past it had been. Now Neil didn't know what to expect, though he should have expected what had happened last night, he thought, as he bypassed the kitchen in favor of the stairs. Alone upstairs, he cast a cursory look at the rumpled covers of the bed and headed for the bathroom.

While shaving he mentally replayed every nuance of the afternoon and evening before, from the time he had walked in the back door and viewed Ellie in all her pregnant splendor, her face radiant and full of color, her eyes dreamily aglow as she contemplated baby items in the department store catalogs, to the way she had looked sleeping drowsily on the back porch, her legs curled up under her, her face resting on girlishly clasped hands that had cushioned her head slightly on the chaise. He'd known better than to come on to her, even to think of making love when their relationship was still so fraught with unspoken tension and anxiety. But he had needed her so badly last night, and when she'd reached out to him verbally in the darkness after dinner, trying so hard to understand his black mood, to help, he had forsaken what he knew was best—keeping his physical distance—and, instead, had given in to the desire that her mere presence evoked.

He stepped into the shower and turned on the pounding spray.

He still wanted her badly. He was still furious as hell. With her, for taking the Middleton case, jeopardizing all they had, and with himself, for not handling her and the whole situation better.

When he ventured downstairs moments later, he found Ellie seated at the kitchen table. In front of her was the "City News" section of the local paper. Her face was inordinately pale as she glanced up at him. Next to her motionless right wrist was an article, with photograph, about the new chief of obstetrics at the Joplin Medical Center. "How long have you known?" she asked.

Neil felt her reaction like a sucker punch to his gut. "That I lost the post? Officially since late Thursday, though I think it really didn't sink in until yesterday, when it was announced to the rest of the staff." Neil spoke casually as he reached for the coffee. It was hard to explain what that had felt like, losing a post he had initially considered his.

"Neil, I'm sorry."

Neil felt some of his irritation returning. He didn't want her pity. Curtly, he advised, "Don't be. As you can see, my rival for the position was eminently qualified. Dr. Vaughn's got ten years experience on me, has headed up residency programs at other hospitals. I have no doubt she'll bring much to the Joplin Medical Center. Certainly, I'll do everything I can to see that she's made to feel at ease." Neil meant what he said. He still felt the disappointment.

Ellie sat very still, looking almost afraid to speak or make a move. Hating her pity even more than he had despised her lack of trust, he said, "It's over, Ellie. Finished. There won't be another election for the position for at least two years."

She nodded her understanding, said finally, "Have you met Dr. Vaughn?"

"Not yet, no." Neil glanced at his watch. "I've got to make rounds at the hospital. I'm on call for the rest of the day. If you need me, I'll be at the hospital." Giving her no chance to respond, he said levelly, "About last night, I'm sorry. As you can imagine—" he indicated the newspaper article in front of her "—I needed...consolation. It won't happen again." He wouldn't push himself on her, wouldn't put her in the position of having to say no. Because desire without trust and love was meaningless, empty. A vehicle for later regrets and recriminations, and Ellie and he had had enough of those between them as it was.

"If you had confided in me..." Her voice trailed off lamely. She still looked stricken.

It was too late for her guilt, her sorrow. He wanted none of it. Pushing her away emotionally as cruelly as he knew how, he said, "What are you trying to say, Ellie? That you would have made love to me out of pity? Offered me a shoulder to cry on? I don't want your forbearance. I don't need it. So save your compassion for someone who does."

In the meantime, Neil would give all he could to his patients. At least there he'd be able to get some return on his emotional investment. He left, unable to get out fast enough. But the vision of Ellie, her face pinched with regret, stayed in his mind.

FOR THE NEXT SEVERAL WEEKS they were like strangers inhabiting the same hotel, Ellie thought. They saw each other coming and going. They spoke with increasing politeness. Yet there was a distance between them that seemed unbridgeable. When the time came for Ellie to go to St. Louis, she went with relief.

"So, how long will you be gone?" Mimi asked when she learned of Ellie's plans.

"I don't know exactly," Ellie replied honestly as they walked leisurely around the high-school track. To their right and left they were being passed by joggers. "A day or two at most."

"When are you leaving?" In an effort to burn off extra calories, Mimi was carrying small weights in each hand. Ellie was glad to see that her sister-in-law's steady efforts to slim down were paying off. She looked trimmer, healthier, every time Ellie saw her, and, as a bonus, happier, too. With effort Ellie concentrated on what they had been saying and answered Mimi's question. "I'm leaving tomorrow morning, first thing."

"Is Neil going with you?"

"No." Ellie looked away, suddenly at a loss for words. She and Neil had promised each other to keep their marital discord from their respective families. Answering as honestly as possible, she kept her voice light. "It'll be a quick trip. I've been asked to represent a woman who's been hospitalized there."

"Another malpractice case?" Mimi looked stunned. She might only be fourteen, but she was plenty old enough to be aware of the disruptions Ellie's taking the Middleton case had caused within the family.

"Could be," Ellie replied carefully. "I won't know until I get up there and talk to the people in person if I even want to take the case."

"But you think you will want to take the case," Mimi ascertained readily.

"I think it's worth checking into. At this point that's all I know." And to be truthful, she was looking forward to the reprieve from the tense situation with Neil.

Mimi skipped ahead several steps, still energetically waving her weights up and down, back and forth, like a prizefighter getting ready to step into the ring. "Didn't Neil used to go with you whenever you had to go out of town?"

"Yes, but...generally, in the past, I've had more notice when I had to go out of town. And he wasn't quite as busy." Or hellbent on avoiding her and the home situation altogether. An outlandish occurrence, since he'd been the one so gung ho on having them continue to share quarters for appearance's sake.

"The two of you haven't been together much lately. How come?" When Ellie was silent, Mimi guessed cheekily, extrapolating, "Don't tell me. It's back to his schedule again. He's been at the hospital around the clock."

Ellie managed a wry smile. "You know as well as I do that erratic hours are typical of an obstetrician." Resentful of his frequent absences herself, Ellie was surprised to find herself defending Neil. He'd been an absolute bear since losing the hospital post, a fact that she assured herself firmly made her almost glad they'd already signed the informal divorce agreement and gotten it out of the way.

"Yeah. But does that mean he has to work as constantly as he does?"

Inadvertently Mimi had touched on Ellie's fear that Neil wouldn't be there for either the baby or her. Even when their marriage had been intact, she'd known essentially that she'd have to be prepared to go it alone at times. Because the minute one of Neil's patients went into labor, off he went to the hospital. Intellectually, she understood and respected his responsibility, though if they were in the middle of an intimate discussion or dinner, it was less easy to accept the never-ending demands of his profession. To her knowledge, she'd never given Neil a clue to her inner resentment of the demands made on him incessantly. She hadn't wanted to make him feel guilty about working. She hadn't wanted to burden him with any extra worries. Now that their marriage was, in essence, over except for the final legal dissolution, she told herself she should feel relieved that soon she wouldn't have to worry about his lack of time for her anymore.

Mimi continued, with a frown, still concerned with Neil's hectic schedule. "Mom has called him about one hundred times since you two found out you're going to have a baby, so she can have a party for the two of you, invite all the friends, some relatives—you know, have a real shindig. Neil keeps promising to get back to her, but he doesn't. Whenever she calls him about it, and I know she's talked to him at least three times altogether, he always makes up some excuse."

"Maybe he doesn't feel like socializing now," Ellie guessed.

"Because of his losing the position at the hospital?"

Solemnly, Ellie acknowledged, "He was disappointed."

"Yeah, but he'll have other chances."

"I hope so," Ellie mused. Jim Raynor, she knew, had held the position for twenty years.

"Is everything all right between the two of you?" Mimi asked.

Again, Ellie smiled and evaded with every bit of lawyer's skill she possessed. "We're both very happy about the baby. Now," she switched the subject adroitly, "tell me more about those school clothes you wanted to buy for yourself. Have you and your mom come to any conclusions about what type of clothes you'll get?"

Mimi rolled her eyes heavenward. "Are you kidding? Mom's tastes are still in the Dark Ages. Every time we go shopping...well, let's just say I come out looking like a miniversion of her.''

Ellie laughed. She knew the feeling. But in this case, what was good for the mother wasn't good for the daughter, or vice versa. There were too many years—and miles of fashion distance— between the two women. ''Maybe I could mediate for you this year,'' Ellie suggested. Mimi had been so good for her lately, getting her mind off her own troubles. And she was close enough now to Neil's mother to know that Adele wouldn't resent the offer to help, but would welcome Ellie's willingness to come to Mimi's aid in the role of big sister.

''Really?'' Mimi's eyes were shining. ''You'd really do that for me?''

Ellie smiled and squeezed her sister-in-law's hand. ''I'd like that very much.'' She and Mimi were getting to be very good friends. Ellie knew it was strange to be getting close to Neil's family just when the marriage was breaking up. But she had no regrets. She was only sorry the friendships hadn't evolved sooner.

THE TRIP TO ST. LOUIS was a tiring one, and, unfortunately, Ellie's business mission there proved fruitless. It was after seven o'clock when she checked into her room. To her surprise, Neil was there, waiting for her. Hands clasped behind his head, he was stretched out on the bed. The shock of seeing him so unexpectedly faded quickly into aggravation, which was doubled by her long, wearying day and by his recent treatment of her.

''What are you doing here?'' Ellie asked in her coldest, most dispassionate voice, removing her key from the lock. Didn't he realize one of the reasons she had come to St. Louis was to get a reprieve from him?

''I heard you were hot on the heels of another malpractice case. Naturally, I couldn't wait to hear all about it.'' His eyes were glittering with an anger she neither liked nor trusted.

She made herself look at him, made herself hold his frank gaze steady. ''Mimi told you?''

''Who else?'' He paused. ''It's true, isn't it?''

''Yes. That's why I came to St. Louis. I had an appointment

to meet with a potential client. Normally, the first meeting takes place in my office, but this time it wasn't possible."

He started to say something, then bit down on it. It was all she could do not to flinch, to run. He kept staring at her as if she were a stranger rather than the woman he had married, the mother of his child. "Well, are you going to take the case?" he asked finally with just a little too much patience.

His cynical, accusing manner made her angry. Why had he come if all he wanted to do was fight? "No," Ellie said shortly, stubbornly offering no details, except to say, "It didn't work out." She paused, unable to help adding defensively, "Contrary to your low opinion of me, Neil, I'm not an ambulance chaser."

He made a nonconcurring sound in the back of his throat. "But you could become one."

Which showed just how little he really knew about her, Ellie thought. "Well, now that you've found out what you came for, I suggest you leave." She was exhausted.

"I'm not leaving, Ellie. Neither are you. Not until I've finished what I have to say."

She could hardly wait. She raised and lowered her brows in silent discord. "I could have you thrown out."

"Now, that would make an interesting headline," he theorized, folding his hands behind his head and settling more comfortably on the pillows. "'Malpractice lawyer fights doctor husband over jurisdiction of St. Louis hotel room.'"

"Very funny." But even as she spoke, she felt an unwilling smile curve her lips. She tossed her purse and briefcase down on the surface of the nearest bureau.

He paused, his temper cooling as what she had told him finally penetrated. "You're really not taking the case?" He heaved a sigh of relief.

"No, I'm not."

His eyes flickered over her, as if he were assessing her. "Was the case without merit?"

Ellie sat on the edge of the desk. "No, it was similar to what happened to the Middletons. Negligence on the part of the hospital when it came to consulting a patient's history. The plaintiffs wanted even a smaller portion of their bill paid by the hospital's insurance company—the twenty percent their own medical insurance didn't cover."

"So why didn't you take the case?"

Because she had other priorities now, Ellie thought. Her baby. And because she was beginning to see that she didn't want to handle any more malpractice cases. Not because they weren't justified, but because she didn't enjoy the work. And because she hated hurting Neil. Not wanting him to know how her emotions were beginning to affect her professional judgments, however, she concentrated on more impersonal reasons. "Primarily, because it would have been just as easy for the plaintiffs in this situation to allow their own medical insurance company to battle it out with the other insurance company, for no fee to the plaintiff."

Ellie sighed, using the opportunity to touch on something that had been bothering her for weeks. "But there was another reason, too, Neil. Raising one child in a loving, stable atmosphere is going to be hard enough, with us being divorced soon after his or her birth, without my complicating matters further or adding additional tension to the situation. We haven't talked about this, Neil, but I assume you'd be willing, because of your erratic schedule and hours, to let me have full custody of the child. You could see the baby whenever or however much you liked. But I think it's important that our child not be dragged around unnecessarily."

Briefly, Neil was shocked into silence. "I'll agree to whatever you want in that regard. When the time comes to...decide," Neil finished with difficulty, looking away.

After a moment he rose lithely to a sitting position, putting his feet flat on the floor. Ellie tried not to notice his suitcase, resting on a rack beside the coat hangers next to the door. He sent her a level, censuring look, but his voice was gentle as he spoke. "I wish you had told me you planned to drive up here, alone, before the fact."

"Why?" Her heart was pounding at his nearness, but Ellie affected a casual manner as she proceeded into the center of the room. Instinctively she feared that if she didn't close some of the distance between them, he would. Casually she took off her suit coat, placed it neatly on a hanger and, after kicking off her pumps, walked serenely across the carpet. She chose the chair nearest the window and farthest away from Neil. Momentarily she pretended to focus on the children splashing in the hotel pool. She turned back to Neil, giving as good as she got. "Why should I have cleared my plans with you?"

"Because it's my baby, too, you're carrying. And St. Louis is two hundred and eighty-two miles away."

She grinned at the exactness of the measure. "I drove, not walked the route barefoot," she said dryly, crossing her legs at the knee.

"Anything could have happened." He watched as with one hand she leaned forward and massaged the swollen arch of her left foot.

"It didn't." Finally feeling some relief in her left foot, Ellie recrossed her legs and started massaging her right foot.

To her discomfiture Neil was still watching her, looking as if at any second he might jump up to help. "And it won't on the way back, either. I intend to drive with you."

If only he'd been that caring and accessible when she'd first taken the Middleton case, Ellie thought. But he hadn't. And now she was getting used to going it alone again. She didn't want to come to depend on him only to have to quit. She took a moment to shore up her defenses. "I checked with Dr. Raynor beforehand. He didn't see anything wrong with my plans." She wasn't prepared to handle Neil in small quarters. Especially when he was determined to protect and watch over her—and his baby.

"Jim's a fine obstetrician. The best. But it's not his baby we're talking about here."

Ellie realized wearily that there was no fighting the possessive, fatherly note in Neil's voice. Especially when he was acting the way she would have expected any red-blooded American man to act, the way she had wanted her own father to, and he never had. "How did you get up here?" She sat back in her chair, forced herself to focus on the trivialities of their current predicament.

Neil grimaced. He rolled to his feet, stretched as if very stiff. "The bus."

She knew how Neil hated public transportation. The fact that he'd taken the bus signaled his determination to stick to her like glue, both there in the city and en route home. It didn't explain his concern. Not well enough, anyway.

"Why didn't you tell me your plans, Ellie?" he asked more gently. "If I'd known what you intended to do, I would have arranged to drive up with you."

"I didn't think you'd be interested," she said after a time, determined to keep up the sophisticated front if it killed her. She wanted Neil to see that she could handle whatever he dished out. "You haven't been around much lately."

"My mistake," he said gravely.

Her mistake was in letting him stay in her room for even a minute. "How did you get in here?" she asked offhandedly. She wanted to see that it never happened again, and forewarned was forearmed.

"I talked to the hotel manager. I told him I was your husband, that I'd unexpectedly gotten time off and wanted to surprise you. I offered my driver's license and credit card for ID."

Determined to be adult about this, she said sedately, "Neil, I want you to get another room."

"I figured you'd say that."

"And?"

"And it would be all right with me, except—" he sighed heavily, as if perturbed about that much himself "—the adjacent rooms are all taken. And I wanted to be close by just in case..."

She swallowed a mystified laugh. "In case what?"

"Traveling can be hard on a woman in your condition. Sometimes it can aggravate morning sickness, which you've already had your fair share of. I...wanted to be within shouting distance just in case you needed me. I already asked the hotel desk if they had any adjoining rooms available, but they're all booked up. We could change hotels, of course. But that seems a little ridiculous, considering we're married and are already managing to live together platonically."

Not to mention the fact that the room had two double beds, Ellie thought. She wouldn't even have to sleep with him.

Neil raked his fingers through his hair, rubbed the back of his neck. "Ellie, I'm tired of living in an armed camp. Don't you think it's about time we sat down and talked again? If not for our sakes, then the baby's. I'd like to take you out to dinner. Please say you'll go with me.''

Ellie took a deep breath. Part of her wanted that, too. But she was still hurt, mistrustful, very aware that it was all too easy these days for them to argue. ''Neil, I'm exhausted.''

''We'll order room service, then. We don't even have to go out.''

That option seemed all the more dangerous. ''Just give me a few minutes to freshen up,'' Ellie bargained finally. He nodded agreeably.

Ellie walked into the bathroom, locked the door behind her with shaking hands. Taking her time, she repaired her makeup, brushed her hair. Seeing Neil had upset her. Part of her had wanted him to come after her, she knew. But now that he was there, she felt oddly vulnerable. She'd hated the anger between them, the pain, the distance Neil had willfully put between them. She knew she still loved him, that she probably always would. She wasn't so sure he loved her, not enough to withstand the pressures of a dual-career marriage and the added complexities that would be created with the addition of a child. If they couldn't handle their lives now, how would they handle the addition of a child, too?

''IS YOUR HEART SET on the hotel restaurant, or do you have it in you to try something more adventurous tonight?'' Neil asked before they left the room.

''What did you have in mind?'' Ellie reached for her suit jacket, slipped it on. Neil was behind her, to help pull her hair from the collar, smooth it over her shoulders.

He named an expensive restaurant, situated across town. With Ellie wearing her business clothes and Neil in suit and tie, they were dressed well enough to be admitted to any of the fine restaurants in town.

''That would be fine.'' She raised a warning index finger, trying without success to ignore the tingling sensations his touch had generated. ''As long as you're paying.''

He grinned with boyish acceptance. ''I'm paying.''

"Then I'm going."

To her surprise the evening was very relaxing and enjoyable. Neil was the perfect gentleman. And by carefully steering the conversation to neutral matters, they were able to talk with ease once again. Outside the restaurant the evening was soft, beckoning, as they waited for the valet to bring Ellie's car around. "Tired?" he asked, sliding behind the wheel.

"Yes." But she was still too keyed up to sleep. Especially with Neil sharing the same hotel room. He held her glance steadily. She knew he realized instinctively how much it bothered her that they'd be sharing the same hotel room for the night. The two double beds, the purposeful blandness of his behavior, helped not one iota. Being alone with Neil made her think intimate thoughts, remember times she no longer wanted to dwell on.

He looked past her, toward the quiet streets. "I know a place where we can hear some great Southern jazz." He seemed abruptly as discomfited as she.

"I'd like that very much," Ellie said, trying to keep the immediate relief she felt from underscoring her words.

Minutes later, they entered a waterfront club, located on the ground floor of a red brick building. The bar was furnished with simple tables and captain's chairs, pushed together to allow maximum seating arrangement. It was a weeknight, but the club was still packed almost to overflowing. Neil was able to get them a table near the far wall. They barely had time to order drinks, a 7-Up for Ellie and a light beer for Neil, before the lights dimmed and the seven-piece band took up the small squared-off area that served as their stage.

Neil reached over and squeezed her hand as the sweet sounds of an authentic Dixieland rag filled the club. "What do you think?" he asked when the first set had come to a close and the waiters were serving the tables, getting drinks for those who desired them in the interim.

Ellie gave the musicians a very positive rating. "It reminds me of the trip we took to New Orleans—the time we spent strolling in the French Quarter." Because Neil and she both had been so crazy about jazz, it had seemed there was only one place for them to honeymoon. And their time there had been sheer heaven.

Neil's eyes darkened nostalgically in the smoky room. "I know what you mean. It seems like just yesterday that we stood watching the street musicians play on Bourbon Street."

"They were good, weren't they?" Ellie said softly after a minute. And she didn't mean just the musicians, but the times, the early days of their marriage.

Neil nodded affirmatively. "The best."

The second set began. The upbeat tempo made her smile and tap her foot and caused her adrenaline to speed along at breakneck rate. Some of the songs tugged at her poignant, introspective memories, thoughts, feelings. She was always surprised by the myriad emotions that songs could stir within her—soothing, mesmerizing, transporting her from reality into the heart and soul of each tune and maybe each group of artists. Neil seemed similarly caught up, entranced. By mutual agreement they stayed until the bistro closed. As they made their way out of the club, she felt drained, yet strangely energized, ready to face the world with a calmer, clearer head.

Outside, the streets were dark, reflecting shimmering rectangles of lamplight broken by shadows of buildings and cars.

"Well worth the late hour and the sleep you undoubtedly deserve but have just missed?" Neil teased as they walked to her car.

Ellie's heart skipped a beat as momentarily she was wedged beneath his tall, rangy frame and the passenger side of her car. "Well worth it. Thanks for dinner and the club," she said softly.

Neil's mouth crooked wryly. "This is beginning to sound and feel as if we're on a date. Our first one."

In many ways that was true, Ellie decided, happiness welling up inside her. "It's been a long time since we took time out simply to enjoy ourselves," she said, settling back into the seat.

"Too long," he agreed, fitting the key into the ignition.

The drive back to the hotel was accomplished with ease, owing to the absence of traffic. They walked in silence to their hotel room. There were two double beds, Ellie thought. No reason for her to feel in any way threatened, yet she was, more by her own feelings than by any move he might choose to make.

He was suddenly all business as he faced the interior of the room. He glanced at the suitcases, the beds, then back at her flushed face. "You can have the bathroom first," he said gently. "I'm going to see if I can find an evening paper out in one of the machines." He left as quietly and unexpectedly as he'd arrived.

Ellie stared after him, her heart pounding, her hands perspiring. How was she ever going to make it through the night?

Chapter Eight

Neil strolled the darkened pool area restlessly, his hands jammed into the pockets of his trousers. The newspaper machines had been empty. Not that he cared. He'd simply walked out to give Ellie a chance to compose herself privately. He hadn't liked seeing her tremble, or watching her wariness. She made him feel like a stranger to his own wife, something he'd never intended to become. Yet it had happened. How and why were of little consequence. He wanted simply to have her back. To recapture their past closeness, the intimacy they'd mysteriously lost.

Neil sat down in a chaise, watching the overhead lights glitter on the water. He stared down into the aqua depths, aware of the hum of room air conditioners sounding all around him. His mind drifted back to earlier in the day, when he'd gone home shortly before noon to shower and change after a night spent in the hospital delivering babies. He hadn't seen the note she had propped up on the kitchen counter until he was almost ready to leave again. He could still recall how that had felt, seeing the small envelope with his name scrawled across it, coupling it with the empty house and the absence of Ellie and her car. For a split second he'd assumed she had left him. He'd never known a more potent despair.

When he had read the note and found that she'd embarked on a 282-mile business trip alone, he hadn't been much more comforted. To his aggravation, she'd left neither a phone number where she'd be staying nor a definite time when she would return. Immediately he'd worried about her safety, about the baby.

He'd phoned Mimi, sure that if she knew anything at all about the reason for Ellie's trip or where she was staying, it would come spilling out during the conversation.

Mimi hadn't disappointed him. With teenage honesty she'd asked him if he was mad at Ellie for taking another malpractice case in St. Louis. Neil had bitten down on an oath, then assured his sister that, of course, he wasn't angry with Ellie. He confessed he had misplaced the name of the hotel where she was staying. Did Mimi have the number? Mimi didn't, but thought Hazel might. Concluding his call quickly with his younger sister, he then phoned Ellie's secretary. She gave him the number where Ellie was staying, all the while silently intimating that Neil never should have let her drive to St. Louis alone while she was pregnant.

Neil agreed heartily with Hazel's assessment. He phoned the hotel, found out Ellie had arrived safely, but was out and had left no indication when she would return. He knew he could have, should have, left it at that, but he'd been unable to let go of his apprehension and, instead, had conjured up all sorts of danger-laced scenarios about Ellie in vivid medical detail. He knew that if anything happened to her or their baby, he would never forgive himself.

Thus, acting like any other frantic husband and father-to-be, Neil had decided to hell with what Ellie might have wanted, he was going to St. Louis to save the day. And just as swiftly he acted, calling in markers he'd accrued during the past unhappy weeks by covering for other doctors—not as Ellie probably thought, he mused, to avoid her, though that had been part of it, but to build up favors now, done for other physicians so that they might help him out after their child was born. He wanted as much time as possible to spend with Ellie and the baby, especially at nights and on weekends.

Glancing down at his watch, Neil realized that a good fifteen minutes had passed. Knowing Ellie, how tired she had looked, she would have finished in the bathroom and probably be curled up in her bed, asleep. He walked slowly back to the room.

To his surprise she was still awake, sitting on the edge of the bed. She was wearing a simple cotton gown, sitting with a hand flat on her abdomen, looking entranced.

At first he thought she might be in pain, but stepping closer, he saw her eyes were round with surprise and wonder. "Ellie, what is it? Is it the baby?" He knelt in front of her.

She nodded. Her hand moved slightly, seemingly of its own volition, and she smiled again. "I'm not sure but..." Her lower lip trembled. Tears of gladness spilled from her eyes, rolled down her cheeks. "I thought, that is..." She paused. "Neil, there was a flutter!"

Joy and wonder wreaked havoc with his usual self-possession, and he placed his hand over hers. Nothing. A moment passed. Still nothing. He was about to give up when he felt it, first at the right side of her abdomen, then surprisingly, toward the center and a moment later on the left.

"Frisky little fella, isn't he?" she said, her eyes still shining.

"And then some." Neil's brow furrowed, perplexed, as he tried to figure the position of the baby. The infant refused to cooperate, remaining perfectly still. Neil glanced back at Ellie's radiant face. All the love he'd ever felt for her surged inside him. "Is this the first time?" If so, he was glad he was there.

"Yes. Oh, Neil, it's so incredible." She finally took her hand from her abdomen and in her enthusiasm, grasped his shoulders with both hands. Her hands tightened over his shoulders, as if to draw him near for an impulsive hug, then abruptly relaxed. Recovering her composure, she gestured toward her abdomen and revealed softly, enthusiastically, "For the first time, I know my pregnancy is real, that there's a child growing inside of me."

"It's just now seeming real to me, too." Still slightly stunned, yet euphoric, Neil moved to sit beside Ellie on the bed. Without really thinking about it, he put his arms around her and held her close. She hugged him back, then stiffened inexplicably, drew back. Glancing down, he saw that one strap of her thin, lacy gown had fallen down across her arm. Her breasts were filling the high-waisted nightdress to overflowing, her newly maternal curves spilling out of the cloth. Lower, her abdomen was gently rounded. How long had it been since he had seen her undressed?

Neil wondered. How long since he had held her, really held her? Or kissed her? Desire welled up within him, fierce, unstoppable.

"Neil—" Her hands were flat against his chest.

His hands moved across her spine to draw her closer still. He wanted only to lose himself in the softness of her body, to luxuriate in the seduction and surrender of his wife, to feel her yearning and giving against him simultaneously. He touched her hair, letting his fingers first crush then sift through the fragrant shampoo-scented ends. "Ellie, I love you," he said softly, before he could think. His hand cupped her neck, guided her closer, until their breaths were meshing. "We're having a child together. Please don't turn me away."

Her mouth opened as if to protest; he gave her no such opportunity. She moaned softly, low and deep in her throat. The sound was cut off by his lips touching hers, tenderly at first, then more rapaciously.

He was achingly aware of the fresh, sophisticated musk of her perfume when combined with the scent of her skin, the softness of her. The taste and texture of her mouth pliantly yielding and molding to his drove him further into the mindless loving abandon he sought for them both. He drew back to look at her once, wanting to memorize her that way for all time, with her cheeks flushed, her lips parted, her eyes bright and needing—needing him. He heard and felt her second deep intake of breath, and then he was crushing her to him, falling back across the bed until he lay beside her, one hand tracing the rounded curves of her shoulders, the other slipping up behind her to cup the nape of her neck. "God, Ellie, I've missed you so much," he said, raining soft, tender kisses down her face. Her breathing was very erratic. Her hands were still gripping his shoulders, but more than holding him at bay, she seemed to be urging him closer.

"Neil," she whispered again, her voice sounding as if it were coming from out of a fog. She seemed in that moment as lost and vulnerable as he felt without her. "Oh, Neil."

The soft murmur of his name was all the encouragement he needed. His mouth found hers, his hands traced the softness of her skin, kneading over the soft material of her gown. Slipping the straps from her shoulders, he easily pushed the cloth lower, until her breasts were bared to his admiring view. Tenderly, gently, he caressed her, welcoming the lushness of her breasts. He kissed her cheeks, her chin, blazed an erotic trail down the long slope of her neck to her shoulder, to explore further the soft, womanly curves. Dimly he was aware through the fog of sensual sensations that he wanted her as never before. She arched against him, as if consumed by fire. His hands moved to the hem of her nightdress. And it was then, as the fabric slid upward and his fingertips caressed, then closed, over the inner slope of her thighs, that she seemed to change her mind, seemed to become aware of what was happening. "No, Neil." Her struggle began in earnest.

Reluctantly, feeling dazed and unbearably frustrated, Neil released her and sat up.

"Neil, I can't." With shaking hands, she arranged the bodice of her gown.

The power of his own yearning held him fiercely in its grip. "Why?" He was angry. With himself, for having started something he knew subconsciously would very likely never come to fruition. Not that night.

She took a deep, halting breath. Her eyes were glittering with suppressed hurt and the considerable effort it was taking for her to deny him. "I don't want to get involved again," she said finally. For a second he thought she was going to cry. That he didn't want. She steadied herself, then said in a hoarse, tortured whisper, "Damn it, Neil. You promised me a divorce."

The reminder acted like ice water on already inflamed nerves. Neil sat beside her a moment longer, gathering his composure, then he stood up. His jaw felt as if it had abruptly been encased in granite. He pushed the words through tightly gritted teeth. "Is that really what you want?" His words were terse, impatient and in direct contrast to the sensual images of her still whirling around in his mind.

"I don't have any choice!" Her jaw grew as stubborn as his. Her eyes misted, but she studiously avoided his glance.

Neil glanced at his watch. It was almost 3:00 A.M. They were tired, exhausted. "All right," he said finally. "All right."

He headed for the shower. The water was icy. He stood under

it for long minutes, but it did nothing to quell the fire burning within him. Like it or not, he still wanted her, and it had nothing to do with sheer physical desire. It had to do with loving her, the fact that she was carrying his child—and should have been loved by him then, more perhaps than at any other time. It had to do with the fact that they were still man and wife, the fact that he wanted their relationship to return to what it was before the Middleton case and his opportunity for advancement had ever come into the picture.

But none of those problems would be worked out that night, Neil knew. Sleepily he toweled and strode back into the darkened room. Too tired to search through his suitcase for clothes, he climbed naked into the opposite bed.

ELLIE WOKE UP around dawn, feeling exhausted, stiff and extremely embarrassed about what she had allowed to get started the evening before, but had been—at the last minute—unable to give in to. She still loved Neil; that much was clear. But she saw no way that she could bring a baby into the mess they had made of their marriage, and hence couldn't permit herself to make love to Neil now, not when she knew that in the course of a few months their marriage would end.

Rising, she saw Neil curled up in the sheets, still asleep. His skin was exposed below the waist. He'd kicked one leg out of the covers. He was bare from his foot past his thigh and hip to his waist. Feeling another dull flush inundate her face and a wellspring of memories and erotic images flood her mind, she rose and tiptoed around, showering and dressing quietly. When she emerged from the bathroom an hour later, fully prepared to face her day, he was lying in bed, wide awake. Hands propped behind his head, sheet drawn up past his waist, he was watching the news.

"Finished in the bathroom?" he asked, his tone was neutral.

Ellie kept her eyes low, to where she was rummaging through her purse for her hotel key. "Yes. I, um, thought I would go have some breakfast."

Neil nodded. "I'll join you."

Twenty minutes later, Neil sat down beside her in the hotel

dining room. Without preamble he handed her a folded piece of paper. "Your secretary, Hazel, called. The lawyers for Memorial's insurance company have called. They're ready to meet with you and have set it up tentatively for the day after tomorrow."

Ellie glanced down at what he had jotted. The time and place looked fine with her. "Thank you for taking the message." She was sorry he'd been reminded inadvertently of what they'd both been striving so hard to forget.

"You're welcome." His tone was gruff, slightly grumpy. He studied the menu with more than usual interest. Ellie could tell that he didn't want to talk about the Middleton case, so she let it drop. She hoped that they would settle out of court and that would be the end of it. In the meantime there was something they needed to discuss. She didn't want the issue left unexamined, to cause trouble between them. "About last night," she began with difficulty, after he had placed his breakfast order with the waitress, "Neil, are you angry with me?"

"No," he said, surprised, as if that were the furthest emotion from what he felt. He looked away, his jaw hardening slightly as he continued, in a low, gravelly tone, "But if you want me to say I'm glad we didn't make love—I can't. Ellie, I still want you."

And she wanted him. "We're getting divorced." She dispassionately reminded herself of the distance between them.

His eyes scanned her, turned away. They finished their breakfast in silence, strangers once again.

NEIL WAS SILENT on the drive home. Ellie was drowsily contemplating the tree-covered hills. Her head tipped back against the seat, she had never seemed more beautiful to him, nor more vulnerable.

Her rejection of him hurt. But worse than the physical frustration he felt, the need burning inside him like molten lava, were the barriers she was putting up between them. She was more remote now than on the occasion of their first date in some ways. Much less open. It was as if she were guarding her every thought, every feeling, censuring what she would or could say to him, what she would or could let herself do with him. He hated the way she was shutting him out, yet at the same time he couldn't blame her. Because wasn't that, in essence, what he had done to her when he'd been angry because she'd taken the case and, later, when he'd lost the position as chief of obstetrics?

Now he knew what it felt like to be shut out. It wasn't a situation he wanted to continue. Yet for the moment he had no recourse, for he was afraid that Ellie might really panic, if backed into a corner, and take their private agreement one legal step further to an official separation. He didn't want that. He didn't even want a divorce, he never had.

So how was he going to get around it?

By wooing her, winning her again? The more he thought about it, the more it seemed like a good idea. If Ellie were certain in her heart that he still loved her, she would be more willing to tear up the divorce agreement, let things between them return to normal. He wanted them to sleep and eat and talk together, to share and to love—and, yes, even fight once in a while—without this damnable tension between them, the fear that their marriage really was over pervading every moment.

Because Neil knew now that their marriage was far from over. The love was still there, the caring. He would find a way to bring them back together. He surely had no intention of letting her back into circulation again. Ellie's heart belonged to him, whether she admitted it or not. And his belonged to her. He would simply have to win her back, that was all, and after that they would work out their problems together. In the meantime there was the meeting with Memorial and the Middletons the following day. He hoped it would be settled then. Then once and for all they could end the concurrent tension between them.

THE DAY OF THE MEETING with Memorial's insurance company dawned rainy and humid. Ellie's mood was similarly gray as she made her way to the hospital conference room.

Seven grueling hours later, to her vast relief, it was all over.

The Middletons talked briefly with reporters, as did Ellie. Together, they walked to their cars. "Thank you so much, Ms. Cavanaugh," Audrey Middleton said, her relief almost palpable. Though regaining her health more every day, the young woman still looked thin and fragile as a result of her ordeal. Every time Ellie was near her, she felt an overwhelming desire to protect her, as apparently did Stu. They had left their baby with a sitter, in anticipation that the meetings to work out a settlement would be long and fraught with legal battle. But now that it was over, both young people were anxious to get home to baby Ryan again. Hence their steps were swift, purposeful.

Stu echoed a similar sentiment. "I don't think any other lawyer could have done as well, certainly not as gently," he said. "The way you handled those doctors…you were so nice to them."

"So matter of fact," Audrey added approvingly.

"I didn't want it to turn into a circus any more than you did," Ellie said. Despite everything, she had much respect for the work the doctors did, the hours they put in, the time and effort they gave. She hadn't wanted to hurt anyone or have the situation become any more difficult than it already was. "I'm just glad we were able to get the insurance company to pay the medical bill," Ellie said, forcing a wan smile. She was exhausted. A tension headache was throbbing at her temples.

Stu agreed. "Thank goodness we won't have to worry about paying that off." He hesitated. "I did feel sorry for Dr. Talbot, though. He was so nice to us all during Audrey's pregnancy— kind of like a father-figure, you know? And now he has to face Memorial's medical review board."

"From what I understand, that's standard practice in cases like this," Ellie said. "Part of the medical community's efforts to police itself." But she knew how the Middletons felt. Dr. Talbot did look as if he had aged a great deal during this ordeal, as if he were filled with self-dissatisfaction. It had been all Ellie could do to walk into that conference room and fight the battle she had agreed to wage for the young couple. As it was, she'd had to remind herself constantly that Dr. Talbot had personally okayed the administration of a life-threatening drug to Audrey. The fact that he had done so unintentionally didn't really matter, not when the cost could very well have been a human life. *I'm still very much a doctor's wife at heart,* she thought. And that meant, in cases like this, that her loyalties would always be split. She hadn't realized how much so, though, until she had taken on this case.

"Well, thanks again," Audrey said. Ellie nodded. They said goodbye. Glancing at her watch, Ellie noted that it was after five o'clock. Hazel would have closed up shop, turned on the answering machine and left for the day. Ellie wavered briefly, trying to decide whether to go home or back to the office. The office won, and minutes later she was letting herself in the door.

Her desk was piled high with phone messages, the day's mail, legal briefs that had been typed but needed to be read, contracts waiting for her perusal. Ellie walked over to the storage room, got herself a cold drink from the refrigerator and settled down to get caught up. Half an hour later she heard a key turning in the front door. Neil sauntered in.

"Well, how'd it go?" he asked.

"Our side won," she said, trying not to let herself be affected by his presence. Her emotions were turbulent, disturbing, nonetheless, and it was all she could do to present a dispassionate facade. Briefly she explained the terms of the settlement, the Middletons' relief.

"How did Dr. Talbot and the intern take it?" Neil asked, standing back against the wall. He jammed his hands in his pockets, restlessly jingling his change.

"They were both very remorseful. I think they were glad the Middletons hadn't asked for a million dollars—which we all knew damn well they could have gotten, too."

Neil grimaced at the passion that unexpectedly flared in her tone. Jaw tautening, he looked away. "Then it's over?"

"For me, yes. Both physicians involved still face a review by the hospital medical board."

Still looking very grim, Neil nodded his acknowledgment.

A silence fell between them, intensifying the awkwardness that hung in the room. Both of them were acutely miserable. Ellie realized abruptly that she needed to talk to him and had for some time, that she wanted to tell him everything about the case, not just the facts, but about her emotions from beginning to end, her justifications, and, yes, even her self-recriminations for allowing herself ambitiously to get involved in the matter at all. She needed absolution, forgiveness from him, some sign that he understood what she had done and supported her in that endeavor. But nothing of the kind was forthcoming. With disappointment she realized nothing had really changed. She needed his respect, but he couldn't give it to her.

"The doctors will probably be let off with a reprimand," Neil theorized broodingly at last, his mind still on his colleagues. He looked past Ellie, out the window. She wasn't sure whether he was still angry with her or not. It was hard for her to tell what he was thinking, and he made no effort to share his thoughts with her. "So, that's it, then?" He turned back to her, as if he were waiting for the next bomb to drop.

Hurt welled up within Ellie. Deliberately she suppressed it, meeting his probing, impersonal look with equal aplomb. "As far as the Middletons go, yes." Ellie gestured toward her desk. "As you can see, I've got a long way to go before I'm caught up." Now she wanted him to leave. Much more of the third degree, and she suspected that she would cry. But, maddeningly, he showed no such inclination.

"Busy?" He turned toward her, his spine stiff as he moved away from the wall.

"Yes, very." She watched him pace the room restlessly, and it was all she could do to stay in her seat and look tranquil. "I'm in the position of having to turn work down now. Before, it was all I could do some days to stay busy and pay the overhead."

"The recovery fee from this case should help you financially." He waited for her reply, a cynical curve to his mouth.

"Yes." That sum alone would pay for her maternity leave, Ellie thought. "It was standard—twenty-five percent of the money they recouped. The insurance company paid that for them, too."

"That was on the low end, wasn't it? Can't you charge up to forty percent?" Neil asked, something new in his voice. Respect? she thought. Or maybe wonder?

"Yes. I chose the lower sum." It felt in some respects as if she were taking advantage of others' unhappiness by taking even that. Ellie couldn't explain it or even rationalize it to herself very well; she only knew that the satisfaction she usually felt at winding up a case had been dampened, presumably, she thought, by the rift between her and Neil and the thoughts nagging at her that no case had been worth the breakup of her marriage. But that realization hardly mattered now. The situation was as it was. Who was to say that something else—another issue—wouldn't have come along and broken them up? she reassured herself pragmatically.

"Well, paying the bills shouldn't be a problem for you now."

"No, I don't think it will." That much pleased Ellie. She had a child to support now, and though she knew Neil would contribute, she wanted to be able to do it all herself.

"So, are you planning to stay here much longer?" he asked finally.

"An hour, maybe two. What about you?" She was curious as to why he inquired.

"I'm on my way over to my folks' house. My mother's been after me about throwing a party for us."

"Mimi told me." To Ellie's relief, he didn't look any more eager to participate in a deepening of their charade than she did.

Neil nodded, taking a deep breath, then plunging on distastefully, "Well, I've been putting it off for weeks now. Finally, today, I told her it was out of the question, and to save it until after the baby is born, that we're both far too busy now. She was disappointed, naturally, but agreed. Anyway, I'm on my way over there to dinner. I thought maybe you'd like to go."

After the day she'd had, Ellie didn't think she could face playing the loving wife. "No, I can't, Neil. I'm sorry. Give her my regrets, please."

He nodded, looking not at all surprised she had refused him. He pivoted to go, then turned back at the last moment, almost as an afterthought. His gaze met hers. "Ellie? Congratulations. About the Middleton case. I'm glad you were able to settle."

"Thank you," she said hesitantly at last.

"You're a damn good lawyer, Ellie. You're not afraid to go out on a limb for something you believe in. I respect that about you. I always have."

"Even after all the trouble my actions have caused?" She

raised her brows questioningly, wondering just how far this new attitude of his went.

He gave a rueful grin. Which led her to believe that it was obviously not as far as she hoped.

"I'm working on it."

Ellie searched his face. He meant what he said. "That's a start," she said softly. Neil might not be anywhere near as "enlightened" as she wanted him to be, but at least he was trying now, at least thinking about changing his unfair views. She smiled. He grinned back and tentatively held out his hand. They linked palms for several long and satisfying moments. It was a gesture of friendship, of peace. Ellie smiled happily again. Maybe, somehow, they would manage to work out their problems after all.

Chapter Nine

"You're still gaining weight at a faster than normal rate, Ellie," Dr. Raynor announced as he finished her fifth-month exam.

"I know," Ellie lamented. She could feel her cheeks suffusing with heat. She hated this weighing in every time she went to visit the doctor. It was embarrassing.

"And the measurements for your abdomen are exceeding what I would expect."

"I feel like a blimp."

He grinned, bantering back, "You're a very pretty woman, especially now that you're pregnant, and if Neil were here, I'm sure he'd back me up one hundred percent."

Would he? Ellie wondered. Since the Middleton case had been settled, he'd been more distant emotionally than ever. He was overly polite. It had gotten to the point where she felt she was constantly walking on eggshells whenever she was around him, and vice versa.

Dr. Raynor put her chart aside and folded his arms across his chest. "Ellie, I would like to do an ultrasound test." At her puzzled glance, he explained, "It's a high-frequency, acoustical way of getting X rays of what's going on inside the mother's uterus, with no harm to either mother or baby."

"How does it work?" Ellie asked.

"High-frequency sound is projected into the body and the sound waves return to produce a reflection of the fetus on a televisionlike screen. Sometimes—and I stress sometimes—we can even make out the sex of the baby. At any rate, I'll take a black-and-white Polaroid photo for you to take home.''

Ellie grinned, immediately cheered. "When can we do it?"

Dr. Raynor glanced at his watch. "Since you're my last appointment for this afternoon, we could do it right now, if you like. It'll take about half an hour."

A picture of her baby! Ellie thought incredulously. "I can't wait." If this was her requital, she didn't care that she had gained so much weight so quickly.

Dr. Raynor reached up into the cupboard above his sink and pulled out a large paper drinking cup. He filled it with water. "Drink this. In order to get a clear picture, we need you to have a full bladder." He headed toward the door. "In the meantime, I'll page Neil and see if he can get down to see the test. I know he won't want to miss it."

Before she could comment further, Dr. Raynor was gone.

Twenty minutes later Ellie was moved to another examining room. Neil was there, as was Dr. Raynor. Dr. Raynor's nurse had gone home as scheduled, since Neil was there to assist.

Neil seemed very nervous, Ellie noted right away, as if he were both anxious and excited. To her further consternation, he didn't meet her eyes straight-on once.

She had no more time to puzzle over Neil's behavior, because Dr. Raynor was turning on the machine. Matter-of-factly Neil lifted the dressing gown above her waist to just beneath her breasts. The sheet draped across her legs was gently drawn down to her hips. While Neil worked in a thin coating of mineral oil across her abdomen, Dr. Raynor worked with the controls.

"All set?" Jim asked, adjusting the knobs on the television screen.

"Ready," Neil said. And again, Ellie noticed how brightly lit were his eyes. It was almost as if, she mused, he knew something she didn't.

A transmitter was run across her abdomen. Ellie turned her head toward the television screen and watched with interest. To her, it all looked like a lot of black-and-white blurs.

Jim and Neil grinned simultaneously. "There's one!" Jim said.

"Uh-huh." Neil grinned. Ellie couldn't be sure, because her own vision was suddenly, inexplicably, misty, but she thought Neil's eyes were glistening.

"Nice healthy heartbeat," Jim murmured approvingly. Ellie could see the white blur moving slowly, in and out, in and out. Together, Jim and Neil mapped out the location of the fetus in the uterus, recorded its size.

Oblivious of Ellie, Neil was still peering intently at the screen. "There's a leg, an arm and...what do you think, Jim?" Neil asked.

"Definitely a male," Jim decided, looking at the shadowy, blurry picture. While Neil took over the transmitter, Jim snapped the Polaroid photo.

Ellie squinted at the screen again. "I don't see anything. Well, not really. It just looks...so blurry."

"It takes time to be able to read an ultrasound screen," Neil said. With that, he moved the transmitter again. "Let's just check out the right side here while we're at it." Neil grinned hugely. So did Jim. Ellie saw more white blurs on the screen.

"What is it?" she said. This feeling of being constantly left out was getting irritating.

"Twins," the men said in unison.

Joy flooded Ellie's heart. She didn't think she could be any happier if she had won a Nobel Prize.

But minutes later, they found that they had underestimated the situation—again.

"Triplets!" a stunned Neil said as they left the doctor's office a full hour later.

"Three babies. Who would have thought?" Ellie murmured. She was leaning against Neil. His arm was wrapped securely around her waist. And it was a good thing, too, she mused, or she surely would have fallen to the ground in a solid faint.

"Thank heaven they're all developing normally," Neil said, ever the obstetrician.

"At least I know now I'm not gaining too much weight."

"On the contrary, now you know you're going to have to start eating more."

They turned to each other simultaneously. Abruptly, they were both standing there with tears running down their faces. "I really don't believe this," Ellie whispered.

"Neither do I," Neil said and hugged her harder.

Ellie paused. "The fact that it's triplets, it isn't due to the medication I took, is it?"

Neil shook his head. "No, there was no indication that you suffered excessive ovarian stimulation because of the medication. The fact that we're having triplets...well, I guess we're just lucky. One of the rare five percent."

"I always knew you were special." Ellie grinned.

"Ditto, Mrs. Cavanaugh." Linking hands, they continued their walk to the parking lot and their cars.

"I DON'T KNOW ABOUT YOU, but I'm famished," Neil reported a half hour later. As it turned out, they'd gotten only as far as a phone booth before they'd decided to call his folks and her mom. They'd turned down invitations to dine with both families, wanting at that moment, Ellie thought, to share their news together—and alone, without having to act the loving couple or pretend their marriage had never been better. Regardless of the troubles still wedging distance between them, though, she was happy. Buoyantly so.

"I'm hungry, too," Ellie admitted, putting a hand to her abdomen.

They stopped on the sidewalk, trying to decide where to go next. Both their cars were in the parking lot. "Let's take my car. We'll come back and get yours later," Neil said authoritatively. Ellie happily handed over the driving chores to him.

Minutes later they were cruising down the boulevard. "Want to go someplace special?" Neil slanted her a sideways glance. Ellie thought that if he smiled any more broadly his face would split.

"I'm too excited to sit still." And she still felt as if she'd start crying again any minute. Her arms hugging her waist, Ellie whispered. "I still can't believe it. Oh, Neil..."

"I know." His right hand slid over hers and squeezed it tightly. "I know." Without warning, he pulled his car into the nearest parking lot, next to a supermarket. He put the car in park, left the motor running and turned to face her. For several minutes they just sat in happy silence, sharing their joy, their surprise, their contentment without speaking.

Ellie realized the intimacy they had shared during the early days of their courtship and marriage was still there, as potent as ever despite all their recent troubles. It was a disconcerting notion.

"I still don't know where we're going," Neil said softly at last. "Where would you like to have dinner?" Ellie shrugged indecisively, and he listed several of the city's small, cozy night spots. Under the circumstances, she wasn't sure that it would be wise to go to some place dimly lit, or reminiscent of happier days. "And, of course, there's always the country club," he continued.

Ellie's response to that was immediate. "No. We'd...I don't want to see people tonight."

"I don't know how we can avoid it unless we eat in our car."

Ellie grinned, inspired. "Now, there's an idea."

Neil followed her gaze several blocks up the street. Half of his mouth lifted as he drawled, "The A & W root beer stand?"

Ellie sighed her longing. "I've been so good about following the food lists the hospital dietitian gave me. That's why I was so concerned when I still seemed to be gaining so much weight. And it's been so long since I had any decent junk food." She wasn't sure how Neil, ever the physician, would react to her idea.

Happily, he seemed not only game but even pleased with her choice. "A & W it is, then." Neil put the car into gear and pulled back onto the boulevard.

Minutes later they were both eating foot-long hot dogs smothered with chili and cheese. "This is great," Neil said, taking a sip of his frosty mug of root beer.

Ellie nodded, taking a crusty fried onion ring from the paper bag on her lap. "Reminds me of all the times we used to meet for lunch when we were dating."

Neil smiled, then his brow furrowed. He looked at her, perplexed. "When did we stop doing that?"

Ellie reflected for a moment. When had the laughter, the urgent need to be together—however or at what inconvenience, whenever they could manage it—gone away? "I guess when we got married," she said slowly. "We could always catch each other at home, or at least we tried to catch each other at home," she said wryly, reflecting on all the times they had missed each other in the coming-and-going process.

"Maybe we didn't succeed in meshing our schedules as often as we should've," Neil said softly. Regret and the desire to do better was mirrored in his eyes. Ellie's heart was pounding. *Don't let him do this to you,* she thought. *Don't let him make promises his schedule and the demands of his practice won't ever let him keep.*

Hardening her resolve against the mute pleading in his eyes, she directed her thoughts to the joyous news they had received and the complications that would now ensue. "You realize, don't you, that we're going to have to get three of everything now?" She pleated and unpleated the paper napkin in her lap.

"Yep." He seemed to be looking forward to the idea with relish.

"Three times the diapers. Three times the sleepers. Three cribs! And three strollers—"

Neil groaned, finishing off the last of his onion rings. "And still unassembled. Putting them together is going to be quite a challenge."

Ellie laughed softly, amused. Neil might be thoroughly adept in a delivery room, but he was a total washout when it came to anything that needed to be put together or taken apart or adjusted in any way in a mechanical or operational sense. Trying to hide an automatic smile of knowing amusement, she asked seriously, "Want me to hire someone to do it?"

His eyes met hers. Stubbornly, he shook his head. "No. I insist. I'll do it."

"You're sure?"

"Positive."

She grinned, relenting whimsically. "Okay. But if halfway through it you get frustrated trying to find part ABX to plug into BGC..." She held up her index finger in a lecturing sense.

Neil's brows rose and lowered with mock reproach. "I'll let you say I told you so."

"Really?"

"Really."

They finished their meal. Neil drove her back to the hospital parking lot where she picked up her car. They met at home fifteen minutes later. As usual, Neil was first inside. When Ellie walked in, he was in the kitchen reaching for the antacids. "I thought I was supposed to be the one with heartburn," she joked.

"My digestive tract doesn't know that," he said with mock solemnity. He peered at her closely, his eyes dropping to the rounded surface of her abdomen beneath the maternity blouse. "Have you been having heartburn?" Without warning, he was suddenly all caring physician.

"Not a lick of it. Even the morning sickness has disappeared."

He made a faintly disgruntled sound, then followed the antacids with a glass of water. "You always did like junk food."

"Yes. And especially to celebrate." She watched as he came around into the living room, rummaged through their records and put a whole stack of Duke Ellington and Count Basie on the stereo.

"How come?" He kicked off his shoes, stretched languidly.

"Hmm. I guess that goes back to my childhood," Ellie theorized, tossing off her suit jacket and kicking off her shoes. She sank down on the sofa, adjusting a pillow behind her back. She propped her stockinged feet up on the coffee table. Neil sat next to her on the sectional sofa. Soft, melodic sounds of jazz wafted pleasurably through the room as Ellie continued to mull over the "why" behind her instinctive preferences. "My mother worked, so whenever we had something to celebrate, we always went out to eat. And to appease me, she usually let me choose the restaurant. Naturally, being a kid, I always chose McDonald's or Pizza Hut or Kentucky Fried Chicken."

"Admit it. You were spoiled rotten."

"And you weren't?" She raised her eyebrows goadingly.

He looked abashed and rubbed his jaw ruefully. "Well..."

"What did your family do to celebrate?" Funny, they'd never talked about this, Ellie mused. What had they talked about in the past? Work, and only that.

"Generally, for birthdays and anniversaries, holidays, we

stayed home," Neil related. "Occasionally, we would go out as a family. Generally, though, my father just took my mother out. They, um, wanted to be alone some of the time."

"Good for them." Ellie applauded their sense.

"Yeah. Good for them," Neil said. There was a pause as he sent her a searching, sensual glance. Panic shot through her, coupled with the sensation that things were moving much too quickly between them.

Abruptly, she was on her feet. The strength of his desire was laced through his velvety soft plea. "Ellie—"

"Neil, it's been a wonderful evening." She was stepping back away from him in a panic, turning and picking up her shoes. He followed her slowly, walking as soundlessly and effortlessly as a predator stalking his prey. Turning toward him, she held her shoes in front of her like a shield. "But I've got a heavy schedule tomorrow. Lots of clients."

His brow furrowed. "More than usual."

"Yes." She swallowed around the knot of apprehension in her throat. "Business has picked up quite a bit."

"Because of the Middleton case?" There was no approval in his face, only mild irritation.

Ellie nodded, not really sorry that she had inadvertently brought the subject of her law practice up. She needed to remember how things were between her and Neil. She needed to keep recalling the reality of their situation, not the way she wanted them to be again because of the news of the triplets. "Good night, Neil." To her faint surprise he did nothing to stop her flight. But it was hours later before the music wafting up from the first floor of the house stopped, hours before Ellie finally fell asleep.

"HELP ME, ELLIE. I can't figure out which is part A and which is part XWT." Neil sat cross-legged in the middle of the children's bedroom. He was surrounded by instructions for three separate cribs, and myriad screws and coils and long metal rods. Ellie, meanwhile, was overseeing the various wooden rails and headboards.

Carefully she tiptoed over to him and sat down beside him.

Within minutes, with her help, they were on their way to assembling the first crib. "You know, if you hadn't taken all three of these cribs out of their boxes at the same time," Ellie said teasingly, handing him the Phillips screwdriver, "you just might have been able to handle the task alone."

"I didn't mean to get everything mixed up," Neil lamented with a heartfelt sigh. "But when I looked at the first set of instructions, I was sure the next set would be easier, and if not them, the third. With three totally different cribs, you'd think there would be one I could put together by myself."

"You'd think that, yeah." Ellie grinned, ducking as he tossed the closest set of instructions over her head. "Face it, Neil, a handyman, you ain't." She tossed the directions back at him.

"You think not, hmm?" He grinned engagingly. "Maybe all I needed was a helper."

Just then the doorbell rang. Ellie, still seated cross-legged on the floor, groaned. She didn't relish another trip up and down the stairs.

"Stay put," Neil said, standing and dusting off the seat of his pants. "I'll run down and see who it is."

He was gone a long time, or so it seemed to Ellie. She finished assembling one half of the crib, then, restless to continue, got up and began lifting the lightweight side rail. Behind her she heard footsteps, then a high-pitched female gasp, followed by her mother's recriminating voice. "Ellie Jensen Cavanaugh, you put that rail down right now! What are you trying to do to yourself?" Viv rushed forward to wrest the rail from Ellie's hand. Viv turned indignantly to Neil. "Did you see what she was doing?"

Neil's hand was busy rubbing his jaw. He was smothering a grin, Ellie knew. "Yes, I sure did." He nodded solemnly, then turned helpless eyes to Ellie.

She felt that she knew what was coming.

Viv continued, "Ellie, now that you're pregnant, you know you mustn't lift anything. Isn't that right, Neil?"

"Uh..."

"Honestly, I should have known you'd be doing things you're not supposed to."

"I'm fine, Mom."

Viv made a disagreeing sound. "I suppose you've been stand-ing on chairs, too. Putting things away in high cupboards." Hands on her hips, Viv faced her daughter sternly.

Unable to lie, Ellie looked skyward. The truth was that she hadn't slowed down one iota since becoming pregnant and had taken pains to stay as physically fit and active as possible.

Viv frowned and sighed her exasperation. "Ellie, pregnant women should not stand on chairs or haul cribs around. You could injure the babies. Isn't that right, Neil?"

"It's true. Ellie could injure the babies if she were to fall off a chair or try and lift a piano. But as long as she uses good judgment—and she has—with reasonable caution, she can move about as freely as she wishes." He wrapped his arm about her waist, held her possessively at his side. Glad for his protection in this instance, Ellie made no move to draw away.

Viv looked at them both with such exasperation that Ellie couldn't resist saying, "See, Mother? I'm perfectly safe, doing what I've been doing. The idea that I'm not is an old wives' tale."

"It is not," Viv countered stubbornly, folding her arms against her waist. "It's simply common sense. An old wives' tale is what my mother told me."

"Which was?" Ellie asked curiously.

"If you lift your arms about your head, you'll cut off the baby's breath!"

Neil was shaking with laughter beside her. Ellie joined him, admonishing, "Mother, you didn't believe that!"

"At the time I wasn't quite sure it was *all* superstition. Some small part of me wondered. So I was extra careful. I didn't want anything to happen to my precious little girl. And so should you be, Ellie."

"I am careful, Mother."

"Hmm." Viv looked as if she would reserve judgment about that until later. "You also reject out of hand any advice I have to give." She seemed to wonder why that was.

"That's because you always taught me to be self-reliant, to depend on myself and no one else." Ellie broke free of Neil to cross the room and give her mother a hug. "I've always appre-

ciated that. Without your example I might not have become the
strong woman I am.''

Viv looked touched by Ellie's remarks as they drew apart.

''Honey, I'm glad you're independent. You know I always
wanted you to be that way. But that doesn't mean I want you
lifting anything more while you're carrying those grandchildren
of mine. And you had better do your darndest to stay off any
chairs!'' Viv turned to her son-in-law for support. ''Neil, for
heaven's sake, don't just stand there. Tell her what will happen
if she continues doing things she shouldn't,'' Viv demanded imperiously.

Neil looked back at Ellie seriously. ''Your mother will be very
upset.''

''Darn right I will,'' Viv continued, waving her hand for emphasis.

''Mom—''

''Promise me, Ellie. No more dangerous activity. No more
reaching and bending and climbing over things and heaven
knows what else. Promise me, Ellie!''

Ellie swallowed. She couldn't deal with her mother when she
was like that. But if Ellie didn't promise, she knew that Viv
would continue arguing with her incessantly and that every old
wives' tale that had ever been spun in the backwoods or in the
current crop of health-food stores would be dragged out into
evidence of Viv's correctness. In addition, Viv would probably
stop by daily to check up on her. ''I promise, Mom.''

Viv loudly exhaled her relief. ''Well, thank goodness,'' she
said. Turning to Neil, she continued, ''And you see she behaves
herself, Neil.''

''Yes, ma'am.'' Neil grinned back at Ellie and didn't say a
word. There were times when neither of them could handle their
parents. This was one of them.

Viv stayed only half an hour more, long enough to see what
they were doing to the nursery and to make Ellie rest and drink
half a glass of juice. Ellie loved her mother dearly; nonetheless,
she was relieved to see her go. Shutting the door behind her, she
and Neil trudged wearily back up the stairs to finish assembling

the cribs. "Your mother really does believe in all those old wives' tales, doesn't she?" Neil asked, faintly amused.

"Yes, she does. Every bit as much as your mother believes that tennis and swimming are necessary to a child's development. Can you imagine what it's going to be like after the babies are born when the two of them get together?" Ellie asked with a sigh, rubbing her persistently aching back. "My mother will want the triplets to eat only organic, homemade baby food. And your mother will want them taking swimming lessons at the country club before they can walk." Ellie wondered what both mothers would think when they learned that Ellie had no intention of following either plan.

"Something tells me that there will be some spirited discussions over how to manage the first three grandchildren," Neil said.

"Thank goodness our families will only be over to visit. If both sets were here at the house full-time, I don't think I could cope," Ellie lamented, picking up the assembly instructions again.

Neil looked faintly troubled, but said nothing more in response as they once again became immersed in their chore. Hours later they had finished. Standing back to survey the room, they saw that they had room enough for three cribs and three dressers and not much else. The second spare bedroom had been set aside as a playroom. They could only hope the arrangement would work. "What's scheduled for next week?" Neil groaned, looking at the boxes stacked in the playroom. "Strollers?"

"And automatic baby swings," Ellie nodded. "Think of it this way, Neil; when the babies arrive, we'll be all ready for them." She touched her back again. Neil glanced down at the place her hand was rubbing.

"You've been massaging your spine all afternoon," he said. "Has your back been bothering you?"

Ellie nodded. "It seems to ache constantly. Probably all the extra weight I'm carrying."

Neil nodded solemnly. "Why don't you go lie down and rest? Put the heating pad on, and maybe that will help. I'll go down and fix supper."

"You're sure?" Ellie asked. He had been working hard. She didn't want to burden him with cooking after he had spent all of his Saturday afternoon and early evening working around the house.

Neil nodded. "No junk food tonight, Ellie. Now, go rest. I'll be back up shortly."

Ellie did as directed, glad for the respite. To her surprise, she dozed off. He woke her almost an hour and a half later. Reaching behind her, he propped up the pillows, adjusted the heating pad and put a tray before her. "Aren't you going to eat?" Ellie asked, looking at the steaming bowl of vegetable soup, chicken salad sandwich and glass of milk he'd prepared for her.

Neil shook his head. "I ate earlier." He smiled with gentle affection. "When I came up earlier to tell you that supper was ready, you were asleep. I decided to let you rest and went downstairs to eat and watch the news."

"Thanks." She met his glance shyly. Though she was dressed in maternity jeans and a long, striped cotton smock top, he was looking at her suddenly as if she were the most beautiful, desirable woman on earth. "I'm going to have to stop drifting off to sleep like that, though," she admitted sheepishly, beginning to eat.

"You need the rest, Ellie," Neil said tenderly. "Now more than ever."

"I know." But she didn't want to seem so fragile around him. It made her feel helpless, an unfamiliar sensation that she despised.

"In a few months you won't be getting any sleep."

Ellie figured that that was true enough. At the present time she had no idea how she was going to manage when the babies did arrive. Because there were no easy solutions in sight, she pushed it from her mind. One step at a time, she told herself. She still had plenty of time before the babies were born, over three months. She would handle caring for the infants when the time came, hiring help if necessary.

"People at the hospital have been asking if we intend to dress the children alike," Neil said at last. He lounged beside her on the bed, stretching out his long legs.

"I vote for different outfits," Ellie said, trying without success not to notice how his jeans molded the sinewy contours of his thighs, the rounded muscles of his calves.

Neil nodded agreeably. He turned toward her, propping his head up on his hand. Through the window, they could see the orange and yellow leaves as the last of the daylight faded softly into dusky evening. September, Ellie thought. Where had the summer gone?

"Good. At school they'll automatically be put in different classes. So maybe, somewhere along the way, we should prepare them for that."

"Nursery school?" Ellie turned inquisitively to Neil. He was three feet away from her, not touching her at all, not trying to. There was no reason for her to be so nervous.

"And whatever else we can come up with that will allow them separate time with each of their parents, separate experiences." His glance moved down to her abdomen approvingly. When he looked up at her, his handsome face was fairly glowing. It was as if he was enthralled with the pregnancy, the changes in her body. Maybe expectant mothers weren't the only ones who glowed, she thought. Maybe, just maybe, expectant fathers were every bit as radiant. Neil certainly looked it. The thought made her smile, and he smiled back. The feeling of intimacy between them increased. *I still love him,* Ellie thought. *After all that's happened between us, I still want him in my life. Am I a fool? Or a realist?*

"Are you planning to hire someone to come in and look after them?" he asked.

Ellie nodded, forcing her attention back to the discussion of the children's future. "I also want to put an office in our—my home," she corrected herself awkwardly. "Maybe work here mornings so I can be around to supervise, only go in for appointments in the afternoon. I really haven't figured that out yet." She glanced again at the window. Darkness had fallen like a black velvet cloth. The wind whispered through the trees, rustling the dry autumn leaves. The warmth of the day was dissipating, being replaced by a cool breeze that she unfailingly associated with autumn.

"Sounds like you're getting it all worked out," Neil said finally in a neutral tone.

Ellie couldn't tell whether he approved of her farsightedness. Not wanting to pursue the subject, though, she started talking about possible color schemes for the triplets' rooms. "I favor doing the playroom in a washable rainbow-print vinyl wallpaper," she said.

"Fine with me, but I think we should stick with a neutral color for the bedroom until after they're born. Remember those ultrasound tests are not positive proof of the sex of the children."

"You think we're going to have at least one girl?" Ellie teased. She herself was positive that Neil and Jim Raynor had been correct in their initial assessment, that she was going to have three boys.

"It's very possible," Neil stressed. His look became darkly intent. "I would like to have at least one girl. And if we did, I'd want her to be just like you."

She beamed at his praise. "But whatever sex children we have, we'll love them just the same."

"Yes. We will." His voice was threaded with fatherly pride.

They chatted on amiably as Ellie finished her dinner. Rising to put the tray aside, she winced again at the pressure on her lower spine.

"Your back is still hurting you, hmm?" Neil observed. Rising, he crossed to the master bathroom and returned with a bottle of lotion. Flexing the fingers of his free hand, he motioned for her to roll over and said, "Let's see what the old doc can do for that."

"Neil—" Ellie found herself blushing with embarrassment, to her chagrin.

"Come on, Ellie, it'll only take a minute. And think how much better those little fellas inside are going to feel."

She sent him a mockingly enraged glance. "Them! They're the ones who are causing me all the discomfort," Ellie said, rolling over obediently on her side as Neil dropped down beside her onto the bed. Deftly he lifted the hem of her shirt and began expertly massaging lotion into her back. The warmth was soothing, the limbering effect on tired muscles heavenly.

"I bet they're inside there saying the same about you," Neil tossed back, using both hands to minister to her spine.

Ellie heard the laugh in his voice. She shut her eyes, just letting herself feel the magic of his hands. "How do you know that?" She drifted on a sea of sensation, loving his touch, his gentleness.

"Hey! As your mother says, I'm the expert around here."

"Maybe medical," Ellie allowed, as her limbs turned to Jell-O. "Do you really think babies are aware of what's going on when they're in the womb?" she said. "Do you think the triplets know one another exists?"

Neil paused, as if he hadn't given it any thought. "I would imagine so, although just how well their intellect is developed at this point, we don't know. Studies have shown newborns recognize their mothers' voices when they're just a day or two old, though. So that must mean they hear our voices in utero."

"So they'd know if we were upset," Ellie said, turning toward him halfway.

Neil's hands slowed to a stop, rested warmly against her skin. "Or happy or amused." His hands circled her abdomen, rolling her onto her back and then toward him. "If they're truly aware of anything right now, I imagine they know that they're loved," he said softly. "By you and me." His husky voice dropped emotionally another note. "And that we're going to do our damnedest to take care of them."

His face was very close to hers. She found herself noticing without wanting to how full and sensual his lips looked, how soft and inviting. "Neil..." Why was he looking at her like that? she wondered. As if he knew and understood her every thought. As if he knew firsthand the strength of the desire pouring through her. It had been so long since he'd really held her, she thought. So long since they'd made love. And she wanted him almost more than life.

"I love those children, Ellie," Neil said softly, brushing back the golden-blond strands of hair from her face. His hand cupped her chin. His thumb traced the parted surface of her lips. "I love you."

His lips touched hers, lingered. The sharp urgency of desire melded with the surprise and wonder at finding themselves undeniably drawn together again—in heart, in soul, in loneliness and friendship and simple, searing need.

Her senses awash with a dizzying anticipation, her heart hammering in her chest, Ellie could no longer remember what it was that was keeping them apart. Their eyes met, held. With a singularity of purpose she found exciting, he drew closer. "Ellie." Her name sounded throaty in the enticing silence of the room, arousing her further. He buried his lips in her throat. His grip on her was shaky. His whisper was the softest plea. "Let me hold you in my arms again. Let me love you as you need to be loved." His open mouth moved over her cheek, roaming, touching, until she was aching with the yearning to be really kissed.

Ellie might have been able to deny him in anger, but she had no defenses against the vulnerability, the need, she saw in his expression, especially when his feelings so closely mirrored her own. Her eyes slowly shut and she opened her mouth to his, first inviting the drugging kisses that quickly followed, then savoring the unique taste of his mouth, the shifting pressure of his kiss. First rough, then tender, then softer, more demanding, his caresses were both expert and inflaming. With an anguished cry, she pressed closer against him, learning anew the sweetness of his touch, and with her own seeking palms, the hard contours of his chest. Impatiently, almost mindlessly in her need of him, she reached for the buttons on his shirt. His hand captured hers, held it still. In that moment he seemed to be telling her that she had a choice—then. Much more and she wouldn't.

"Yes," Ellie murmured. A languid, sensual weakness stole over her. It seemed as though she had waited an eternity to experience his kiss again, his gentle loving. "I want you." God, how she wanted him. Every part of her was burning, aching, needing to be soothed, loved, adored in the way only Neil could cherish her. And more, she needed to hold and celebrate him, too. She needed to love him, the father of her children. Her husband. Her life. She needed to show him that she still cared about him, to discover if he cared for her.

His hand relaxed over hers. He gave her a tender, crooked grin. "And I want to make love to you, Ellie, more than you could ever know.'' His voice was husky. It floated through her senses, urging her on to the velvet-edged oblivion, to the glory, of their love.

Ellie finished unbuttoning his shirt. Her fingers combed through the hair on his chest, just as his hands found the front clip to her bra. Ardently he left a trail of kisses down the nape of her neck to her navel. He caressed her tenderly, the pads of his fingers cupping and stroking her breasts. Her hands gripped his shoulders, curled tighter about the warm, firm flesh.

Desperate to return some of the pleasure he was giving her, she let her fingertips move slowly, erotically, down his spine in a way she remembered he had always liked. He drew in a ragged breath. She felt the quiver of taut muscles beneath her palms, heard him hoarsely murmur an accolade.

Selfishly she struggled to control the pleasure. She wanted their loving to go on forever, to stretch into an eternity, but driven by needs out of her control, she moved restlessly against him. Her hands slid down to his waist, lower, beneath the waistband of his jeans. His skin felt like hot silk, stretched tight over corded muscle. He groaned as her hands swept lower, touching, skimming. And then everything was raging passion, out of control. Her mouth sought his in a wanton kiss that made him give a soft moan. And then there was no stopping it. He was turning her toward him so that she lay slightly on her side. His arm was sliding beneath her neck, to cushion her head, to hold her close. His other hand was freeing her of her unbuttoned smock, dispensing with her jeans, skimming over her thighs, upward, melting into the softness, caressing her tenderly, making her ready. He came to her with a long, low contented sigh. Ellie wrapped her arms about his neck and lovingly whispered his name, once, twice. She knew only pleasure—a passion of which he was in full control. He held her there, poised on the edge, for only a moment. And then the last of his reserve was tearing away, the barriers between them were tumbling down, and all was lost in the swirling, sensual magic.

ELLIE LAY ON HER SIDE, turned away from him. She'd never felt more vulnerable in her life, more helplessly, hopelessly in love.

He'd been gradually withdrawing from her, too. She'd noticed it soon after the lovemaking had stopped. He'd held her less tightly, said nothing. She wasn't sure that he knew what to say, but she knew she had to extricate them both from this inelegant situation. So they'd made love. So what? It did not lessen or alter the problems they'd been having in their marriage. It didn't negate their agreement to divorce. Plenty of separated people made love. It happened all the time. Usually she'd hear about it from a tearful client, how they'd never meant to, but it had happened—they'd been together…and yet nothing had changed; the divorce was still going to happen, after all. Those clients had been devastated. Ellie felt devastated now and so very alone, so very afraid. As if she could break into pieces at the slightest touch, the slightest word.

"You're sorry I made love to you, aren't you?" Neil asked. He was lying on his back, his hands folded behind his head. He was staring at the ceiling.

Ellie rose and slipped on a robe. "I don't think it was wise for either of us, under the circumstances." She looked down as her hands fumbled with and finally managed the belt.

Neil rose and went to the closet and slipped on his own robe, a velvety-brown monk's robe that brought out the darkness of his eyes, and the perenially tanned hue of his skin. He gave her an assessing look that seemed to slice right through to her soul. "Is it because we're…getting a divorce?" He said the words with difficulty.

Ellie nodded, turned away.

He strode forward, closing the distance between them implacably. When she moved as if to avoid him, his hands clamped down over her arms. He held her there wordlessly, until she was forced to look at him. "I'm sorry if you felt I took advantage of you—the situation," he said finally. As if realizing how tightly he was holding her, he dropped his grip on her arms and moved away. His jaw was like granite when he spoke. "But a divorce is not what I want, Ellie, not anymore. And especially not with three children on the way."

"What do you want, then?" Ellie sat down on the chaise in

the corner of the bedroom. Her knees felt weak, as if they would no longer support her.

He sat down on the bed opposite her and rested his forearms on his knees. He rushed on, as if he'd already given the subject considerable thought and was delivering a well-rehearsed speech. "I want us to stay together, at least for the first year. If you..." He stopped and wet his lips and went on with difficulty. "If you don't want me to make love with you, fine. But at least let me stay and be a part of the children's lives. The triplets are going to need us both. With one child, maybe you could have managed. But not with three. Please, Ellie. Let me stay here."

Realistically she knew that what he said made sense. And she couldn't deny that she'd feel better with a doctor on the premises. "It's what you want?" In the back of her mind she knew she was already hoping for a reconciliation with Neil. Despite the fact that they still had problems, their relationship was improving daily. She was beginning to feel close to him again.

"It's what I want," Neil said firmly.

"For the children's sake, I'll agree to continue our arrangement for a little while longer than we'd originally agreed," Ellie said cautiously at last. One step at a time, she reminded herself firmly. She'd seen too many couples rush into reconciliation too swiftly, without working out their basic problems first, to disastrous result. When Ellie got back together with Neil, she wanted it to last. Only by continuing to go slowly could they hope to achieve truly lasting results in any medium as difficult as marriage.

"You won't regret this, Ellie." He flashed her an engaging grin. "I promise you I'll be the best father around."

Ellie smiled back. She didn't doubt his assertion for a second. Her high spirits restored by his equally cautious reassurances, she linked hands with him. "Neil, I think one way or another we're going to make quite a team."

Chapter Ten

"Can you believe this?" the staff nurse grumbled to her subordinate. Her strident voice carried down the hall to where Neil was standing at the vending machine just inside the staff lounge. "I've already checked this patient's medical history three times, but the doctor of record is forcing me to check it again."

A can of caffeine-free soda clunked into view. Neil reached for it and carefully opened the tab, took a sip. He didn't really want to listen to the grumbling about medication rechecks, but as he still had business to attend to at the nurses' desk, he had no choice. His only consolation was that the two nurses obviously didn't know he was on the floor. Beyond, the voices continued, "You can't blame him, really. The trouble over at Memorial has made everyone extraordinarily careful nowadays."

And maybe not all to bad result, Neil thought, walking casually toward the nurses' station. "Yeah, but if it hadn't been for Cavanaugh's wife—she shouldn't have sued the hospital, no matter what. Come on, a doctor's wife? If it had been me, I wouldn't have jeopardized *my* marriage for a lousy..."

That was the difference between the women, Neil thought, surprised by the vehemence of his desire to protect and defend his wife. Ellie acted on principle. These women were clearly self-serving. Thank God the majority of nurses at the Medical Center were truly selfless and caring, devoted to their work and their patients. The nurses who had been gossiping paled, looking up at Neil.

"Dr. Cavanaugh—" the first said weakly.

"Mrs. Murdock's chart, please," Neil requested with quiet civility. The fact that staff members were gossiping publicly bothered him; the mention of his wife's name had made him livid, particularly when he knew how much Ellie had already suffered inwardly for what she had done. He maintained eye contact for a good half minute more. All was quiet as he wrote out the new orders for his patient.

Jim Raynor sauntered up just as Neil was leaving. In the elevator down to the ground floor, Jim asked, having picked up on the tension at the desk, "Trouble?"

Neil sighed, glad he was able to confide in his mentor. "More gossip about Ellie."

"Don't let it bother you," Jim counseled. "It will die down in time. Though I must admit I am sorry you didn't get the position as my replacement."

"Next time, maybe," Neil said. His glum mood faded as he thought of the triplets. "With the brood I have coming, I'm going to want all the time I can get to spend at home."

Jim smiled, agreeing. "Are you going over to Memorial for the seminar on the latest laser-surgery techniques?"

"Yes, I am. In fact, I'm on my way over now. Can I give you a lift?"

"I wish—" Jim grinned "—but one of my patients is en route to the hospital. Possible hemorrhage. We may have to do a D & C. So, it looks like I'll be in the emergency room for a while. Maybe on to surgery after that. Do me a favor and take notes, pick up the literature for me that I'll miss?" The elevator stopped, and Jim stepped out into the corridor.

Neil followed him, preparing to head out the opposite way. "Will do."

Minutes later Neil was parking in the Memorial lot. Since Ellie had taken the Middleton case, he'd hated driving over to the rival hospital—maybe because he was afraid of running into the physician Ellie had brought up on malpractice charges, a colleague Neil knew only slightly, but what he had known of the man, he had liked, even admired. Neil found himself wondering what was going to happen to his career.

No sooner had Neil entered the auditorium than he saw Dr.

Talbot. The seminar began seconds later. When the lecture concluded, Dr. Talbot surprised Neil by walking over to join him. They exchanged pleasantries, mutual comments about the lecture they had just witnessed as Neil paused to pick up extra literature for Jim Raynor, as promised.

"Got a few minutes?" Dr. Talbot asked.

To Neil's relief Dr. Talbot looked relaxed, not angry. "Sure." The two men ambled toward the senior physician's office. The conversation did not take the expected turn, though, until the two men were alone. "I want you to know I have no hard feelings toward you," Dr. Talbot began.

"Because of what Ellie did?" Neil guessed at the direction the conversation was heading. He was disburdened to finally have the conflict out in the open.

"Yes. Although I can't say I'm glad I have the mark on my record—" Dr. Talbot forced a smile and a bit of self-effacing humor into the grim situation "—I do feel a responsibility for what happened to Audrey Middleton. I should have caught that error in medication. I would have five, ten, even two years ago. I've had to face the fact that age has slowed me down, made me a little less sharp, and that slight inattentiveness is something none of us can afford. I'm retiring from the practice of clinical medicine, Neil. Unofficially, I've already stepped down from my rotation here at the hospital. I'm going to be concentrating on administrative work from now on, spending more time with my family and grandchildren."

Neil stared at the physician, unsure what to say. "I'm sorry," he said finally.

"Don't be," Dr. Talbot counseled firmly, meeting Neil's gaze forcefully. "I should have retired on my own, without this happening. But I didn't. And a price was paid." Dr. Talbot sat down on the edge of his desk. Behind him the walls of his office were papered with various awards, service commendations, diplomas. "Your wife conducted herself admirably during the arbitration. Frankly, it could have gotten very nasty. I expected it to. I credit Ms. Cavanaugh with the fact it didn't."

The meeting drew to an amiable close.

As Neil walked to his car, he realized to his own amazement

that subtly his feelings were beginning to change. And most of it had to do with Ellie's taking the Middleton case. True, he still had a gut-level dislike of malpractice suits of any kind. He still felt a sympathy for Dr. Talbot and what the distinguished man and his family had been through, but he also harbored a nagging aggravation. Why had it been left to come to that? he wondered. Why hadn't Talbot retired sooner on his own? If his judgment had been impaired, why hadn't his colleagues noticed it, taken steps to make Dr. Talbot aware of it?

Suppose it had been Ellie and not Audrey Middleton in Dr. Talbot's care; suppose Ellie or their babies had died because of a careless mistake in medication? Neil would have been furious and probably not nearly as understanding as the Middletons had been.

For the first time what Ellie had done seemed not so wrong to Neil. The attention given the case had made them all more careful in checking patient histories and prescribing medications. That was for the good.

He was tempted to find Ellie immediately and tell her how he felt. He didn't, because he knew her next question would deal with the subject of her taking another malpractice case. How would he feel? And about that, Neil didn't know what to say. He couldn't lie to her. She wouldn't want to be deceived; she'd see through it. Unhappily, his gut instinct was still to request that she not get involved in any cases slanted against his profession. How could it not be, when even members of the American Medical Association had recently banded together to combat what they considered a national medical malpractice problem of crisis proportions. And yet now, because of Ellie, Neil wondered if physicians were right to keep lawyers out of the issue altogether. If Ellie hadn't helped the Middletons, who would have? Not the hospital. Not Dr. Talbot.

Much as Neil wished otherwise, his and Ellie's was still a difficult situation, the possible ramifications of malpractice hopelessly complicated. He could only hope that, given time and a willingness to solve the conflict on both their parts, a solution would be found yet. One that would satisfy them both. Until then, he would just have to keep working on it, keep thinking.

Surely an answer was there to be discovered, if he just looked hard enough.

"YOU'VE GOT TO SLOW DOWN, ELLIE," Jim Raynor said, concluding her sixth-and-a-half-month exam. "Neil needs a break, too. Neither of you took a vacation last summer. You need to relax."

"Are you speaking as a doctor or a friend of the family?" Ellie teased back, not willing to reveal the reason why neither of them had vacationed.

"Both." Jim's look was unexpectedly grave. "Neil's had a rough time of it the past few months."

Guilt flooded Ellie, that she'd made Neil's life harder when lately he'd done everything in his power to make hers easier. "Because of the Middleton lawsuit?" Ellie asked.

Jim nodded. His gaze was frank. "Neil's had to endure a lot of grumbling from the staff about you. Frankly, I think he could do with a little tender loving care. As could you. So, with the weekend coming up, maybe the two of you could do something about it. Take a night off, cook a special dinner just for the two of you, get some extra rest. If you see to Neil, I'll cover for him here at the hospital Saturday evening."

Ellie pleated the sheet on her lap. "That's very nice."

"Yeah, it is, isn't it?" Jim grinned immodestly before sobering again. "Take care of him, Ellie. He's had a rough couple of months. You both have. And you won't have too much more time alone, with the babies coming in a couple of months."

Jim was more correct about that than he knew, Ellie thought. She forced a smile. She did owe Neil a lot. "I'll take care of him. Don't you worry."

"I'm not."

Despite her casual confidence, Ellie was apprehensive, however. She fretted about how Neil would take a romantic dinner prepared by her. Three weeks had passed since they had made love. As per her wishes, he hadn't approached her again. He had been home as often as possible and, when there, had been loving and gentle and attentive, yet at the same time remote. They were still walking on eggshells around each other. She wasn't sure how much more of the strain she could take. Maybe, she figured pragmatically, it would be better if she and Neil tried harder to become friends again. If not lovers or man and wife, maybe they could just be friends. Heaven knew, the children needed them to be at peace with each other, not at war.

"HEY!" NEIL EXCLAIMED appreciatively as he walked into the house Saturday evening after a long afternoon at the hospital spent tending patients. "What is this? Am I in the wrong house?" For a second his dark eyes glinted with amusement. He glanced around at the roaring fire Ellie had built to take the chill off the unseasonably cold October evening. The aroma of simmering beef Stroganoff, one of Neil's favorite dishes, and crusty homemade bread lingered in the air.

"Jim Raynor said you needed some tender loving care. I decided to act on his assessment." Ellie forced lightness into her tone. She looked at Neil as she would at any other friend, male or female.

Picking up on her overly casual attitude, Neil surveyed her for a long second. "Well, this is great. Really great, Ellie. Thanks." He followed her into the kitchen. His eyes stayed on her as she flitted from table to sink to stove, nervously checking the progress of their dinner.

Ellie turned toward him. For the first time in weeks, she noticed how tired he looked, how...lonely. She felt that way, too, more than he knew. "I'm glad you approve."

Neil went upstairs to wash up and change his shirt. Ellie put the finishing touches on their meal while he was gone. When he rejoined her, they carried their plates into the living room and ate by the fire. "I noticed you've been doing some more work on the nursery," Neil commented.

Ellie nodded. "I wanted to get some diapers in, have some sleepers and T-shirts and so forth ready in the dresser drawers. Your mother and Mimi are having a baby shower for us in a few weeks. Hazel and my mother are planning another with colleagues and employees and friends from Temporary Solution."

"That's nice."

"It will certainly help in terms of buying baby things. Although not everything will be new. I was surprised to find out that both of our mothers have saved some of our own infant clothes and will be donating them to the cause.''

Neil seemed simultaneously amused and touched by this bit of information. ''Hmm. Maybe our mothers have more in common than they know.''

''Maybe,'' Ellie agreed. They were lounging on their sectional sofa, a distance of several feet apart, out of touching range, yet Ellie hadn't felt so close to Neil in weeks as she stared dreamily at the fire. It was the food, she thought, the relaxed atmosphere, an ambience in the room almost like old times.

''What are you thinking about?'' Neil asked at last.

''The babies.'' Ellie's lips curved in a smile. ''I want to do so much for them, Neil. Take them places, show them things, open up the whole world to them.'' She held her arms wide. ''Does that sound silly?''

''No. I want to give them happy memories, too. I want them to have a happy childhood, free of strain and turmoil.'' Neil stared down into his glass, then drained the last of his wine.

''Like your childhood?'' Ellie stared into her glass self-consciously.

''Yes.'' Neil was silent. ''I know you had a miserable childhood, Ellie. You must have, with your parents getting divorced when you were seven, and your mother struggling to survive after that. But you never talk about it. Why is that?''

Just that quickly, Neil had ripped open old wounds. Pain sizzled through her as she recalled the heartache of long, desperate days, one after another, so many years ago—days when she had stared out the window, watching for her father, wishing he would come home again, wishing he would telephone to say he had changed his mind, and nights spent wide awake, alternating crying and staring at the ceiling, wishing her father would come through the apartment door. And worst of all, the times she had heard her own mother cry herself to sleep. No, those had been ugly times, painful years. She didn't want to go back, didn't want to contemplate them, not ever.

''What point would there be in discussing it?'' she asked coolly, getting up to pour herself some more mineral water. She paused to twist lemon into it and gave it an unnecessarily vehement twist. Finished, she carried the wine bottle back to Neil, watched as he poured another serving into his glass.

"Plenty, I would think. If it made you feel better." He set the wine bottle on the table and looked up at her.

"Thinking or talking of my father never makes me feel better." She stood there, angry tears blurring her vision. Part of her resented Neil intensely for ever bringing the subject up; part of her was glad he had. She had to start dealing with it, somehow get to the point where those memories, that time, didn't hurt her anymore.

Neil was beside her. His hands were on her shoulders, gently reassuring. "I'm sorry. I didn't mean to upset you."

Ellie took a long, deep breath and moved away from him. She sat down in her original place on the sofa. "It's all right. I know you can't understand." The caring in his voice had been unmistakable. "You love your father, and he cares very much about you. So much so that he was even willing to interfere in our marriage—a task I know he found loathsome—if he could try to spare you pain. But my father was—is—totally different from that. He never cared about me, never wanted me. I haven't heard from him in years. I'm not sure I want to."

After a moment, Neil also assumed his place adjacent and away from her. "Is he still alive?"

"Yes, living in Los Angeles, last my mother heard. He fled the state so he wouldn't have to pay child support, and back then, when I was little, he was able to do it. They didn't have the kind of legislation they're pushing through now. He's lived there ever since, works for the regional distribution center of a large oil company. Ameritex Oil, I think it is."

"Have your parents been in touch since the divorce?"

"They corresponded, off and on, over the years. Mostly about matters related to breaking off the marriage. It seemed that there were always details surfacing—an insurance policy that needed to be changed or revoked, a question on one of their past joint income-tax forms. And then, of course, there were my mother's somewhat persistent attempts to get or keep him involved in my life."

"Didn't work?"

"No. Those letters he never answered. Only the ones about money or legal matters did he answer. Maybe that's why there were so many of them that kept cropping up over the years." Ellie smiled sadly, reflecting on her mother's resourcefulness. "Anyway, the last time—and the only time I was in touch with him personally—was when I was in college and law school." She'd contacted him because she'd had no choice and found it every bit as difficult as she had imagined it would be. "I was applying for scholarships, student loans, and in order to qualify for them, I had to give legal proof that my father did not help support me, never had, never would."

"What happened?"

Ellie shrugged uncaringly, swilling down the mineral water as if it were gin. "I sent him some forms in the mail. He returned them filled out. Undoubtedly he was happy that I wasn't asking him to support me through school."

"Would he have?"

Her laughter was bitter, unexpected. "I hardly think so. No, my father wouldn't have done that for me. He wouldn't have done anything. So now you have it." She set her empty glass on the table. She felt miserable inside, aching again for something she could never have, a father's love.

"His rejection still hurts you, doesn't it?" Neil asked softly. He seemed to remain where he was with effort.

Ellie nodded. She couldn't lie to Neil about it. Bravely she forced a more neutral, unaffected tone, but still her emotions came through as honestly as her words. "I tell myself it doesn't matter. But it does. There's a part of me that always feels so bereft, so unlovable, because of what he did, the way he left."

"There's nothing unlovable about you," Neil said fiercely. This time he was on his feet, coming over to sit down beside her.

Her head lifted accusingly. "Yet you were able to leave me, to just walk away and sleep nights at the hospital."

"I was a fool. And I've paid for that mistake, Ellie, more than you'll ever know." His voice was husky with hurt, yet with all her self-preserving instincts coming to the fore, she stalwartly resisted the urge to comfort him, too.

The question was, could they go back, pick up where they had left off? Ellie didn't know. She nodded slowly, weighing the validity of his emotions. Would his love of her last or disappear again at the first sign of trouble? "Or maybe you were just more right than you knew," she finished calmly, bringing their attention back to the actions of Neil's that had started the all-out war between them in the first place. Pain was throbbing in her temples. Ellie moved away from Neil. "Look, I don't want to talk about this. I don't want to think about my father. It always upsets me, to no purpose."

Neil studied her a moment longer. He was sitting with clasped hands hanging loosely between his knees. "Ellie, I wish there was something I could do." That much was genuine.

Ellie stoked the fire, then pivoted toward him. "There isn't. Except maybe drop it?" Within her, she felt the babies kicking, then moving as if doing loop-the-loops. Her hand moved to her abdomen unself-consciously. She stroked it involuntarily through the loose and long, embroidered smock.

"All right," Neil consented.

But even as he spoke, he seemed willing to do anything but that, Ellie thought. A shiver of fear raced down her spine. She knew how Neil thought, that with patience and love anything could be resolved. But in this case he was wrong. "Neil, the man was not loving, not caring, not tender, not anything a person would ever want in a father."

"Maybe you just remember him that way."

Tears blurred Ellie's eyes, as even sharper pictures came to mind. "I didn't imagine his coldness. He left for good without even saying goodbye. Never once can I recall him kissing or hugging me or even so much as giving me a present or taking me out for an ice cream cone. He just didn't love me."

Neil was silent, apparently giving up trying to dissuade her. Ellie continued, waving her arms wildly and sharing more of her thoughts about her father than she ever had. "Sure, I wish things had been different then. I wish he could get to know and love his grandchildren. But that's not going to happen, Neil. I know it. I've accepted it. They'll still have my mother and yours and your father. The children won't lack for anything." Except maybe, she thought, two parents who loved each other, who had a normal marital relationship, a solid marriage.

Neil grinned, suddenly cheering. Without warning, he issued the next bit of information. "You know, I did see a sale on baseball gloves and bats and balls the other day!"

Ellie laughed, easily imagining Neil standing mesmerized in front of a hardware store window. "Don't you think you're jumping the gun a bit, Doc? Buying athletic equipment already?" She moved forward, cautiously lowering herself onto the sofa. They were sitting adjacent to each other again, this time with their positions reversed.

"You think I should wait until they're two years old, hmm?"

"At the very least. Otherwise, we'll end up hosting our own version, in triplicate naturally, of Pebbles and Bamm-Bamm on *The Flintstones* cartoon."

He grinned. "Okay, the baseball equipment is out. But there was also a soccer ball that came with a special net...."

Ellie groaned and covered her ears with her hands.

Neil lifted her hands away from her head. "Maybe baby footballs or children's croquet?"

"You mean Neil left you alone?" Viv asked incredulously as Ellie tried ten different ways to get comfortable in an easy chair. "Now? When you're seven months pregnant?"

Ellie tried to cross her legs but couldn't. "*Barely* seven months pregnant, Mom." To her dismay and increasing frustration, none of her contortions worked. No matter how she sat or arranged her loathsome weight, she still felt as though her back were going to be sawed in two and her legs would go numb. Finally she stood and paced restlessly around the living room. "I told you, Mother, Neil hasn't had a vacation all year. And I can't travel now."

"But to leave the state?"

"Neil had Dr. Raynor check me just before he left. According to him, I'm miles away from delivering." Though how she was going to manage to lug around those three babies for two more months, Ellie didn't know. She was exhausted now, always tired, and even had trouble concentrating for more than an hour or two at work. And it was all but impossible to sit still for any length of time.

Careful to avoid stepping on the heavy canvas drop cloth upon which Viv was seated, Ellie watched with minimal interest as her mother carefully repotted several houseplants.

"Even so," Viv clucked disapprovingly. "Neil never should have left."

"A medical-school friend of his is getting married in Chicago. He had to go. And besides, he's only going to be gone one night or two. Three days at the very most. After that he has to be back at the hospital."

In truth, Ellie wanted her husband home now. It wasn't like him just to leave like that, no matter who was getting married. Yet by the same token, Neil had been very up-front about where he was going, and had promised to call her twice daily to check in. He'd even given her a chance to object to the trip, as if half hoping she'd refuse to let him go and beg him to stay home and take care of her. But disinclined to give him the satisfaction of seeing her grovel, she hadn't. Instead, she'd wished him well and told him to stay away as long as he liked. After all, she had her work to keep her busy during the days, and she could always dash over to see her mother in the evenings. If anything came up medically, she could call Dr. Raynor, who had promised, as a friend as well as Ellie's obstetrician, to be available instantly for any emergency.

On the surface, everything was fine. Yet Ellie couldn't shake the feeling that Neil was lying to her, or at the very least suppressing something. About a special bachelor party the men had planned, maybe? He had been living like a monk lately, and with the exception of the one time they'd made love... No, she wouldn't let herself think that. Neil wouldn't be unfaithful to her!

What was she thinking? What right did she have to ask him to remain true to her? They had no commitment to each other. Still, the whole idea of his leaving so suddenly annoyed her. Why was it, she wondered, that this trip and the wedding had just come up out of the blue? She didn't recall any invitation arriving in the mail. Or even Neil's running out to buy a gift. Nor had she ever heard him mention this particular friend before. More incriminating yet was the fact that he seemed not to want to tell her much about the so-called friend of his. And Ellie had been too proud and too stubborn to ask.

Viv finished patting the soil around the plant's base. "Well, maybe it is good Neil got away for a few days," her mother decided finally, pulling off her gloves. "He has been under a lot of pressure. And he won't have much chance for partying once those triplets are born."

Ellie sincerely hoped not. Drinking and carousing were two activities she wouldn't put up with, even if he did go out of state to do it!

Viv laced an arm around her daughter's ever-expanding waist. "How about some carrot juice? You look like you could use a glass."

Ellie almost choked. She felt as if she could use a drink, but she'd sworn off alcohol since early in her pregnancy. "I don't suppose you have anything carbonated or calorie-laden?" She shot her mother a hopeful glance.

"Not a chance," Viv smiled, knowing her daughter's beverage preferences well. Without warning, she relented, becoming the soft touch Ellie remembered from her youth. "However, I suppose, if you're craving it, Ellie..."

"I could just die for a cherry Coke," Ellie said swiftly, taking advantage of her mother's momentary weakness.

Viv laughed and shook her head in fondest exasperation. "Grab your purse, Ellie, and we'll go get one for you."

"Onion rings, too?"

Viv studied her only child fondly. Instead of refusing to indulge Ellie's dietary vices, as usual, Viv said gently, "Honey, after what you've been through the past few months, you can have a double order."

Chapter Eleven

"Mr. Jensen?" Neil asked. "I'm Neil Cavanaugh, your daughter Ellie's husband. May I come in for a moment? I'd very much like to talk to you." Neil had tracked Ellie's father down at Ameritex Oil, only to find that Ted had taken advantage of the company's flextime policy; he had come in inordinately early and had already gone home for the day. The company had refused to give Neil his father-in-law's home address. But that hadn't mattered much. Neil already had gone through Ellie's private papers when she wasn't around and found what he had been looking for without ever having to involve either his wife or his mother-in-law in what he hoped would be the best surprise Ellie had had in a long time. Unhappily, though, it wasn't turning out at all in the way Neil had envisioned.

After a moment's hesitation Ted Jensen swung open the door to his apartment fully, and recalcitrantly ushered Neil in. He was a plump, soft-muscled, ill-groomed man. Neil felt uncomfortable with him on sight.

Unfortunately it didn't get any better. The interior of the room was slovenly. Old newspapers and battered magazines littered the room. Dishes were piled high in the sink. The whole place smelled faintly of garbage several weeks old that Ted had apparently been too lazy to take to the dumpster out back. A small portable color television blared from a stand in the living room. "What do you want?" Ted Jensen asked, making no move to switch off the evening news.

With effort Neil ignored the man's blatant lack of hospitality and sat down on the edge of a chair. He hadn't come all the way to California to find Ted Jensen, only to be put off by a less-than-hearty reception or quarters that showed a disgusting lack of both taste and cleanliness.

"It's my understanding that you haven't seen your daughter in quite some time. I thought you'd like to know how she's grown up," Neil said simply. Was it possible that Ted Jensen had given up on ever being a part of his daughter's life out of guilt over what he'd done years before? That was what Neil had originally hoped. Or had he just stepped out of her life after realistically assessing his own limits as a parent, to spare Ellie pain? Whatever the truth, Neil felt instinctively that Ellie hadn't missed much by not having Ted Jensen around. The problem now was how to let her know that.

Still, Neil had come to California to tell Ted about his daughter, perhaps to forge some bridge of communication between Ellie and her father. Despite the disagreeable surroundings, he felt honor-bound at least to try to manage that. Before Ellie's father could react, Neil had reached into his coat pocket and produced a picture of Ellie, taken the first year they were married.

Ted looked at it, studied it briefly, impassively, then handed it back. No emotion registered on his face. Undeterred, Neil launched into a complete rundown of all Ellie's accomplishments. Ted cut Neil off before he could be given news of the triplets. "Look, why are you telling me all this?" he demanded roughly, pacing agitatedly back and forth. He lit a cigarette and clamped it tightly between his teeth.

"I thought you'd at least be curious as to what your daughter was up to," Neil said, with effort stifling an urge to stand up and punch the ungrateful lout in the face. Didn't he realize all he had given up, stepping out of Ellie's life that way? How could he not feel something for his wonderful daughter? Even pride?

"I don't want to know anything about her, never did." It was a simple statement of fact, cold-bloodedly issued. "Maybe her mother mentioned I never wanted kids?"

"No." Neil's jaw clenched. Neither had Ellie. But it certainly was clear enough. Was this what Ellie had lived with? Neil wondered savagely. How had she managed? How had Viv?

Valiantly Neil made one last try to wedge some sort of peace between father and daughter, to find something in common, something Ellie could hold on to. "Ellie's going to have triplets," he said calmly.

Ted's eyes registered neither joy nor surprise. "So?"

So that makes you a grandfather, you bastard, Neil thought savagely. With effort he kept his acerbic thoughts to himself. His jaw tautened. He was finding it increasingly hard to hold on to his temper, but he knew he had to try for Ellie's sake.

Ted did some rapid thinking of his own and came up with his own assessment of why Neil was there. "Wait a minute. If you think I'm going to pitch in financially, young fellow—"

"Hardly," Neil said icily.

"You're well off, then?" he asked with faintly discernible interest.

"No." Neil wasn't about to offer Ted Jensen any money. "Except maybe in the fact that I have Ellie and the children." He'd never appreciated his own family more.

"Well, you're welcome to them." This was said without malice or feeling. Apparently feeling that Neil was about to punch him, Ted held out both hands in front of him defensively, "I meant I had no claim."

"You'll stay away from her?" Neil found himself asking. He'd gone there to effect a reunion and found himself warning the man off. He was glad now that he'd followed his instincts and not involved Ellie in this effort of his in any way. It would only have hurt her. Nothing of Ellie's joie de vivre, wit, intellect or compassion had ever come from that man. There was no connection between them and, sadly, never would be. It wasn't an ideal situation, but one perhaps that Ellie could eventually learn to live with, given time and understanding and much support and love from Neil, her mother, her own children.

"Haven't I been staying away?" Ted Jensen asked, a contemptuous curl to his lips.

"Your word," Neil demanded tersely, his hands curling into

fists at his sides. At the moment he wanted nothing but to get away from the selfish bastard.

"You got it."

Neil left, never feeling more dissatisfied and unhappy in his life.

When he returned to Joplin late the next afternoon, Neil immediately sought out his father. He found him at the country club, just finishing up a game of golf with one of his clients. At Neil's request, Herb and he entered the club for a drink. Within minutes, Neil had told his father about the visit with Ted from start to finish.

"And Ellie doesn't know you saw her father?" Herb ascertained finally, taking a sip of his beer.

"No, I didn't want to tell her about it in case it didn't work out. She's been emotional enough as it is lately. I guess it's a good thing I didn't." Neil stared into his glass. The depression that had plagued him since he left Los Angeles was even more intense now that he was home. He had an inkling of how Ellie felt now and his desire to help his wife increased.

Herb's brows drew together as he regarded his son bewilderedly. "Where did you tell her you were?"

"Chicago. A friend's wedding. I know I shouldn't have lied, but if I'd said California, she would've known what I was going to do, would've tried to stop me." And he hadn't intended to let her do that, any more than Neil intended to let her raise their children alone, no matter what he had agreed to. If it came down to it, which he hoped it wouldn't, he would fight Ellie tooth and nail to oppose the divorce. Hell, he wouldn't even agree to a legal separation. And he knew that his feelings would only deepen once the children were born.

"Why is it so important that you make peace between Ellie and her father?" Herb asked, unwrapping a saltine from the basket on the table.

"Because the sleazy piece of garbage hurt her badly when he left her when she was a kid. I thought going out there that any relationship with him at all would be better than nothing, but now I don't feel that way. I think she's better off keeping him out of her life completely."

Herb was silent for a long moment. "Still, you should tell Ellie," he said finally.

Neil knew that—in theory at least. Doing it was another matter indeed. "Normally, I would, Dad. Normally, I wouldn't have had to deceive her. But she's been so fragile lately. Dad, I don't want to hurt her." He'd already wounded her enough inadvertently.

"Lying to her isn't helping."

"I know." Neil ran a hand across his jaw, feeling the stubble of evening beard grate against his open palm.

"So, level with her," Herb encouraged, reaching for a second cracker.

But Neil couldn't do it. Nor would he give lip service to something he didn't sanction, and Herb knew it. He and his father were both silent for several more moments.

"So how is Ellie now, anyway?" Herb asked finally, evidently figuring he'd pushed his son hard enough. "You know, your mother and I haven't seen the two of you together in...I don't know how long. Months."

Neil took a long swallow of his drink. "We've both been very busy at work."

"Everything okay?" Herb's eyes narrowed into contemplative slits.

"Yeah." Neil scanned the crowd in the country club bar evasively, looking for people he knew. Seeing another doctor from the hospital, he nodded a silent hello.

"You know, son, I never should have gone to see Ellie that day, asked her not to take the Middleton case. Not that I've changed my mind about what she did. I still think she was wrong. But I shouldn't have interfered. Your mother made me see that. I promise you it won't happen again. So, if Ellie's still irritated with me over that—"

"She's not," Neil interrupted.

"You're sure?" Herb still seemed concerned.

"Positive." Neil spoke with a conviction he seldom felt anymore when it came to the subject of his wife. He glanced at his watch, gestured for the check. "Listen, Dad, I've got to go." When the waitress arrived, there was a moment's grappling for the tab. Finally both men shelled out several dollars, split the tip and let it go at that.

"Give Ellie my love," Herb said as he walked his son out to his car.

"I will," Neil promised, slipping behind the wheel. Now, if only he could get Ellie to accept his own love as well.

NEIL HALF EXPECTED a fight when he got home. He knew damn well, if Ellie tried to call him at his friend's place in Chicago, she would have gotten a prearranged runaround. But, apparently, she hadn't called his friend, she hadn't checked up on his whereabouts, and she wasn't the least bit happy to see him. Instead, Ellie looked tired and worn-out as she folded a laundry basketful of clothes.

"Aren't you going to ask me about the wedding?" Neil found himself irked that she wasn't at least a little bit inquisitive about where he had been.

"How was it?" Ellie shot him a bland, disinterested look as she smoothed and folded a plush pink towel into a neat square.

"Fine." Neil peered closer. Ellie's face looked faintly puffy, as did her fingers and wrists. "Ellie, are you feeling all right?" She'd been fine when he left. More than fine, actually. Yet, as a physician, he knew how quickly a patient's health could take a turn for the worse, as Ellie's condition apparently had.

"I'm tired a lot," Ellie admitted spiritlessly at last.

"Anything else?" Neil found himself sitting beside her on the sofa. He reached into the laundry basket and began silently and swiftly to help her fold the clothes.

She shook her head, sweeping the silky blond hair off her face with the back of her hand. "No, I'm just tired of being pregnant, I guess, anxious for it to be over."

"And that's it?" Neil asked, hardly able to tear his eyes from her face. She had been on his mind incessantly for days now. Weeks, actually. And he had been forced to keep busy, just so he wouldn't seek her out in a marital sense. Still, he had spent time with her, watched over her. And the minute he turned his back for an instant, or in this case less than forty-eight hours...

"What else could there be?" Ellie's low, haughty voice was like a douse of ice water in his face.

Something in the way she looked at him made Neil realize that she knew in her heart that he'd been lying to her. But as depressed and exhausted as she seemed, now was not the time to go into his discoveries about her father. He would have to tell her eventually, but it could wait, he decided, until after the babies were born. The most important concern now was her health.

He studied her a moment longer, not liking her lack of color. "Maybe it's time you stopped working," he said.

"I've already cut back on my office hours." She jerked a silky beige bra and half-slip from his hands.

"If you're this tired, Ellie..." He watched as she shoved her lingerie down on top of the stack of clothes. Despite her agitation, no more color had come into her face.

Her eyes glistened with moisture that was more, he thought, a sign of fatigue than sadness or anger or frustration. "Neil, I don't want to argue with you. I'll work as long as I want to, okay?" Her chin assumed its most stubborn tilt. Putting a hand to the back of the sofa, she slowly levered her way to her feet.

He gave her a hand up, which she promptly shook off, the action nearly causing her to lose her balance. He gritted his teeth in aggravation, finally planting his hands on his hips. He deliberately blocked her way, refusing to let her go past him before she heard him out. "No, it's not okay, Ellie. Not if you're endangering the health of my babies." His voice carried an undertone of steel.

She looked at him furiously. "Of course. I should have known you'd say that." She picked up the laundry basket, shoving it between them.

Neil reminded himself that pregnant women were often highly emotional and irascible in the last trimester of pregnancy, as a result of a combination of worry, lack of sleep, unceasing physical discomfort and hormonal changes. He moved to let her past, not attempting to wrest the laundry basket from her, though admittedly he would have preferred to carry it up the stairs for her.

Ellie appeared not to appreciate his gallantry at all. Walking stiffly by him, she announced, "I'm going up and go to sleep."

Neil followed her at a distance as far as the stairs. "This early?" It was barely 7:00 P.M.

"I've already eaten and I'm tired. Okay?" She didn't turn to look at him, but there was a pleading note in her voice that cut straight to his heart. She seemed at her limit, physically, emotionally. Neil backed down, again suppressing the urge to try to help her with the basket of clothes, light as he could see it was. "Okay. But if you need anything, Ellie..." His offer was low, husky with genuine concern.

"I won't." She looked at him directly as she reached the top of the stairs, the fierceness of her gaze signaling the end of the conversation, then turned away.

Neil could have sworn there were tears in her eyes.

He considered for a moment taking her to the hospital then and there, then decided he was overreacting. There would be time enough to call Jim in the morning and tell him about the depth of his worries. Right now Ellie needed sleep. And he would be here with her, in case anything came up. But tomorrow morning, first thing after she woke up, she was going into the hospital, Neil decided. Even if he had to carry her there kicking and screaming.

Still, the harsh words between them bothered him. *I should have gone after her,* Neil thought minutes later when she was still on his mind, but he hadn't. He'd let her bad temper come between them, because that had been easier than answering questions or lying to her about where he'd been. He wanted to help her; he ended up hurting her. Weariness overcame Neil, too. Muttering a few choice words, he kicked off his shoes and lay down on the sofa and went to sleep.

WHEN ELLIE WOKE, sunshine was streaming into the room and Neil was carrying a tray to her bed. "Breakfast is served, madam." He looked fresh and rested. He was wearing a dress shirt and slacks, no tie.

"Why aren't you at the hospital?" She yawned sleepily, sitting up. Glancing at the clock, she was alarmed to see that it was almost eleven o'clock. Had she really slept sixteen hours straight? She'd known she was exhausted, but... "Who turned off my alarm?'' Her brows knitted together unhappily. She watched as Neil fitted the tray over her lap and wordlessly plumped up pillows behind her back. She could smell the faint scent of the shampoo and after-shave and soap he used—all scents that combined in a fresh fragrance that was uniquely his.

''I did. I also called Hazel and told her you wouldn't be in to the office at all today,'' Neil announced imperiously. As her senses were still reeling at his nearness and unexpected attention, he straightened and folded his arms across his waist in his best no-nonsense manner. His eyes were incisive, direct. ''I'm taking you to see Jim Raynor. Your appointment is at one.''

Ellie had half expected him to insist that she see her obstetrician. She'd planned to call Jim herself and see him a few days earlier than scheduled. ''Why?'' Why was he being so wonderful to her, after he'd taken off like that, leaving the state? Not that it was his fault she wasn't feeling well. No, that downturn in her physical well-being had been as much a surprise to her as it was to him.

''You don't look good, Ellie. I want him to have a look at you, that's all.''

She didn't like his careful tone. Ellie ignored the tempting array of hot cereal, toast, juice and coffee before her. ''That's not all.''

''All right. If you want me to be honest, I think it's going to be necessary to put you in the hospital for a few days, but that's up to Jim. So, eat your breakfast. Get dressed and we'll be off.'' He turned and left the room before she could comment. Ellie ate her breakfast dutifully, then swiftly showered and dressed.

Ellie was scared, more scared than she dared admit. The truth was that she hadn't been feeling well for the past few days, and for Neil to have seen it so swiftly... Was there anything wrong with her or the babies? They were still kicking quite actively in her womb. Still, she put her hand to her abdomen as Neil drove the familiar route to the hospital. ''Contractions?'' He glanced at her sideways.

''No.'' She flushed guiltily.

''But you have been having them,'' he ascertained, looking grimmer by the minute.

"Just *false* contractions, a few every now and then." She emphasized the difference between what she'd been feeling and real labor.

"How often?" he asked as he pulled into the doctor's lot and parked in the space assigned him. Shutting off the ignition with a snap, he turned toward her, letting his arm snake possessively across the back of his seat. "Every day? More than once? Perhaps when you've been on your feet too long?"

Deciding primly that Neil was acting like an anxious husband rather than a physician, she clamped her lips together firmly. "I'm not discussing this with you. I'm talking only to Jim Raynor. He's my obstetrician, Neil. You're not." She reached for her purse and stepped stoically out of the car. Her back was rigid as she took steps toward the sidewalk.

"Ellie!" He slammed out after her and caught up with her before she'd made it past the next car. He caught her by the elbow, and swung her ever so gently around to face him. His eyes were glistening with a depth of emotion she'd never before seen him exhibit. "I know I'm acting like an idiot," he said with such velvet softness that ripples sped down her spine. "I know I'm exasperating. I see other expectant fathers, and I can laugh at their overprotectiveness. I see you, carrying my babies—" his voice dropped huskily another notch "—and all I can think about is taking care of you, making you happy. Damn it, Ellie, I care about you. Don't you know that by now? Can't you cut me some slack? Humor me a little, as I'm trying to humor you?"

How could she shut him out when he was like that? When all she really wanted was to make love to him and hold him close and never ever let him go? But that wasn't their agreement, she reminded herself firmly. Still, she nodded her understanding of his position with a sudden lump in her throat. The seconds drew out. He seemed suddenly very close to kissing her, right there on the sidewalk in front of the hospital. Ellie wanted him to do just that, and yet she didn't. It was hard enough to keep her emotional distance from him as it was, without adding fuel to the already roaring fire. "We're going to be late," she reminded in a thready tone.

He said nothing in response, just fixed her with an intent,

deeply sensual look. "We're not finished here, Ellie," he said. "We're going to talk about this." His light grip on her arms tightened momentarily, then dropped.

Talk, and let him find out how much she still loved him, still yearned foolishly and unrealistically for their marriage to work against all odds, when they'd already proved their relationship was in dire trouble? If she'd fatuously had hopes before for a reconciliation, his trip to Chicago, his evasions, had dashed them. No, they weren't going to talk about her feelings for him, Ellie thought with new desperation. They weren't. She wouldn't allow it. She'd been hurt enough already.

"NEIL, THIS IS RIDICULOUS." Ellie grumbled two hours later, walking slowly into the private room. "I don't belong in a hospital."

Neil closed the door behind him and put Ellie's suitcase on the floor. "You heard what Dr. Raynor said. Complete bed rest. If you don't have it, there's a very good chance that you could go into premature labor." Still, Ellie was reluctant. And he could hardly blame her. If he'd been ordered suddenly into the hospital, he would no doubt feel just as bewildered and unhappy.

"But—"

"No arguments, Ellie. This is what's best for you and the babies."

Without warning all the fight went out of her. She sighed tremulously, leaned against him. He tightened his arm around her possessively.

"Do you need some help getting into a gown and robe?" Neil asked gently.

She turned toward him, scowling, moved away and raked a hand through the tousled ends of her hair. "No. And don't start on me. I'm so confused that I don't know whether to laugh or cry as it is."

"Then do neither," he advised sagely. He reached for her suitcase and opened it up on the bed. Lifting the first available garments, he handed them to her. "Just undress and get into bed."

He'd known from the moment Jim told her that she had to be

put into the hospital for the duration of her pregnancy, that she was going to make trouble. Blessedly, she hadn't said much to her obstetrician. No, she'd saved all her recriminations and complaints for Neil and was currently looking at him as if her hospitalization were all *his* fault, not an occasional hazard of carrying triplets, as Jim had explained to her. Unfortunately, he knew that she still had questions about his trip out of state. He saw her distrust in her eyes every time she looked at him. But that didn't alter his determination not to discuss what he'd done, or discovered about Ted Jensen, with her now. Every instinct he had told him that would be a mistake. It would be better to let her think he had simply been inconsiderate and inattentive—two sins he could easily rectify—than for her to know the truth in her present vulnerable state.

Ellie exhaled. "Can't I just stay in street clothes for a while and lie on top of the covers?"

He fought down a smile. "Into your nightgown, Ellie." He kept both his tone and steady appraisal stern with warning.

Her jaw jutted out mutinously. She didn't reach for the garment he held out. Neil thought idly about pressing them into her tightly compressed fists or undressing her himself, the latter of which appealed to him more, then decided on a lighter, more taunting approach. He regarded her motionlessly for several more challenging seconds, in which neither gave an inch. "Already out to prove the axiom true, Ellie?" he asked in the softest of possible tones.

Her eyes narrowed suspiciously. "What axiom?" She correctly sensed a trap. Grabbing the clothes he held in his hands, she tossed what he'd selected back into the suitcase, pulled out a second gown and robe of her own choice.

"That the only patient worse than a physician is a physician's wife?"

She blushed to her roots, turned away, muttered something unprintable about his lack of character, understanding and finesse—a tirade he found highly amusing.

Neil allowed himself a wide grin. "Hey, lady, don't look at me as if I'm the villain!" He spread his hands wide in a helpless gesture, defending himself to the limit. "I'm just saying what I know the staff is going to be saying. What they always say when an admittedly difficult doctor's wife is admitted.''

She slammed shut the lid of her suitcase and stalked haughtily by him toward the private bath and shower in her room. ''Don't feel you have to wait around.'' She pushed the words through a wall of white teeth.

Neil said nothing in reply. The door slammed after Ellie with a resounding bang. The show of hot temper made Neil smile. Ellie was feeling better already, just knowing that actions were being taken to bolster and correct her declining health.

While she was in the bathroom, Neil emptied her suitcase, putting personal belongings, her makeup and hair dryer in the dresser drawer next to the bed, and hanging her clothes in the closet. When she emerged, she looked at him, as if stunned to see that he was still there. Her eyes were slightly red, as if she'd started to cry out of sheer frustration, then stopped. Pretending not to notice her tears, Neil reached for the street clothes she'd just taken off. ''I'll hang those up.''

For a moment he thought they were going to play tug-of-war. Finally she let go of her clothes. Still, she made no move to get into bed. He walked back to her side. She was staring out the hospital window at the traffic on the busy city streets below. She was wearing a wine brushed velvet robe and lacy white gown.

''I hate this,'' she said softly.

''I know.'' Not caring whether she wanted him to hold her or not, Neil reached for her, held her as close as was possible, considering her advanced stage of pregnancy. Against him, he could feel the kicks of the babies moving about in her softly rounded abdomen. ''Active little buddies, aren't they?''

His affectionate assessment of their children made her smile. ''Yes, they are.'' Again, she looked as if she was going to cry. Deliberately she turned back toward the bed. There were light violet shadows beneath her eyes. Her face beneath the light, despite the deftly applied makeup, was very pale, showing the signs of physical and emotional strain she'd been under.

''Look, is there anything you want? Anything I can get you?'' Neil asked finally.

''No, I...no. I am worried about my work, though. The office.

I can get other attorneys to cover for me or take over my cases. But I'm the only one who can sift through my calls."

"Would you like me to talk to Jim?"

"Would you?" She'd been so stunned with the initial prescription that she enter the hospital that she hadn't thought to ask. Later, as they'd driven home to pack her suitcase and promptly return, Neil knew that her work had been on her mind.

"Yes."

"Great." She tremulously smiled her relief. "If I could have Hazel come here in the mornings and maybe again in the late afternoon..."

"One hour a day, tops, Ellie. That's it."

Thankfully, she realized when there was no room for negotiation. Hopefully, she asked, "Do you think my time with my secretary could be increased?"

"It depends on how you do, Ellie. If we can get the slight increase in your blood pressure taken care of, reverse the slight swelling in your hands and feet and stop you from dilating any more than the one centimeter...we'll just have to see. I'll talk to Jim about letting you work with Hazel, one hour every morning, but only if you get into bed now and rest for the duration of the afternoon."

Her mouth curved wryly, alerting his attention anew to how really beautiful she was. Some of her radiance came back. Her breath came out slowly. The set of her shoulders relaxed slightly. "Maybe I will take a nap," she said finally. With highly exaggerated complicity, she sat down on the edge of the bed.

"Atta girl," Neil patted her on the shoulder and smiled his approval. "Should I draw the drapes?"

She turned back to him with a warning look, arching her fair brows. "And darken this room to a nice sickroom aura? Don't press your luck, Neil. I'm on the bed. I may even get under the covers and close my eyes. That's about it." She wasn't about to let anyone turn her into even the suggestion of an invalid.

Ellie, Neil thought. *Vintage Ellie.*

Chapter Twelve

"It's a good thing I've turned fourteen; otherwise they wouldn't let me up to see you," Mimi said several days later, moving closer to Ellie's bed. Ellie put down the magazines she had been restlessly thumbing through. The first day in the hospital had been fine. She'd slept almost the whole day. After that it had gone downhill. Her time with her secretary was all too short, and she hated having to refer so many cases to other lawyers when she'd worked so hard to attract clients in the first place. But she supposed that was a hazard one took when one went into business alone.

"How are you feeling?" Mimi asked, tilting her head sideways to survey her sister-in-law better.

"Not so hot," Ellie admitted with a heartfelt sigh.

"How come?" Mimi rummaged in her purse for some sugarless chewing gum, which was what she munched on now between meals.

"Oh, little things. I can't sleep, can't do anything comfortably." Ellie took advantage of her chance to complain to someone who appreciated her misery and could understand how stifling it was for her. "And worst of all," Ellie finished several minutes later, exhausting her litany of complaints, "I look like a beached whale washed ashore and draped with white sheets."

Mimi laughed uproariously. "And I thought Neil was a grump when he was sick! You two sure are alike! Come on, now. It's really not so bad being here, is it? You know you don't look like a whale...a porpoise maybe!" Mimi held up her hands and laughingly dodged the pillow Ellie threw at her. Coming up for air, Mimi finished, "And that white nightgown is pretty."

"And conservative. I don't know. Normally, I like the old-fashioned white lacy gowns, but wearing them all day and all night, day after day, I just feel frumpy." Ellie frowned again.

"At least you don't have to wear those stupid hospital gowns all the time," Mimi pointed out.

"True," Ellie said glumly, only slightly cheered. "But you look terrific, Mimi."

"Thanks. I miss walking with you, Ellie."

"I miss it, too."

Mimi curled up in an armchair by the window, tucking her newly slim legs beneath her. "Great news. I have a date to go to the Homecoming Dance."

"That's wonderful!"

"We're doubling with another couple, and we have to be in early. You know my dad. He's so conservative! But, still, it's a real date and a real dance and I'm going shopping with my mother this afternoon for a dress to wear to it. I wish you could go with me. I really liked it when you helped me pick out my school clothes."

"I enjoyed myself."

Ellie looked up to see Neil standing in the doorway, just outside in the hall. He'd obviously overheard much of the conversation between her and Mimi. He looked pleased to see them together.

Seeing her brother, Mimi jumped up, found her purse and popped her gum. "Well, listen, I better be going. Neil made me promise I wouldn't stay long."

Ellie shot Neil a glum look. "Thanks." Her tone said she was anything but appreciative of his efforts to protect her.

He only grinned and stuck his hands in the pockets of his trousers. "We don't want to tire you out now, do we, Ellie?"

"The only thing *we're* liable to die of is boredom."

"So you keep saying." He grinned again, suddenly all rogue. "However if you really want to remedy that..." He had plenty of ideas.

Ellie succeeded in fighting down a blush. He was incorrigible!

Because Mimi was looking all too interested in discovering Neil's theories, Ellie changed the subject adroitly. "Spare me your ideas about making ceramic keyholders. And I'm warning you, Neil, if you start again on that old axiom about doctors' wives making bad patients..."

"Boy," Mimi said, scooting sideways toward the door. "You sure can tell the two of you are married."

Ellie shot her teenage friend a startled glance and started to blush despite herself. But Neil was grinning from ear to ear. "We do sound as if we've been together for a long time, don't we?" He liked the idea.

"Yeah." Mimi raised and lowered both brows. To Ellie, she said, "I'll, um, come back and see you sometime soon. Maybe next time I can bring you something." Before Ellie could protest that it wasn't necessary, she was gone.

"WELL, WHAT DO YOU THINK?" Mimi asked the following Saturday as Ellie stared in awe at the maternity black-silk-and-chiffon gown and matching shirred lace bed jacket Mimi had picked out.

"I think it's gorgeous and it must have cost a fortune." Ellie eyed the lush fabric and plunging neckline with a combination of longing and envy. How long was it since she had worn anything that luxurious against her skin?

"Do you like it?" Mimi was hopeful, apprehensive.

"Yes." It was so racy! "But, Mimi, I didn't want you to spend—"

"Listen, Ellie, you've done a whole lot for me this past year. You helped me lose weight and to exercise and feel better about myself, think about my goals for the future. You've really helped me. Not because I'm Neil's sister, but because I'm me. And that really means a lot to me. Besides, I had some baby-sitting money saved. You do like it, don't you?"

"Well, yes. It's gorgeous." Just perfect for a night at home, alone, seducing your husband, Ellie thought.

Mimi sighed her relief. "Great. I knew you needed something really special, and the saleswoman at the maternity boutique said this would definitely make you look unfrumpy!"

And then some, Ellie thought wryly, holding up the neckline that looked as if it would plunge to her sternum, at the very least.

"Go ahead. Try it on. I want to see how you look."

One look at Mimi's excited face told Ellie that she couldn't refuse. She went into the bathroom dutifully. When she came out, Mimi's face told all. "Wow, that really is foxy."

Ellie nodded. "You're right. It definitely got rid of that frumpy feeling." Even nearly eight months pregnant, she felt as if she were a real siren.

Just then a nurse came in bringing Ellie's medication. She took one look at Ellie's gown and smiled broadly. "Well, well, Mrs. Cavanaugh. What have we here?"

"A present from me," Mimi said proudly, looking back at Ellie and squeezing her hand as Ellie climbed back into bed. "Don't you love it?" Mimi asked, turning back to the nurse.

"That gown is really something. All the hospitalized pregnant women ought to have to wear them," the nurse agreed. "Maybe it would do something for their flagging spirits. And I *know* Dr. Cavanaugh is going to love it."

Neil. Since Ellie had been in the hospital, he'd been in and out of her room scores of times daily. Ironically, she was seeing more of him now than she ever had before.

"Well, listen, I gotta go," Mimi said. "I promised Neil I wouldn't stay long, and tonight is the big night."

"Homecoming?"

"Uh-huh." Mimi paused to describe her dress to Ellie in great detail. "Naturally, it's not as foxy as what you're wearing, but it's okay. It definitely is not from the kiddy department. And the flowers my date is going to bring me...well, he promised they'd match my dress."

"You make it sound like so much fun. I wish I could go."

"Maybe you and Neil will do some dancing on your own."

Ellie only wished. But the time for that had long passed. And, realistically, considering that they'd agreed to divorce, she couldn't expect it to happen at any time in the future. They chatted for several more minutes. "Have a good time tonight," Ellie urged, thanking her again for the gown.

"I will. You, too, Ellie."

Less than fifteen minutes later Neil came charging into the room. One look at Ellie had him reeling. To her chagrin he let out a long wolf whistle that could be heard several rooms away. There was soft female laughter outside the door, and then one of the nurses came forward to hand Neil a piece of cardboard, lettered with black Magic Marker. "The sign you requested, Dr. Cavanaugh," she said formally.

The sign said Do Not Disturb.

"Great," Neil said, taping it to the outside of the door. Finished, he dusted off his hands and fixed Ellie with an unabashed leer before turning back to his co-workers to announce, after clearing his throat, "Now, if you ladies will see that I'm not disturbed..."

Laughing and shaking their heads in mock reproval, the nurses left. Neil shut the door tightly, then stalked back rakishly and pulled up a chair.

"Was that necessary?" Ellie asked.

"I have my reputation to think of."

He'd certainly earned it just then, Ellie thought.

"So where did you get the gown?" Neil continued playing the rake on the make.

"Mimi," Ellie explained.

"That was sweet of her." He looked her up and down again, his eyes lingering on the deep cleft between her breasts, on the silky Empire bodice clinging to her curves. "The two of you have become rather close, haven't you?" His tone was gentle and serious as his gaze returned to her face. She was reminded of what a tender, considerate lover he could be and how much she had missed getting the benefit of that tender loving expertise.

"There's no stronger bond than that of women who restrict their diets together," Ellie said sagely. "It's a constant struggle for both of us to stay away from junk food."

"But very necessary now," Neil said, referring to the low-salt, high-protein regime the dietitian had put Ellie on since she had entered the hospital.

"I know. I'm not cheating," Ellie said seriously.

"Even if you were, I'd have to say you look sensational." He wiggled both brows in a predatory manner, then advanced, his curiosity deepening his low, husky tone. "What's beneath the covers anyway?"

"Neil!" He caught her hands with both of his, then transferred both of her wrists to one of his hands. There was a brief skirmish, which Ellie lost, as he sat down beside her, shifting playfully closer. Ellie's breath caught rapidly. He surely knew how to chase away the doldrums, she thought.

Neil's teasing leer became more pronounced, then disappeared altogether. He leaned closer, until his shoulders blocked out the rest of the room, and all she could look at were his eyes, dark, intent. She wanted to get lost in that determined gaze; she wanted to get lost in his love. Threading his hands through her hair, he arranged and rearranged the silky tresses. "How long has it been since I kissed you, Ellie?"

Was it her imagination or was his breathing becoming more erratic, too? Ellie hung on to the threads of her composure with effort. "Every day, at least one hundred times." A quick hello and goodbye. He never seemed to miss an opportunity to deliver a brief peck on the cheek or temple. And he'd kept up his attentiveness until her anger over his unexplained trip out of state had faded.

"I mean really kissed you." His eyes were darkening. He moved his mouth slightly to the side, then slowly lowered it to hers.

Ellie wanted to run, but there was no place to go. He let go of her hands and the mattress yielded slightly as he shifted his weight beside her.

"You do look sensational in that gown, you know," he murmured admiringly.

Her hands came up to rest on his shoulders. She'd meant to push him away, or at the very least hold him off, but she only ended up bringing him closer. "I really didn't want to put it on." She felt a strange lassitude in her limbs. His muscles beneath her palms were taut, so very male.

His hands slipped beneath the lacy bed jacket, smoothed over her bare shoulders to the thin spaghetti-strap ties. "But Mimi left you no choice?"

"After the trouble she'd gone to, I didn't want to hurt her

feelings." Ellie was tingling everywhere he touched. "But I didn't want you to think I was coming on to you." What a mess they'd gotten themselves into. She couldn't approach him, couldn't forget him.

He let that register a moment, then said simply, honestly, "I wish you would come on to me."

He lowered his head, until his mouth fit perfectly over hers. His lips moved across hers, back and forth, back and forth, until her mouth was open, receptive to the inflaming, tormenting glide of his tongue. She caught the stubble of his beard, pleasurably rough against her face, and the faint taste of mint. Lazily, thoroughly, his hands swept beneath the bed jacket, moved around her, tarried across her spine. Contentment flooded her senses and she realized how much she had missed his touch and how much, despite everything, she needed him still. He paused for a moment. She knew she should say something, but nothing came to mind. She only knew that she didn't want anything to spoil the moment; she didn't want him to stop. Their breaths mingled in a long, low sigh and he leaned forward to resume the kiss. Moments spun out, one more golden than the last, as he tantalizingly disabused her of the notion that she could ever forget him or how wonderful his lovemaking made her feel—how cherished and adored.

The kiss lasted until her heart was pounding erratically beneath his hands. He explored the silken skin spilling from the neckline of the gown, his caresses not at all "married" but those belonging to a lover, a seducer. And it worked damnably well. She trembled with the intensity of the pleasure soaring through her, but he made no move to further the embrace. Physically they could go no farther, not without risk to the pregnancy. And it was something they were both clearly aware of as he drew away slowly, his yearning as fierce and fevered as her own. "I don't think this is what Jim had in mind when he prescribed 'bed rest,'" Neil said ruefully at last. He moved forward to hold her close a moment longer. With infinite gentleness he kissed her eyelids closed.

Ellie reveled a moment longer in the luxuriant wealth of sensations his nearness afforded. "I won't tell if you don't." Her voice was husky, equally bantering. Yet confusion flooded her senses, compounded by an attraction for him she didn't want to recognize.

Ellie could handle the euphoric, congenial Neil, the moody stranger or the preoccupied, exhausted physician. She could even handle the frustrated male. But Neil was acting as if, without warning, all their troubles were over. What was worse, there was a part of her—the part that believed in fairy tales and happily-ever-after endings and winning the grand prize in a lottery—that believed it, too. Yet she couldn't allow herself to get carried away. She had to remain practical, realistic as to what the future held. He had agreed to stay on for a year, for the babies, not because he loved her or was sorry or determined not to let work come between them ever again. But because, like her, he wanted to give their children a solid, stable environment, the kind of two-attentive-parents environment Ellie had never had. She couldn't let herself hope for anything more. Yet, despite all the pep talks she had with herself, she found that she was hoping for more, and as the days in the hospital passed, her yearning only grew stronger.

"WE'RE GOING TO HAVE to stop meeting like this, Doctor," Ellie said nearly two weeks later—the longest two weeks of Neil's life.

"You only wish." Neil stopped just short of her bed. He was relieved to see that she was calm, though the news they'd both just had in individual sessions with her obstetrician wasn't good. "Seriously, how do you feel?"

He wished he could spare her some of the agony she was going through, wished he could have somehow made their marriage indestructible before she'd entered the hospital. But he hadn't. And since that afternoon he'd nearly made love to her against all common sense and concern for her health, he'd forced himself to go slowly where she was concerned—to show her he loved her, but not in a sexual way. Not in any way that would make her feel pressured. In turn, she'd responded with a neutrality that let him know that they were and could always be good friends. But anything more...? Sometimes he had the feeling that he had let her down one time too many. That maybe she would never trust him again. And after the cold, indifferent way he'd behaved toward her for days on end, understanding fully now the force of the rejection she'd received from her father, he wasn't sure theirs was a marriage that could be repaired. He only knew that he wanted to try and didn't intend to give up, not for a long, long time. But first things first, and, for now, that meant seeing Ellie through this increasingly difficult pregnancy with as little emotional turmoil as possible.

"You mean, aside from the swelling of my fingers and toes and ankles?" Ellie asked wryly. On her lap were some briefs she'd been going over, but as per Jim Raynor's directions, she'd been remarkably good about staying off her feet and resting as much as possible.

"And the constant back discomfort and slightly elevated blood pressure," Neil commented quietly. They'd been able to control these complications only by keeping her on constant bed rest. In addition they'd done blood counts, checked for kidney infections, run routine urinalyses and a second ultrasound test to determine the position and approximate size of the babies. Sometimes he wondered how she stood it, being cooped up for so long. Yet, since the first week or two, she hadn't complained, had instead accepted her fate, realized that her body had all it could do to nurture the three infants growing inside her, and had gone on, taking it one day, one hour, at a time. He admired her for that. He wasn't sure that he would have maintained the same composure under the circumstances. But nonetheless she was anxious; that showed in the paleness of her face.

"I'm fine, Neil." She seemed to be trying hard to reassure him.

Neil strode over to the window, cast a look out at the traffic crowding the city streets below. "I've just talked with Jim. He said you've started to dilate even more." His low voice was underscored with worry. For once he wished he weren't a doctor, didn't know by heart all the factors that could go wrong or endanger their children's lives.

"I know. I've had some more contractions, usually at night.

It's as if the babies wait until I go to sleep, then try to mastermind a jailbreak.''

Neil grinned at her apt description. "How long do the contractions last?" He wished he could suffer them for her.

"That's just it. They're highly erratic. Usually, as soon as I'm fully awake, they stop. If I go back to sleep, they start."

"Ornery children, aren't they?"

"It would appear so." She looked down at her hands, knitted tightly together. "Neil, what would happen if I did go into labor?"

"We'd try to stop it, of course. If we couldn't, the babies would be born prematurely." Neil knew that if he gave in to his emotions now and held her, she would pick up on how really worried he was. With effort he remained where he was, his back against the window frame. He forced himself to keep his voice casual, as he had on other visits to her room. "Naturally, the fact that you're having contractions now is not a good sign. But it's not that unusual, either. Many women do begin dilating slightly in the last few months."

"Then why am I still in the hospital?"

"Because you've got high blood pressure and the swelling to worry about, too. It's just easier for Dr. Raynor to control those complications and keep an eye on you if you're here." After her first week in the hospital, they had done an experiment, let her be up walking around for half a day, to see what would happen, if she could go home without ill effect. Unhappily, once she was out of bed, up and around, her blood pressure had gone right back up. Hence it had been decided to keep her in the hospital. Because of her pregnancy, it was safer to give her a minimum of medication and, instead, control complications like high blood pressure through simple rest whenever possible. Unfortunately for the patient, it was a routine much easier to prescribe than to follow. What healthy active adult wanted to lie in bed idle, day after day after day?

"Frankly, Ellie, I think everything will be fine. You've been cooperating thus far. If you could just hold on a little while longer, stick with the prescribed regimen of bed rest and diet until you're all the way through your eighth month and well into your ninth..." The risk to the children would be minimized, if they were born only a week or two prematurely.

"I'll hold on," Ellie said determinedly. She glanced down at the work in her lap. "I'm not overdoing it, Neil, I swear. But if you think it would be better for me to cut out my work completely, even the little I'm doing..."

Neil paused. He had always resented her work when it interfered with anything that had to do with them. But now he was seeing the solace it gave her, the way it helped her get through day after day. The more she concentrated while lying quietly in bed, the better she was later able to sleep. Knowing Ellie, he knew that if she were to lie around watching television all day, she would soon be going crazy with anxiety. And that could be disastrous, as increased tension would most likely only work to elevate her blood pressure more.

"I trust you to be able to decide how much you can do," he said quietly. If only he had trusted her to be able to handle the Middleton case, none of their current estrangement would have happened. But it had. And now he could only deal with it day by day, hour by hour, much the same way they were dealing with the complications of Ellie's pregnancy. For to discuss anything that would burden her emotionally...no, he couldn't do it. He couldn't chance her getting upset. And he was thankful that she was calm now, almost one hundred percent of the time.

"I know I've said this before—" he moved away from the wall "—but if you ever need me, I don't care what for..."

"I'll call your secretary and have you paged." Ellie gave him a searching look and turned away. He hadn't a clue as to what she was thinking.

He walked over to give her a light kiss on the forehead, held her hand between the two of his. The enforced distance was hell on him. "I love you, Ellie." He spoke in the same quiet tone he would have used with a family member or close friend of either sex.

Ellie kept her tone neutrally sincere but unromantic. "I love you." She seemed to be telling him they were friends, but that was all. Disappointment flooded Neil, that she wasn't leaning on him more now, but he knew how she prided herself on being self-reliant.

"Everything's going to be all right," Neil assured her, releasing her hand.

Slowly, still looking to him for gentle assurances and comfort, Ellie nodded.

Neil had meant to be on his way; he found himself staying a little while longer.

Chapter Thirteen

"How much longer before we'll be able to take the children home?" Ellie asked Neil, watching as he shifted Tyler in his arms.

"Their pediatrician said three more days. She wants them all to weigh a minimum of five pounds each before they're released."

It had been six weeks since Ellie had delivered two girls and a boy two weeks prematurely. She'd had time to heal physically from the cesarean section and had just been pronounced fit by Jim Raynor earlier that morning in a postpartum office exam. "We've been through a lot with you children," Ellie said, enjoying immensely the sensation of being able to hold both Lindsey and Caitlin in her arms.

"Not the least of which was three bouts of hyaline membrane disease," Neil said.

For a while it had been touch and go for all three of their children, but, miraculously, they were all fine now, their lungs all working normally. And they'd been moved from special care units to regular nursery beds.

Ellie shifted Caitlin and Lindsey slightly so she could better study their tiny pink-tinged faces. "Do you think they'll all get sick together every time one of them comes down with a cold or flu? I know the hyaline membrane disease was due to their premature birth, the fact that their lungs weren't properly developed."

Neil shrugged. "Hard to tell what will happen, Ellie. But from what I've seen, when one child in a family gets chicken pox, they all get it.'' He looked up. ''Want to switch? I think Tyler's getting restless.''

''Okay, you take Caitlin. You've already had Lindsey this evening,'' Ellie said.

''They're beautiful children, aren't they?'' Neil said, once they were all settled comfortably again.

Ellie nodded. ''Tyler looks just like you.''

''And Lindsey and Caitlin look just like each other.''

Ellie laughed, lamenting, ''How we're ever going to tell them apart, I don't know.''

''I guess we can't leave on those ID bracelets forever.''

''No, we can't. They'll outgrow them. But for a while, we'll have to keep some identifying means on them.''

His eyes met hers disarmingly, reminding her again of all they had been through together, and how much closer she felt to Neil since the birth of their children and the subsequent weeks, when they'd worried and watched over their children's progress in tandem. Neil had been extremely supportive, caring. Ellie didn't know how she would have gotten through those heartrending hours without him—and moreover, he had seemed to need her, too. But nothing had been said about their marriage. Sadly, he'd given no indication to her that he had changed his mind about an eventual divorce. And she wasn't sure that it would have been wise to call it off at that stage, anyway. Neither of them had been thinking much beyond the moment while the children were sick.

''I'll get one of the nurses to make us up some new, larger ones when we leave.''

''Is that allowed?''

He shrugged, grinning. ''Being a physician has to have some advantages.'' They went back to enjoying their babies. ''How are things at the office?'' Neil asked. Ellie had been going in four hours a day and spending the rest of her afternoons and early evenings at the hospital with the children.

Ellie touched her cheek to Tyler's downy black hair. ''I'm catching up. I'm not taking any new cases, though.''

"Why not?" Neil's brows knitted together. His tone was filled with concern.

"I'd meant to talk to you about this." Ellie swallowed, not sure how Neil would feel. "I'm taking a leave of absence for another six weeks. I'll take care of my mail, maybe do a contract or two, but that's all. Once the children are released from the hospital, I...want to stay home with them until they get on a schedule."

"From a father's point of view, I think that's wise. But what about your career? Can your law practice survive without your being there in the office for another couple of months?"

"I don't know," Ellie said quietly. She met Neil's steady look. "Right now I'm still referring cases to other lawyers, just doing simple wills and going over contracts. Because of the way business picked up after the Middleton case, I'm still able to pay the office overhead and Hazel's salary. But I don't know how long that will continue if I don't get back into the courtroom soon." Moreover Hazel was getting restless. With Ellie not doing much, there wasn't much for Hazel to do, either, except answer the phones and take messages. And Ellie didn't want to lose her.

"Well, I'm sure you know what's best," Neil said finally. Clearly, he had an opinion about what she should do with her career, but he was not going to offer it. And Ellie wasn't going to pursue it. She didn't want to chance their disagreeing about anything. "What about until you do go back to work?" Neil said. "Have you thought about child-care arrangements, getting help in any way?"

"I know you suggested that I hire a nurse for the days, but I really don't think it will be necessary until I go back to work on a part-time basis."

"Ellie—" His disapproval came through, loud and clear.

"Well, I'm not going to be working. I want this time with the children." She wanted to get used to caring for them alone. "It's not as if I'm intending to do everything alone. Both of our parents have already helped out enormously. My mother took care of getting in diapers and formula and all the baby supplies. Your mother prepared a whole freezer full of dinners for us and found a cleaning woman to come in three times a week. Between Viv and Adele, we're all set. And they'll all be over to help out with the children whenever I need them."

"All right," he conceded finally, letting the subject drop. "We'll see how it goes."

GETTING THE CHILDREN settled and safely strapped into their infant car seats for the ride home from the hospital was the easy part, Neil concluded sagely several days later. It was the three days that followed that had been utter chaos. A succession of family members, his and hers, had trooped in and out of the house, somehow managing to wake the babies every time.

Tyler had proved to have the best set of lungs. When he was wet or hungry, he let Ellie know it. Lindsey and Caitlin were equally vocal, and hence it seemed that one of the children was demanding attention all the time. He personally didn't know how Ellie was coping, but somehow, miraculously, she was. The physical strain was showing, though, he noted as she rocked Tyler in the living room while simultaneously dictating a letter to Hazel, in response to the sole lawsuit still in her care, one that had recently been placed on the court calendar for later that spring.

Mimi was sitting in a corner of their sectional sofa, cradling Lindsey, looking entranced. Herb was next to her, helping out and giving directions. Caitlin was in the kitchen with both Viv and Adele, being simultaneously cooed over and held. Neil shook his head in exasperation. Crazy as it was, he'd actually seen more of his children when they were in the hospital, and of Ellie, too.

He loved his family; he was glad they were all so eager to be of help, but right now he needed time alone with his wife. With a jerk of his head he motioned to his dad. Obediently but reluctantly, Herb rose from his place on the sofa beside Mimi. "What is it, son?"

"How about some help, bringing in more wood for the fire?" Neil reached for his down jacket, hanging on a crowded coatrack near the door.

Herb shot a look at the cast-iron wood basket next to the fireplace. "But there's plenty of— Oh, yeah, right away. Just let me get my jacket and gloves." The February wind was icy. "So what's up?'' Herb asked moments later as he and Neil trudged toward the woodpile.

"It's Ellie. I haven't seen much of her the past few days. Or the kids."

"Is that bothering her?" Herb couldn't resist teasing, with a twinkle in his eyes.

"No, but it's bothering me, and since I arranged to have the afternoon and evening off..." Neil left the rest of the sentence hanging.

"You want us to leave?" Herb did a bad job of feigning astonishment.

But Neil wasn't clowning around. "Directly after the dinner dishes have been done. Dad, I hope I'm not offending you—"

"No, don't be silly. Hell, son, I want you to tell me what's on your mind. And cute as those kids are, I understand your needing some time alone with your wife."

If only Ellie needed time alone with him, Neil wished. Instead, she seemed to be putting up more barriers between them with every minute that passed, using people and activity with the children as a shield.

"How is Ellie feeling?"

"Good." Another reason Neil wanted to spend time with her. Now that he could finally make love with her again, he wanted to reconsummate their relationship, start all over again as husband and wife. Since the triplets had been born, neither of them had talked about the damn agreement to divorce that they had signed. He was content to forget about it but he didn't think Ellie was. He had the feeling that she was going to hold him to that written piece of nonsense, and it terrified him.

"Is she going to go back to work full-time?"

Neil sighed. That was the question everyone asked. And it was another complication, more vexing than the others. "I don't know, Dad. It's kind of funny. Before the babies were born, she didn't want to take any time off. Now it's hard to get her to go in to the office just to look at the mail. And there's so much chaos here at the house, it's hard for her to get anything done. Yet you saw for yourself that she asks Hazel to come here rather than go in—which, with the wealth of baby-sitting help we have today, Ellie could easily have done. Probably to swifter, less harried result. Hazel doesn't say much, but I know she's worried about Ellie, too." His wife's current behavior was drastically uncharacteristic. "It's almost as if she thinks someone is going to take the children away from her."

Herb considered that for a moment as he and Neil slowly loaded wood into a heavy cast-iron bucket. "Well, that's normal, don't you think, because the babies were so sick and all?"

"I don't know," Neil said.

"What Ellie's going through is normal, Neil. No mother wants to leave her baby. And she's got it three times as bad. They'll break away from one another in time."

"I know. But it's more than that, somehow. When she's not busy, sometimes I'll see her looking out the window. She'll be standing there with tears in her eyes, but the way she looks at me if she catches me watching her...it's like she's just daring me to notice or ask her about it, daring me to try to touch her or talk to her about the melancholy in any way."

"So what do you do?"

"Nothing." He shrugged. "Pretend it's not happening. With all she's been through, I just don't feel I have the right to pressure her now." He felt that if he did, he would be in more danger of losing her than ever.

"You're an obstetrician. You know how emotional women can be after the birth of a baby. It takes time for their hormones to settle down. That's all it is, son. I promise you. A few more weeks and everything here will be back to normal." Herb grinned. "Or as close as it's ever gonna get with triplets in the house."

NEIL DECIDED on his course of action as the afternoon progressed. After dinner, when everyone left, he and Ellie would get the triplets into bed. Then the two of them would go downstairs and talk—realistically—about when she was going to end her leave of absence and go back to work, and how they would manage child care when she did. Whatever arrangements she wanted to make they would begin setting up now, get them in working order, or as close to it as they could manage. From there they would talk about their relationship. Or if that didn't seem palatable, maybe just make love. One way or another, he wanted her back in his life full-time. And he knew she still wanted him, too. Or at least she had the last time he had really kissed her, which had been in the hospital when she'd been wearing that lacy black gown Mimi had given her. She just didn't realize it, or didn't want to admit it. Yet. But that was something that could be changed.

Unfortunately, nothing worked out as he had planned. Minutes after everyone left, Tyler came down with colic, or at least what Neil supposed was colic. He and Ellie took turns walking the piteously wailing infant back and forth across the living room. By the time they finally got him down and sleeping, Lindsey was up for her 2:00 A.M. feeding, and shortly thereafter, Caitlin.

"Well, Dad, how do you like it so far?" Ellie said from her rocker in the combination play-and-changing room next to the nursery. She held Caitlin and Lindsey in her arms.

"I don't think they know the meaning of 'nocturnal' yet," Neil said. "How long do you think before they'll learn?"

"You're the physician. You tell me."

"I don't know." He glanced at his watch. Five A.M. "What do you say we just put them into bed?"

"I don't know. They'll probably cry."

"They need to develop their lungs."

She laughed, not about to do as he suggested. "You can go on to bed."

He shook his head slowly, so there was no mistaking his meaning. "Not alone, not this time. I'm staying right here with you and the children."

She swallowed. Rising, she carefully settled first Lindsey, then Caitlin, in their cribs. He deposited Tyler in his. All was quiet except for faint gurgling noises as they left the nursery. "Think it will last?" Neil said, turning the lamp down to its dimmest setting.

"I don't know."

"Wait a minute, I have an idea." Neil disappeared and came back with a portable radio. Turning to a station that played only jazz, he set the volume on low. Soft blues floated out over the room. The music was somehow soothing, Ellie thought. The babies thought so, too. They didn't make a whimper. Ellie watched surreptitiously from a distance as Tyler found his thumb and shoved it into his mouth, Lindsey found the first two fingers on her left hand, and Caitlin was content to burrow into the soft cotton of her crib sheet.

"I don't believe this," Ellie whispered, backing softly out of the room.

Neil only smiled. "It's the Cavanaugh in them."

Ellie knew that he expected her to head for the master bedroom. Part of her wanted that, too. Since the triplets had been home from the hospital, she'd had very little sleep. Still, she started for downstairs, acutely aware that he was following closely behind her. "Just in case it doesn't work for long, I think I'll put on some coffee."

"Ellie." He caught her arm, turning her toward him. "I want my wife back, Ellie. One hundred percent."

"You mean you want to make love to me." Ellie's pulse was racing. She'd half expected this. She knew it had been on his mind ever since Jim Raynor had pronounced her fit. It had been on hers.

"I mean," he enunciated quietly, "a hell of a lot more than that. I don't want to just make love to you, though I do find you incredibly sexy, always have, always will. But I want to know you're committed to me and I to you." Ellie had waited a long time to hear him say those words. Maybe too long, though, months too long, because she didn't trust them. She only knew how hurt she'd been when he'd turned his back on her. She didn't think she could go through that again. And hence, it was easier to keep her guard up, to not let him close to her.

"You're emotional now, because of the birth of the children..." she began quietly.

"I'm emotional," he said raggedly, "because I've been without you, been without a wife. How can I make you understand that I need you? Not just anyone, not just a lover, but you. I want you to be here for me one hundred percent of the time, and I want to be here for you. I want to know those vows we made years ago count for something, that we truly will stay together through better or worse, and not just for the kids' sake.''

Happiness was brimming over inside Ellie. But it was a quick happiness she didn't trust. ''It's what I want, too.''

''Then why are we still apart?'' His hands ghosted over her shoulders, feeling the tension there, the tautness of her muscles.

''Because I'm scared it won't work again.''

''There are never any guarantees, Ellie. Just the strength of our commitment to each other.''

''That commitment proved almost worthless before we knew I was pregnant.'' The accusing words slipped out. She hadn't meant to say them, wouldn't have if she hadn't been so tired. He saw again the depth of her hurt.

''I'm sorry for that. I promise you it won't happen again. I won't walk out on you in anger, or sleep at the hospital to avoid you.''

Ellie knew he meant what he said at that moment. What she wasn't sure of was if his feelings would last when put to the test—when she began working again, or when one of them encountered or made decisions that might put a strain on the marriage. ''I'll have to think about it,'' she said finally. ''I don't want to rush into anything at this point. Maybe if you still feel this way in a couple of months...''

There was a long silence. ''All right,'' he said finally. ''I'm not going to issue any ultimatums or put conditions on my love. If it's time you need, then it's time you've got. I'm not going anywhere, not this time, not ever again.'' His eyes moved lovingly over her. He held out his arms to her. Slowly, Ellie glided forward into his embrace. He held her to him for long quiet moments, but when he released her, it was to separate beds they retired.

To Ellie, it felt as if she were standing on the edge of a great cliff, with Neil just beyond the drop-off, reaching out to her, the children behind her in safety. She wanted to go to Neil, to the safety and love he seemed magically to offer, but to do so she'd have to risk everything. She wasn't sure she could. She fell asleep dreaming of great swirling gray clouds and a love that seemed to disappear as rapidly as it had surfaced, only to reappear again. She awoke, realizing that they weren't out of danger of losing each other yet. Rather, far, far from it.

Chapter Fourteen

Ellie let the subject simmer between them for a week, undoubtedly the most agonizing seven days she had ever spent. But she had to be sure that she was doing the right thing, not just for herself, but for the children and Neil, too. Because to get back together too fast, for all the wrong reasons, would inevitably be to break up again, and that would hurt them all immeasurably.

Beyond which there was something she needed to do. Something that had been weighing on her. After calling Viv and Adele to sit for the triplets Saturday afternoon while Neil was at the hospital delivering a baby, she went to her downtown law office and made one of the hardest long-distance calls of her entire life. Luck was with her, for once, and the phone was answered on the fourth ring. "Hello, um, Mr. Jensen. This is Ellen Cavanaugh. Ellen Jensen Cavanaugh." She was talking to her father, Ellie thought, and she didn't even know how to address him.

There was a pause, significantly long. The voice that spoke was cold, grating. "I already told your husband I wasn't going to add to the financial support of those babies. I suppose you've had them!" Ted Jensen asked with vague interest, that of a stranger.

"Yes. Two girls and a boy." Ellie twisted the phone cord between her fingers, trying to suppress her shock at what he had just revealed. "Wh-when did you speak to Neil? I wasn't aware you even knew I was married."

"I didn't. Not until he showed up. Your mother and I haven't talked for years, since you were in college." There was another silence, this one even more difficult to bridge. Ellie realized with regret that she would have had an easier time speaking to a repairman. "So, what did you want?" her father asked impatiently.

"Nothing, I just...thought I should tell you." The pain Ellie had known she would feel at confronting her father again after all those years was very real. But it was also as if a weight had been lifted. For hearing his voice again had brought a hailstorm of memories back—none of them good, but all of them vital just the same. And with that, the realization that a father wasn't just the man who was biologically responsible for a child's existence, but a person who cared, who suffered right along with his children, who loved and rocked and touched, and even sometimes lost his temper. Whereas Ted Jensen had always been glacial and remote, less interested in her than even the IRS was. She owed him nothing. Except perhaps the realization of how wonderful a man Neil really was, and how very much she still wanted him in her life.

"Well, you've told me," her father said briskly, anxious to get her off the phone. "Uh, congratulations, but, uh, don't expect a gift, because I told you—"

"You're not interested, I know," Ellie said, unsure whether to cry with disappointment or relief.

"Right." There was another pause and then a click as her father set the phone down, severing the connection.

Ellie stared at the phone for several seconds more. Abruptly, she knew what she had to do. She could only hope it wasn't too late. She called her mother and Adele and asked them if they could somehow sit the rest of the weekend. They agreed, mystified, but applauded her when she told them where she and Neil, too—she hoped—would be. After a few more minutes putting together a romantic treat for later, it was off to the hospital. As she arrived, he was just leaving.

She pulled up beside him, smiling, "Hey, mister, need a lift?"

"I might be going your way." He got in beside her, his long legs nearly pressing up against the dash.

Ellie turned the car out of the lot.

"Where are we headed?" Neil leaned back in the seat. He'd

looked exhausted as she'd pulled up, but there were definite lights of interest in his eyes now.

"The Joplin Holiday Inn." He sat up straighter, nearly coming out of his seat belt at the news.

She chatted on nervously, not daring to take her eyes from the city traffic for a second. After all that had happened between them, the way she had held Neil at arm's length, she wouldn't have blamed him if he'd refused her newly pledged commitment. Had he any idea how treacherously close she was to losing her nerve?

"You told me you wanted a wife again. Neil—" her voice dropped tremulously another notch "—I'm ready to be that."

Neil reached over to capture her hand and bring it to his lips. His eyes were bright. "I'm glad, Ellie. Very glad."

Silence fell between them briefly as she headed toward the interstate where the hotel was located. Nonetheless she could feel his steady gaze appraising her silently, and her cheeks flushed with warmth. Once in their room on the third floor of the motel, he began asking the questions he'd been suppressing. "You want to tell me what changed your mind about us, or how this all came about?"

"I realized today that I've been unconsciously making you pay for a lot of sins, Neil, none of which were yours. This isn't easy for me to admit, but when I went into our marriage, I think I was inwardly half expecting it to fail. I guess I didn't really believe I could hold you. I thought you'd eventually leave me."

"Ellie—"

"Please, Neil, let me say this. I didn't realize how much I was holding back of myself until the Middleton case came up. Some of the arguments we had later—everything you said was true. I was holding your family at arm's length. I guess I was afraid to let myself get close to them for fear the marriage would fall apart and I'd lose them, too.

"I got close to Mimi first because of selfish reasons—because I needed to forget about what was happening with us, needed to concentrate on something else, and maybe, too, because I saw something of myself as a teen in her. She was nervous and insecure, not really sure she was worthy of being anyone's daugh-

ter. You're a tough act to follow. But Mimi's resolving that—
what with the way she's acing her classes at the high school, her
weight loss, boys, the accolades she gets when she baby-sits, not
to mention the financial independence. And I'm confident that as
she gets older her self-worth will increase even more."

"It's not just Mimi, though; you're close to my whole family
now. Even our mothers are friends." Neil watched as Ellie
poured champagne into glasses and handed him a drink. She'd
also packed a picnic hamper of other goodies for them.

"Why not? They have something very important in common,
three adorable grandchildren. But you're right, I am close to your
family. Getting closer to them has taught me how generous and
unselfish love should be within a family. I didn't know that. I
never had anyone to count on except my mother.

"I phoned my father, Neil. I told him about the babies. He
couldn't have cared less."

"I'm sorry."

"Don't be. That phone call taught me something. It made me
realize that he had and always would shut me out. There's nothing I can do about that, Neil; it's not my fault or up to me to
change it. The difference is, I finally know that in my heart."

"I went out to see him, Ellie."

Relief flooded Ellie that Neil was finally leveling with her
about his actions. "He mentioned that." Ellie had been hoping
Neil would tell her that of his own accord.

Neil sighed deeply, his anguish showing plainly on his face.
"As foolish as it seems in retrospect, after what little you'd told
me about the man, I nevertheless hoped he'd want to share our
joy. I didn't tell you because I was afraid it wouldn't work out,
and I didn't want to hurt you. That trip to Chicago for a friend's
wedding was a lie. I went to California instead to see him."

He shot her a level, reassuring glance. "I would have told you
eventually, Ellie, but I wanted to wait until after the triplets were
born; then later, after they'd had time to adjust, get on a schedule.
I wasn't sure how you'd take it."

"I wasn't sure, either. I just knew that I had to do something
to resolve that, one way or another. Talking to him on the phone
brought all his coldness back. But it also made me realize how

very different you are from him. I realized that from the very first I'd been putting up barriers, to keep others a safe emotional distance from me. But that doesn't necessarily work, either, and in fact can end up being more destructive than insulative. I've learned that opening myself up to people doesn't necessarily mean I'll get hurt as I did when I let myself love my father years ago."

"So what are you going to do about your father?"

Ellie shrugged sadly and took another sip of champagne, admitting, "There's nothing I can do, Neil. He doesn't want me in his life. And I've realized, finally, that I don't really want him. What I want is a storybook ending to it, and that's not going to happen, not ever."

"I wish I could tell you differently, Ellie," Neil said sadly, "but I think your assessment is absolutely correct. I was out there. I saw the man. There's nothing of love or affection in his life. He's going to continue to live an isolated, embittered, dispassionate existence."

"I don't want to end up like him, Neil. Alone, unhappy."

"I don't want that, either." He held her tightly. His sense of humor surfaced. "Of course, with triplets in the house, that would be pretty hard to do. Which reminds me, where are the babies, by the way?" He just assumed she had taken care of them.

"The two grandmas have taken charge of our house."

"I'm impressed with your foresight and planning, Ms. Cavanaugh."

"Thank you. Now that I've finally let go of the past, I thought it was high time we gave our marriage a real chance for survival, a no-holds-barred type of commitment."

Neil looked both relieved and euphoric. "Well, I'll certainly agree to that. How long do we have?" He looked longingly toward the bed.

"Till tomorrow evening if all goes well. I hope you won't be called back to the hospital."

"If I am," Neil declared augustly, waltzing her backward toward the bed, "I'm taking you with me. I am curious about one thing, though. What made you decide you could trust me again?"

"The fact that you didn't pressure me this week, that you said you'd wait as long as it took for me to feel secure, and you did, the fact that you're a wonderful father, and you've been a wonderful husband, even throughout all the turmoil we've been through the past year."

"I do love you, Ellie."

"And I love you."

They kissed for long moments.

"Promise me something?" Ellie said. "That we'll never let our work interfere with our marriage again, and that if we do have problems, we'll try to work them out right away, rather than let them escalate into something unmanageable?"

"You have my word," Neil pledged seriously, tightening his arms around her. "I've learned the hard way that nothing can be gained by shutting someone out. The worst part of it is that all along I thought I was doing us both a favor, that by staying away I could keep our problem from getting any worse. And when it didn't work, when we just got farther apart, I didn't know what to do. So then I reacted as I always do under stress. I tried to lose myself in my work. And in the process, I almost lost us a marriage."

"You had help there," Ellie said softly, reflectively. She leaned her forehead against his shoulder. "I was just as much at fault. I didn't want to confront our problems straight on any more than you did; otherwise I would have leveled with you about my taking the case from the start. But I didn't. I ignored it because I didn't want to hurt you—or us—either."

Neil squeezed her again, held her as if he never wanted to let her go. "Since then I've come to the conclusion that no job is worth losing a marriage for," he confessed in a harsh whisper.

"You don't mind losing out on the hospital post?" Ellie reveled in his strength and his warmth. How she had missed him, how she had missed the luxury of holding him close and being held.

"The new chief of obstetrics is excellent, brings with her a lot of expertise." He shrugged, his expression telling her how little the advancement really meant. "I wouldn't have time for it now that we've got the three kids. They're going to take a lot of tender loving care.''

"Don't I know it," Ellie snuggled closer.

With difficulty, Neil located the champagne bottle. He poured them both a little more. "To us," he gently toasted the renewal of their marriage vows.

"To us," Ellie echoed softly. Arms entwined, they drank of the bubbly golden wine.

He held her against him, one hand coasting lazily down her spine. They fit well together once again. "This is nice," she murmured, as his hands reached her hips and directed her forward, against the taut plane of his abdomen and thighs.

"Very nice," he murmured, shifting her forward once again. Urgency overtook them both. Buttons were unfastened, zippers undone, stockings removed, underclothes stripped off. They tangled together on the bed. Ellie had missed seeing his masculine splendor, the hard flesh feathered with coarse hair, the perennially dark skin, the gracefully curved long legs.

He left a trail of kisses from her head to her toes, kisses so fragile and light that she might have thought she imagined them were it not for her thudding pulse and tingling skin. A warm flush spread over her; color highlighted her face as his hands moved over her, learning her anew in a manner that was both exacting and exciting. She made a soft moaning sound when he took her mouth again, then moved his lips over her skin. Then they were turning, rolling, laughing; Ellie was on top and loving it. His hands opened and closed in her hair. And then there was the maddeningly slow flow of events...Ellie once again feeling the mattress at her back, Neil above her, wedging his knees between hers, moving closer. She arched against him, whispering her need. "Now, Neil, please—" Her hands closed compellingly over his biceps.

"Ellie," he whispered her name once and then again. And then she knew nothing but the magic of loving bonding them together, heart and soul.

"WELL, ALL'S QUIET on the home front," Neil said, replacing the phone on the hook several hours later. "I'm not needed at the hospital. What more could we want?''

"Room service?" Ellie prompted as her stomach growled hungrily. They'd long since eaten the snacks and champagne she'd brought with her.

Neil bowed from the waist. "Whatever madam requests."

Several hours later, after a dinner of chateaubriand, Ellie and Neil splurged with a second bottle of wine. Perversely, the talk turned to personal, practical matters as they sat cross-legged on the rumpled covers of the bed.

"You may not believe this, Doctor, but I didn't bring you here just to ravish you. I also wanted to talk to you about my plans, professionally. I've decided to take a longer leave of absence from my work, maybe a year or two. So I've decided to hire an attorney to step in and take over, run the office day-to-day. I'll still go in an hour or so every day, to make sure everything is running smoothly and lend a hand when need be, but I won't be actively involved in preparing court cases or wills on a daily basis. Naturally, this will mean a sharp cut in pay for me. I'll still be able to pay the other attorney's salary, plus office overhead and Hazel's salary, but it won't leave much take-home pay for me.''

"I think we can manage," Neil took one of her hands in his.

"You don't think I'm being foolish?" Ellie searched his face. It was important to her that he still respect her professionally and as a person.

"No, not if it's what you want. That's what life is all about, Ellie—making choices freely to suit yourself. Or at least it should be. Which brings us to the next point of discussion. I've been thinking a lot about what happened to split us apart when you took the Middleton lawsuit. Most of it was my fault. I should have trusted your judgment more. I promise to do so in the future. If you or your new associate takes on another malpractice case, I won't object—or resent your doing so, even silently. I trust your judgment. I know that whatever you do will be fair to all the parties.

"You see, I realized, after the lawsuit was concluded and I had talked to Dr. Talbot, that the issue isn't one any of us can afford to ignore any longer. The American Medical Association has advocated the strengthening of state licensing boards and hospital peer-review procedures, but as of yet, not nearly enough has been done toward that effort. If it had, suffice it to say, the Middletons' traumatic experience would never have happened. I don't want to see anything like that happen in Joplin again. So I've decided to do what I can to see that the A.M.A. suggestions are followed and implemented here in Joplin. So, we'll both be working toward good medical care for the general public. I'll go at it from the inside and a medical viewpoint. You'll work at it from a legal perspective.''

Ellie was silent for a moment. ''Maybe it's time we took it one step farther and really worked together on the issue, Neil, not just individually. I've been doing some reading and thinking, too. Malpractice has gotten rid of some physicians who shouldn't be practicing medicine. But it's also hurt a lot of good doctors, driven up insurance premiums and the cost of medical care in general. And that hurts everyone. That has to be stopped, Neil.''

''How would you go about it?''

''I'd like to go after some of the people bringing 'nuisance suits' against doctors. I'd work to help establish penalties for that. And I'd start by becoming more knowledgeable in the area of malpractice in general. Together, we could read and research cases, use our combined knowledge to considerable impact on the medical community here in Joplin and, if we're successful, eventually even in the state.''

''Counselor, I like the way you think.''

''And I admire the kind of doctor you are. So, do we have a deal?''

''Yes.''

''So, back to square one.'' Ellie sighed happily after a moment. They could go back to being a happily married couple, parents....

Neil drew her down beside him. ''Not quite,'' he corrected gently. ''Because we know now, whatever our career choices, they no longer take precedence over our family.''

''Agreed,'' Ellie said softly, seriously.

''However—'' Neil made a great show of clearing his throat

"—about your taking extended time off from work. Are you sure? Before the babies were born, you were so adamant about continuing. I want us to do what's right for you, Ellie, as well as for the babies."

Ellie sighed reflectively, softly told him what was in her heart. "Before the babies were born, I had no idea how strong the maternal instincts within me would be. I care deeply about my law practice, Neil, but it's nothing compared to the way I feel about the kids. I want to be there for them. Maybe with one child, I could have kept working and still done him or her justice. Maybe even with two, if they'd been different ages. But with triplets, there's no way I could meet all their needs. And these early years are crucial to a child's emotional and intellectual development. It's important for me and for them that I be there to oversee their care. Besides, with us working on this malpractice issue together, and me reading up on it in my spare time, I think I'll be very busy indeed, as well as intellectually quite content."

Neil beamed his approval. "I still can't see you as a stay-at-home mother indefinitely."

"I won't be. I'm sure that by the time they're in school, I'll be back at work, toiling simultaneously as they learn. But if the way I feel about our children now is any indication, I think I'll still want to be there for them most of the time when they get home. Fortunately, because I have my own practice and make my own hours, I'll be able to do that. And when I can't—well, maybe they can come down to the office and do their homework and have milk and cookies in a spare room we'll set up there."

"You have given this a lot of thought!" Neil nodded approvingly, adding pensively, "I agree with you, though. One certainly can't go back and recapture lost time."

It was Ellie's turn to clear her throat and teasingly let her hand drift down his thigh. "Doctor, one can always try."

He reached for her again, not stopping until they were cozily ensconced among the pillows once more. "Hallelujah for that."

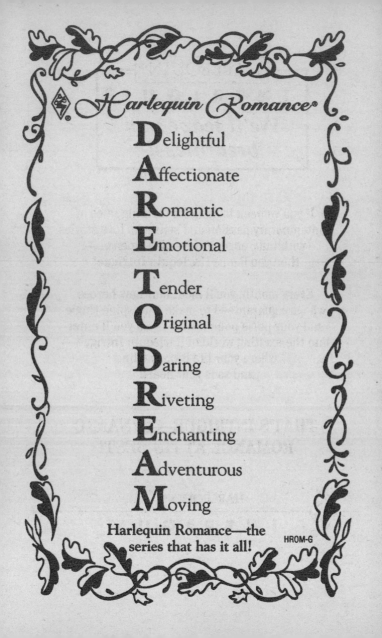

Harlequin Romance®

Delightful

Affectionate

Romantic

Emotional

Tender

Original

Daring

Riveting

Enchanting

Adventurous

Moving

Harlequin Romance—the
series that has it all!

HROM-G

LOOK FOR OUR FOUR FABULOUS MEN!

Each month some of today's bestselling authors bring
four new fabulous men to Harlequin American Romance.
Whether they're rebel ranchers, millionaire power brokers
or sexy single dads, they're all gallant princes—and
they're all ready to sweep you into lighthearted fantasies
and contemporary fairy tales where anything is possible
and where all your dreams come true!

You don't even have to make a wish…
Harlequin American Romance will grant your every desire!

Look for Harlequin American Romance
wherever Harlequin books are sold!

HARLEQUIN ⬥ PRESENTS®

HARLEQUIN PRESENTS
men you won't be able to resist
falling in love with...

HARLEQUIN PRESENTS
women who have feelings
just like your own...

HARLEQUIN PRESENTS
powerful passion in
exotic international settings...

HARLEQUIN PRESENTS
intense, dramatic stories that will keep you
turning to the very last page...

HARLEQUIN PRESENTS
The world's bestselling romance series!

Harlequin® Historical

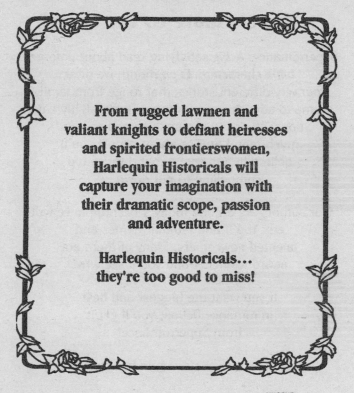

From rugged lawmen and
valiant knights to defiant heiresses
and spirited frontierswomen,
Harlequin Historicals will
capture your imagination with
their dramatic scope, passion
and adventure.

Harlequin Historicals…
they're too good to miss!

HARLEQUIN SUPERROMANCE®

...there's more to the story!

Superromance. A *big* satisfying read about unforgettable characters. Each month we offer *four* very different stories that range from family drama to adventure and mystery, from highly emotional stories to romantic comedies—and much more! Stories about people you'll believe in and care about. Stories too compelling to put down....

Our authors are among today's *best* romance writers. You'll find familiar names and talented newcomers. Many of them are award winners—and you'll see why!

If you want the biggest and best in romance fiction, you'll get it from Superromance!

Available wherever Harlequin books are sold.